Rosie Blake

the HYGGE holiday

sphere

SPHERE

First published in Great Britain in 2017 by Sphere

1 3 5 7 9 10 8 6 4 2

Copyright Little, Brown Book Group Ltd © 2017
Written by Rosie Blake

The moral right of the author has been asserted.

*All characters and events in this publication, other than those
clearly in the public domain, are fictitious and any resemblance
to real persons, living or dead, is purely coincidental.*

A CIP catalogue record for this book
is available from the British Library.

ISBN 978-0-7515-6974-2

Typeset in Caslon by M Rules
Printed and bound in Great Britain by
Clays Ltd, St Ives plc

Papers used by Sphere are from well-managed forests
and other responsible sources.

Sphere
An imprint of
Little, Brown Book Group
Carmelite House
50 Victoria Embankment
London EC4Y 0DZ

An Hachette UK Company
www.hachette.co.uk

www.littlebrown.co.uk

Rosie is an author of comic commercial fiction. She started out writing short stories and features for various publications including: *Cosmopolitan*, *The Sunday People*, *The Lady*, *Best* and *Reveal* magazine. Previously she has had three novels published: *How to Get a (Love) Life*, *How to Stuff Up Christmas* and *How to Find Your (First) Husband*.

She worked in television as a presenter on both live and pre-recorded shows and she makes regular vlogs. She lives in Berkshire with her husband Ben, her son Barnaby and a couple of chickens. She is into making soups at the moment because someone gave her a soup recipe book. When she isn't walking along the river, writing in her shed (an absolute *hygge* haven) or listening to her son sing the 118th round of 'Row, Row, Row Your Boat' she is day-dreaming about the day when Julia Roberts finally rings her and asks her to be her best friend.

To Barnaby – our gorgeous son

Chapter 1

Clara had only been inside for ten minutes when it happened.

It had all seemed like a perfectly normal Tuesday evening. There had been a few people in the pub: a young couple in the corner, the man trying to get comfortable on a narrow wooden pew, his partner opposite him in a chair, understated and pretty in a black cashmere jumper and jeans, her strawberry-blonde hair tied back in a low ponytail. An older woman with thick eyeliner and dyed auburn hair was propped up on a stool at the bar, making her way through a bottle of red wine. The large barman topping up her glass had a tattoo on his arm of a type of bird that Clara couldn't quite make out. Another man, around the same age but about half the size, was looking dolefully into his pint in between snatching glances at the woman at the bar and smoothing down stray wisps of hair over his bald spot. A neon slot machine flashed and beeped intermittently in one corner, beside an empty dartboard and opposite the floor lamp next to which Clara was sitting reading her book.

Suddenly a woman appeared in the doorway, hair wet though it wasn't raining outside, dressed in a turquoise woollen coat and purple wellington boots. Flinging her arms wide, she marched straight into the room. 'Gin and tonic, Gavin, double, hold back on the tonic,' she cried, moving towards the bar. 'I'm done,' she announced. Every head in the pub, including Clara's, turned towards her. 'It's over, I'm shutting it. I was in the shower and I thought, damn it, I can't do this any more. I'm off.'

Gavin paused, his hand on the gin bottle, his mouth open.

'That gin won't pour itself, Gavin,' said the woman, whipping off her turquoise coat to reveal hot-pink thermal pyjamas. 'I'll take it back with me; my bottle was empty and I'm in desperate need of a stiff drink. You need a stiff drink when you've made a difficult decision. I only had Baileys, and that is not a drink that suffices in a moment like that.'

'But Louisa, wait, talk to us ...' Gavin said, reaching underneath the bar to pull out a tumbler.

The woman with the thick eyeliner muttered, 'Drama, drama.'

Clara saw Louisa looking sharply up at her.

Gavin shovelled some ice into the glass. 'Come on, Louisa, love, a problem shared and all that ...'

Louisa walked over to the bar. 'God, you sound like a hideous greetings card, Gavin. Fine,' she rattled on, throwing her coat over a stool, 'I'll stay for one but you won't change my mind. Oh no, I've decided. It's done. I'm going straight back to book a flight.'

'A flight?' Gavin's hand slipped and he splashed tonic on the bar.

'A flight. I'm off. Spain. I can't stay here any more,' Louisa announced, scooping up the drink and taking a first gulp. She smacked her lips in an exaggerated fashion. 'Gin. The greatest of all inventions.'

'But what about the shop?' Gavin asked, looking at her, hands resting on the bar, fingers like ten splayed sausages.

'Closing,' Louisa said after a pause.

'What do you mean, closing?'

'Shutting. Finishing. Kaput. The End. It's over. I'll close it quietly, no one will notice anyway.'

'But it's Christmas soon and—'

'Woman can't do anything quietly,' said the woman at the bar, cutting Gavin off, her thin lips stained red from the wine, her face weathered as if she worked outside.

'Roz.' Gavin topped up her drink, giving her a warning look over the bottle.

Louisa spun round to face her, 'And what is that supposed to mean?'

It seemed the whole pub was holding its breath. The couple at the table nearby were riveted, the man with the bald spot nursing his pint hadn't even realised it was empty and was openly staring. Even Clara, picturing the small bed below the eaves upstairs, her shoulders aching from carrying her rucksack around all day, couldn't tear her eyes away.

'You heard,' Roz said, chin up, staring Louisa down from her stool.

Louisa stood, slicked wet hair dripping, cheeks reddening. 'Just because you're a dried-up prune with no fire in her belly.'

The man with the bald spot called out, a sudden fierceness in his eyes, 'Hey, she's not a prune!' Immediately he clamped a hand over his mouth, as if frightened more words would come tumbling out.

Louisa turned on him. 'Sticking up for your girlfriend, Clive?'

'She's not my . . . ' His cheeks blazed red almost instantly, head lowered so the whole pub could only see the bald spot.

'Don't worry, Clive, she won't do it,' Roz said. 'It will be a passing fancy; she'll go back, dry her hair and change her mind.'

'Oh, I see,' Louisa said, slamming the tumbler down on the bar so that one of the barely melted ice cubes popped out and bounced off the surface onto the floor. 'You think this is just a phase, I suppose, a passion.'

'One of your many.' Roz toasted the words, twisting herself back round to face the bar.

'How untrue,' Louisa announced. 'Gavin, more gin,' she added, still glaring at the woman with the red wine, who

4

was now ticking things off on her fingers, nails painted a deep plum.

'There was the learning-to-knit course, the time you were gluten-free, Nick and that whole saga . . . ' She paused to roll her eyes, 'Reg who replaced Nick, oh, then there was the birdwatching phase, raising funds in here for your proposed trip to Iceland to see puffins that never happened, and Clive gave you five pounds for that one . . . '

'Everyone thinks puffins are related to penguins, but they actually belong to two completely different families,' Clive murmured into his pint.

This wasn't the evening Clara had envisaged when she'd stumbled across the pub by chance a couple of hours ago. She'd been exhausted, had planned to be in bed by now, but this was better than a TV soap.

' . . . the online adult educational course in English litera-ture, the village book club you insisted on starting up – we never even met and I read *Mansfield Park* for nothing; that Fanny Price must the most boring woman in literature, I genuinely thought I might die before reaching the end of it . . . '

She'd thought she had left it far too late to find somewhere to stay that night. She'd been distracted by a stunning sunset over the flat fields, the tea in her Thermos flask still warm as she'd gazed out at the sky cut up into ribbons of orange and pink. The windows of the pub had cast bright pools on the ground outside; the silhouettes of people inside could be seen moving from a hundred yards away.

As she'd approached, she'd stared up at the enormous thatched roof, weighing down the whitewashed walls. A small handwritten sign in the window announced 'Bed and Breakfast' and she had felt relief wash over her. She'd moved inside, hoicking the rucksack up on her back, desperately hoping there was a room free. She'd pictured steak and kidney pie in front of a roaring fire, washed down with a smooth ale, and then reading her book and bed. Not this.

She'd soon discovered the light had been coming from a bare bulb hanging between heavy wooden beams and showing up every stain on the swirled red carpet. Dried muddied leaves littered the floor, more blowing into the room as she stood in the doorway. Food wasn't being served. The bed and breakfast consisted of one small attic room, a miniature packet of cereal and a banana left on a tray.

Still, there was no way she had time to look for another place, and the bar had seemed comfortable enough: clusters of red velvet chairs crowded around walnut-brown tables, the bar in the middle of the room, patrons sitting around in a U shape. She'd ordered some salt and vinegar crisps, two Snickers bars and a pint of the local ale. After the second pint she had forgotten her desire for a cooked meal and was happily ensconced in her book, nestled in a patched armchair next to the only radiator and lamp in the place. Then this wet-haired whirlwind of a woman had appeared, and the night had been transformed.

'... the Pilates classes you never went to, the pottery

wheel you bought on Gumtree because you wanted to make your own ramekins ...'

Louisa seemed to dim as Roz's list went on. Placing her hands over both ears, she shook her head, perhaps hoping it might stop.

'... the time you adopted a baby giraffe in Niger and invited us all to a slideshow of photos from his first year but the projector didn't work ...'

'No,' Louisa piped up in a loud voice, 'no, no, this time I'm going. Spain. I'm closing it; I'm going to book the flights.'

'You love that shop,' Gavin said, pushing a second gin and tonic her way.

'She won't do it, Gavin, it's all talk, talk, talk,' Roz said, getting into her stride.

'You're wrong,' Louisa said, seeming to rally. 'I'm going to close the shop, no one comes in; they don't need me any more.'

Clara wondered what it was that there was no demand for; did Louisa run an internet café, a DVD store?

'Well, off you go then. Book the flight. We'll miss you,' Roz said, rolling her eyes.

The blonde with the low ponytail had stood up and moved across to Louisa. 'Oh, we will miss you. Are you really leaving?'

Roz slammed a hand on the bar, 'She won't go, Lauren.'

The blonde spun around. 'But there's no need to drive her away.'

Roz's eyes narrowed.

The blonde woman's partner had stayed fixed to his pew, looking utterly out of his depth, pushing the glasses up the bridge of his nose. 'Darling, shall we . . .' He glanced at the door, clearly wanting to do a runner before it all ended in a fist fight.

The three women at the bar were still glaring at each other.

'There'll be nothing left open on the high street,' Gavin said, his double chin wobbling. Clara found herself wanting to go behind the bar and give him a big hug.

'I can't carry around that responsibility on my own, Gavin,' Louisa said, throwing her arms wide. 'It's too much for one small woman.'

Roz spluttered into her red wine at the word 'small'.

'Hey,' the blonde said.

Louisa didn't appear to have noticed. 'I just can't go on hoping it will all change; there's nothing worse than feeling depressed in a toyshop that should be full of happy children.' She was becoming tearful, sinking onto a bar stool, her wet curls hanging over her face. Clara was about to stand up and move to comfort her when the blonde did just that, putting an arm around her shoulders and shushing her.

'Oh, bring on the waterworks,' Roz sighed.

'She's upset,' the blonde snapped.

Roz shrugged and drained the last of her red wine. 'Woman's always causing a scene. Nothing's changed.'

'And I suppose you're going to bring up the fete again

8

now?' Louisa looked at the other woman, defiance in her eyes. 'I really didn't mean to do it.'

'Likely story,' Roz scoffed.

'Roz,' Clive whispered from his spot nearby.

She turned towards him. 'Don't you get involved; I didn't see you getting involved then.'

'The fete again?' Gavin glanced at them both. 'Shouldn't you two let bygones be bygones?'

Clara couldn't help wondering what on earth could have happened at a village fete to cause this tension.

'Gavin, drop it,' Louisa said in a low voice, wiping at her face. 'Just leave me the bottle.'

'I'm not sure . . .'

'Well, if you don't, I'm off. I've got a hundred and one things to do anyway, and a full bottle of Baileys.'

And as quickly as she had arrived, she left, in a whirl of turquoise, the cold air sweeping in as she swung open the door, leaving the whole pub staring after her at the empty doorway.

Chapter 2

Clara had always got up early. She could see sunshine straining at the thin red cloth of the curtain over the small window set into the eaves. Kneeling on the bed, she drew back the material.

Blinking at the winter sunlight, a slow smile crept over her face as she took in the view. She pushed the catch, feeling the nip in the air as the window opened. There was frost glistening on the grass of the pub garden, the benches speckled in white. Beyond the hedge at the back was an uninterrupted view over fields, some churned up in uniform lines, some patches of green hidden beneath the thin layer of diamonds sparkling in the morning sunshine. The sky was streaked with pinks and pale blues and Clara felt the familiar thrill of a new day in a different place.

Ignoring her box of cereal and the trickle of the en suite shower, she rummaged through her rucksack, pulling on her jeans and a thick woollen jumper, unearthing a knitted hat, which she pulled on over her hair, hiding the dull blonde in need of a wash. Leaving the rest of her things in the room, she crept down the wooden staircase into the bar area and through the kitchen, letting herself out of the back door.

She knew the shops would be shut at this time but she had a faint hope that she might stumble across some kind-hearted baker who would open his door just for her. She could almost taste the thick warm dough, sniffed the air for a telltale whiff of it. There didn't appear to be a bakery in the village at all. Or a café. In fact, as she moved down the high street she was shocked to see so many 'For Sale' signs, shops with nothing in the windows but a few chairs or rolls of carpet. Other windows were boarded up, even the graffiti half-hearted, illegible squiggles in spray paint, dull colours. There was faded writing drawn into the dust on one window, a notice promising an end-of-stock clearance sale in another.

She tucked her hands into her pockets, the breeze picking up as she continued to take in the deserted high street. She imagined it bustling in the summer months, window boxes bursting with colour, the cobbled side streets holding treasures, secret shops, antiques piled high outside, cafés making up smoothies and juices, people ambling through the village before heading off to walk across the fields, take in the views. What had happened?

It never failed to surprise her, even after all these years of living in England, how quaint the villages could look, all the cottages squeezed together, so different to the city in Denmark that she'd grown up in. As ever, when she thought of home she felt a lump in her throat; she swallowed it back down.

Across the way she stopped, taking in the brightest shop, a burgundy façade, golden letters spelling 'Alden Toys', kitsch but eye-catching, and she frowned as she realised that this was clearly the shop shutting its doors. It seemed terribly sad that in the next few weeks, as people geared up for Christmas, it would remain closed, the dark interior at odds with the cheerful shopfront.

She reached the end of the street, the road disappearing around a tree-lined bend. Opposite stood a small church, entry through a lychgate, fields beyond. The village was a stunning, romantic place, but in that moment Clara felt as though she might be the only person living there. She looked back down the street, closing her eyes briefly and taking a deep breath.

"Gain, 'gain.'

Her eyes snapped open at the sound behind her.

'Really? OK.'

Singing soared out of the side street: 'Five little ducks went swimming one day, over the hills and far away, mama duck said *quack, quack, quack, quack*, but only four little ducks came back ...'

'Why?' came the younger voice.

12

'I've told you why,' the female voice said. 'Because a duck ran off, darling. Hence there are now only four ducks left.'

'What happened to the duck who ran away?'

'Nothing too nasty.'

'Did he die?'

'No, I'm sure he didn't.'

'Did he break his leg?'

'No, no, I don't think so, he comes back at the end.'

'Why?'

'Because he was probably missing his mama, like you would miss me, wouldn't you?'

'Maybe.'

'What do you mean, maybe? Of course you'd miss me. Who would make you pancakes?'

'Daddy.'

'OK, that's a fair point. Who would give you juice?'

'Nana.'

'Rubbish, Nana never gives you juice, she thinks it's got too much sugar.'

'I like sugar.'

'Yes, I know.'

''Gain, 'gain.'

A sigh followed. 'OK, but I'll start when there's only one duck left, because your attention span is . . . RORY.'

Suddenly a toddler burst out from the side street, stopping short to stare up at Clara before his eyes widened in panic and he spun on his heel to dive behind his mother's legs.

'What is it? I told you not to ru— Oh, hello.' It was the

13

woman from the pub last night – Lauren, the strawberry-blonde lady who had comforted Louisa. 'Sorry, we're disrupting the peace.'

Clara looked at her, at her impossibly straight hair, her camel-coloured coat, the freckles on her nose the only sense of disorder about her. 'It's fine. I thought it was a very cheerful song.'

Lauren hid her head in her leather-gloved hands. 'Oh God, how embarrassing.'

Clara laughed. 'No, honestly, it was wonderful. I'd never heard it before, actually,' she admitted. 'We don't have that one at home.'

'Where's home?'

'Denmark. We're more about fish than ducks really.'

'You're a long way from home,' Lauren commented.

Clara nodded, unwilling to add more.

Not noticing Clara's change in tone, Lauren explained, 'Well, it's about five ducks who run away and then all come back. There's not much of a narrative to it. Rory was right to have some questions.'

'Rory right, Rory right.' The little boy started helicopter-ing round his mother.

'The ducks are really not very safety-conscious, but you do have to question the mother's competence – I mean, after losing three of them, you'd think she'd think twice about sending the other two out on their own.'

Clara laughed, the sound seeming to reverberate around the street. 'She does sound quite irresponsible.'

14

'I can't judge, though, I can barely control one,' Lauren said, watching Rory dangle off the end of a bench. 'Rory, careful.'

'Cafful, cafful, cafful,' he said, letting one arm go, his bobble hat dropping to the ground, his light brown hair falling down in a curtain.

'We never really see anyone at this time, but he goes stir crazy if he doesn't get out, and frankly, I hate sitting in the house being reminded that I have a pile of ironing to do and pans to wash up.' Lauren held out a hand as Rory toddled back over on uncertain legs. 'Sorry, I'm Laur— RORY, NO!' she said, the hand she was holding out whipping down to stop Rory picking up an empty chocolate wrapper. 'Lauren,' she finished, scooping up her son. 'And this, as you've heard, is Rory.'

'I'm Clara.'

'It's nice to meet you,' Lauren said as Rory started kicking his legs, wanting to be released. 'Stay on the bench,' Lauren said as Rory roared away in the opposite direction. 'Wow, it's almost like he doesn't listen,' she laughed. 'Sorry. Kids are not great at social niceties. Last week he went straight up to an old man in the supermarket and told him to punch his willy. I literally died in the cereal aisle.'

Clara made a face, unable to stop marvelling at Lauren's energy. 'Do you know anywhere I can get something to eat?' she asked. 'I was hoping for a pain au chocolat or a muffin, or ... well, just a coffee would do.'

Lauren shrugged, her smile fading. 'Only online now,

or the big supermarket in the next town if you have a car. There's a good farm shop, but that's a decent drive too.'

Clara shook her head. 'I haven't got a car.'

'How very environmentally friendly.'

'No, I just never learnt to drive. Cars cost a fortune back home and I used to walk everywhere in . . . ' Clara faded off, not wanting to say the name of her home town, not even wanting to think about it. 'So there's nowhere?'

Lauren sighed, wrapping her arms around herself. 'There used to be Bertie's – an amazing restaurant that did incredible breakfasts, which were so wrong but so right: basically French toast, banana, a heap of bacon topped with maple syrup. I miss Bertie,' she said wistfully.

'Where did he go?'

'Opened up in the next-door village about six months ago; he was one of the last to leave. And now . . . ' Lauren pointed at Alden Toys opposite. 'Although do not tell you-know-who unless you want to see a small person's world end before eight a.m.; it really won't be pretty.'

Clara nodded, knowing that Lauren was trying to make light of things but aware of her sad smile.

'It's horrible,' Lauren said, looking around. 'When we moved here five years ago, it was this gorgeous corner of the world, independent shops, people saying hello in the high street, but now, so many of the familiar faces have gone and the shops, well,' – she indicated the boarded-up windows – 'you've seen. Now it's just the pub left. And Roz sells milk and things from the post office but there are funny opening times and I never seem to get them right. You could try there.'

Rory had run back over, his mittened hand creeping up into Lauren's.

'Roz,' Clara repeated, picturing red hair and thick eye-liner, 'wasn't she in the pub last night?'

Lauren nodded. 'Ah, you were there for that. God, that was pure drama. She and Louisa don't see eye to eye. They're neighbours, but not very neighbourly to each other. There's history,' – she waved a hand – 'I think it dates back to the late eighties. And then there was the saga at the fete, but you really don't want to know about that.'

'Sounds intriguing,' Clara said.

'Let's just say they didn't have the coconut shy back the year after . . .'

'Noconut, noconut,' Rory chanted, spinning in a circle, cutting off Clara's questions.

Lauren was rummaging in her handbag. 'I genuinely thought I might have to act as referee last night. Literally nothing that dramatic has happened here in forever.' She pulled out a tissue and tried to wipe at a mark on Rory's face. 'We go out about once a month, so it was deeply exciting that it happened on date night; it stopped me talking in detail about Rory's vaccinations and his intense bromance with George.'

'George?' Clara queried.

'Peppa Pig,' Lauren explained. 'Which is basically my world now . . .'

At the mention of Peppa Pig, Rory had looked up, almost head-butting his mother, who had given up with the tissue. 'George, watch George. Home, George.'

'Oh God, what have I started?' Lauren said as he tugged on her hand. 'I'd better go.'

'Well, it was nice to meet you,' Clara said, bending down. 'You too, Rory,' she added, which made him squeal and hide behind Lauren's coat.

'Are you staying here long?' Lauren asked, resisting Rory's urgings.

'I was planning to head to Cambridge,' Clara said.

Lauren nodded. 'That's a nice place. Good for punting. It's a shame you're not sticking around – I could have done with a new friend.'

'I'm friend,' Rory said, tugging at the bottom of her impeccable coat.

'Hmm, you are,' Lauren said, ruffling his hair. 'I actually meant a friend who can drink wine and bitch about my other friends,' she muttered to Clara.

'Ditch?' Rory repeated. His hearing was obviously pretty good.

Lauren grimaced.

Clara looked at her, a slow smile creeping over her face. 'It is a shame,' she repeated, suddenly knowing exactly where she was headed next.

Chapter 3

Joe was standing with his back to the door, brushing at the sleeve of his suit. He had them tailor-made and the fabric was straining slightly between his shoulders. He knew he needed to get back into the gym. He stood taller, studying his reflection in the window.

Beyond the glass, London was sprawled below. He could make out the dirty grey of the Thames as it snaked around the corner, the top of the London Eye in the distance. The sun had yet to fully rise, so half the city still seemed shadowy, the glow only hitting the offices above him. He stared down at the rooftops of east London, the mishmash of streets beyond, the tops of people's heads as they moved beneath him. What would they see if they looked up? Just the sleek outside of the office building, all chrome and steel and floor-to-ceiling windows. He was too far away for anyone to see him standing there in his navy pinstripe suit, his polished shoes, his tie in a Windsor knot. It made him feel taller, the fact that they moved around below, unaware that they were being watched.

He saw the thin strip of light in the reflection, the shadow of someone entering the room, and he swallowed, ready for action. Turning into the room, he thanked Pam with a curt nod of the head as she went to leave, briefed already that he did not want her to offer them coffee. She took one last look at the man who'd just walked in, biting her lip as she turned to shut the door behind her.

'Joe, morning,' the man said, striding across the room. There was a dirty mark on the shoulder of his well-cut Armani suit; it gave Joe a renewed confidence as he shook his hand.

'Matt, thank you for joining me.'

Matt raised an eyebrow, 'It's all very cloak-and-dagger. Pam was waiting for me as I got in, whisked me away before I could even turn on the computer.' He stifled a yawn with his hand.

Joe looked away. 'Yes, she had to wait half an hour for you.'

Matt didn't react, eyes on Joe's half-eaten croissant on the desk across the room. He licked his lips, which annoyed Joe further. 'Pam was telling me about her new grandson, same age as my Nancy. I told her we could have them betrothed . . . ' His voice tailed off, the first frown settling on his face.

Joe stared at him, head cocked to one side. He'd had no idea Pam had any grandchildren. He launched into his planned spiel. 'I expect you know why I've asked you here?'

Matt's frown deepened, the normally smooth olive skin between his eyebrows puckered. 'Not to tell me about this year's squash ladder, I assume.' His voice had dropped, becoming duller with each word.

Joe didn't raise a smile. 'Your team, they've been carrying you. Jules has brought in two new clients in as many months, Paddy is getting into the office at four thirty to make up for the slack you're creating . . . '

Matt stepped back as if he'd been slapped. His mouth opened, no words coming out.

'The bosses upstairs' – Joe glanced up – 'have had enough excuses from your team. You used to be a producer but you haven't brought in any new business for months. And the screw-up over Anderson was the final straw.'

'I told Karen: my associate – he messed up the pitch book. Our figures were out.'

Joe cut him off, one hand raised. 'And in the old days you would have spotted that.'

Matt fell silent. Joe looked away, not enjoying himself, suddenly remembering one day last year when Matt had covered for him. They were taking an important new client out for lunch and Joe had overslept, arrived over dessert. Matt had made a joke out of it, hadn't told anyone. Other guys would have used it to stab him in the back. He shook his head, dismissing the memory.

'So you're firing me,' Matt said, palms out flat, his voice weary. 'Is that it?'

Joe cleared his throat, tried to get back on track. He wished Paul had taken this meeting. He lived for this sort of stuff. He shifted on one foot, started listing reasons on his fingers: 'Consistently late into the office, often unable to be present at meetings, a shortfall on the figures, ineffective team management...'

Matt listened, his cheeks reddening as the list went on.

Joe stopped, looked at him. 'It's a warning, mate.'

'We're not mates.'

Joe cleared his throat again. He deserved that.

'Look, we just need you to sort things out and get back on top. We want to see you producing again, bring in some business.'

Matt's eyes were dull as he looked at Joe. 'God, I got you wrong. I thought...' He paused, then straightened, chin out. 'You're one cold bastard, you know that?' Joe didn't flinch as Matt continued: 'All you and the rich twats upstairs want is profit, profit, profit.'

'You used to want that too.'

'And I still do.' Matt threw up both his hands; Joe took a step back. 'So I've been spending a few more hours at home. We've got our first kid, Joe. You know how long we tried for a baby. God.' He stopped, raking a hand through his hair. 'I practically fucking cried on you in the bar that night, telling

22

you what we'd been through. It's been hard, but it's getting easier; she's sleeping through now, almost. I want to help Suzie, she can't do it on her own, Joe.'

Joe held up a hand. 'I know, and I'm sorry, but—'

'You're not bloody sorry.'

Something inside Joe snapped. He didn't want to be here, he didn't want to be doing this. It made his voice harsher as he tried to justify himself. 'We're under pressure, Matt, you know that, you know what's happening here at the moment. You lost us that merger with Anderson Corporate, the Kline Brothers got in before us. We were too slow. We need to be better. So take this as your first formal warning.' He paused, before adding, 'You're lucky.'

'Lucky? Oh yes, how decent of you, *mate*, thank you so much,' Matt said, his voice flaring up. 'Just a first formal warning. You know they'll find an excuse to fire me. You know that.'

Joe looked away, not wanting to hear it, knowing as he did that Karen would want him to report back, knowing how these things worked. Matt had a target on his back. 'You'll be all right,' he said, his voice smaller, his confidence ebbing.

Matt glared at him, 'Well, if that's all, I'd better take my ineffective arse back to my useless team and start work.'

Joe looked back at the windows.

'You'd better hope you never need to be cut some slack,' Matt said, turning to leave. He walked across the room, Joe following his reflection in the glass. He paused at the door before turning back. 'You know there's more to life than this job, mate.'

Joe shrugged once, didn't answer, brushing at his sleeve again as he watched Matt leave, the strip of light disappearing as the door shut behind him.

The sun had risen fully now, its rays on the office building opposite dazzling Joe for a second. He pulled his phone out of his pocket, checking for new emails, an update on their latest deal. He looked at the screen. A missed call from his mother. She was probably on one of her early-morning walks and wanted to tell him about the sunrise. He sighed. He hadn't got the energy for that now. With a small spark of guilt, he put the phone back in his pocket. He'd ring her back later.

Chapter 4

Louisa threw the phone in frustration. It landed amongst the two huge bundles of rejected clothes.

'Stop staring,' she said to the cage in the corner of the room. 'You know I can't take you with me. It's a bird flu thing.'

The parrot gave her a withering look down its beak and moved deliberately along its perch, one careful foot over the other. 'YOU'RE FIRED,' it called out before turning to face the corner.

'Fine, be like that,' Louisa said, holding up a mustard-yellow cardigan and throwing it onto the left-hand pile. A large ginger cat stretched out in front of the log fire paused in cleaning its paws. 'God, not you too? Will you both stop! I'm feeling guilty enough already and I don't need you adding to it.'

Her suitcase was open, towels, swimsuits, books and clothes in an enormous haphazard heap inside. It had taken her an hour to find her passport and she was now impossibly rushed, the clock in the kitchen utterly useless as it had run out of batteries about a year before and was giving her a heart attack every time she thought it really was 11.05 a.m. She knew she was muttering again, but since the previous night in the pub and bloody Roz being all high and mighty, she hadn't been able to stop. She'd been telling Lady CaCa all about it, but now the bird had got the hump on seeing a suitcase.

'Can you please turn back around, I want to finish the story,' she said to the cage. 'I'll let you out for a few minutes.' At this, Roddy the ginger cat looked up, fur instantly raised, yellow eyes wary. 'Oh hush, Roddy, don't be silly.'

The promise had worked and the parrot had turned back round and moved down the perch towards the door of the cage, waiting with an imperious expression on her face as Louisa reached up to open it. 'LOVELY JUBBLY, LOVELY JUBBLY.'

The buzzer rang and Louisa swore, dropping her hand before she had touched the cage. The parrot gave an angry caw.

'Oh bugger. Hold on, darling.'

Lady CaCa padded back to her spot, furiously spinning round to stare at the corner once more. 'YOU'RE FIRED, SHITHEAD.'

Louisa rolled her eyes; she really was the most diva-like

26

parrot. She wavered as she stood next to the intercom. She couldn't see the high street from any of the windows. It wasn't long until the cab was due, though, so she pressed the button tentatively.

'Reg? If that's you, you're early,' she said.

A voice she didn't recognise responded. 'No, it's Clara, you don't know me but, um ... well, it's Clara.'

Louisa released the button and turned to look at the cat, who had returned to cleaning his paws. 'Who's Clara?' she asked. He didn't look up.

Louisa shrugged and turned back to press the button. 'Come up,' she said, looking round at the flat, which was littered with her entire wardrobe.

She heard footsteps on the narrow staircase as she went to open the flaking door. A young blonde girl appeared, dressed in jeans, a soft woollen jumper and a purple knitted hat. Impossibly smooth skin, bright blue eyes already lit with a smile, her face vaguely familiar. Louisa frowned.

'Thank you. I'm so sorry just to burst in,' the girl said, reaching the top step. 'God, I am so unfit,' she laughed, holding her sides. 'One flight of steps and I need to sit down.' There was something about her that made Louisa feel a warm glow. She found herself smiling straight back at her.

'Come in, come in,' she said, closing the door. 'But, um, who are you exactly?'

The girl straightened up, her cheeks flushed from the cold outside. 'I'm Clara, I'm staying in the pub; I was there last night.'

'Oh God.' Louisa threw her hands in the air. 'What a night. Carrot cake?' she offered.

'Ooh yes please. I was looking for a café or something just now. I haven't had any breakfast.'

'You'll be hard pushed to find a café,' Louisa said, picking up a fuchsia sarong and throwing it in the direction of the suitcase. 'It's on the counter. I made it yesterday, it's Lady CaCa's favourite.' She nodded her head at the cage. 'Cut yourself a slice – actually, cut me one too, do you mind? I'm right in the middle of packing – my flight, you know . . .'

'Oh, of course, of course.' Clara crossed the room, picking her way round the piles of things, jumping as the parrot called out 'YOU'RE FIRED!'

Louisa waved a hand as she scrabbled in the back of the wardrobe. 'Sorry about that, and the mess. I'd love to say it's because I'm packing, but actually it often looks like this.' She pulled out a pair of bronze flip-flops and grinned. 'Hurrah! I knew they were here somewhere,' she said, holding them aloft.

Clara looked at the succulent orange sponge and picked up a knife. 'So you are really going? Where are you off to?'

Louisa, bent over a drawer under a divan bed, didn't look up. 'Madrid,' she called out.

Clara moved a slice of carrot cake onto a plate. 'How romantic,' she sighed, picturing winding cobbled streets, bright flamenco dancers at every turn, large jugs of sangria, people laughing in sunlit squares.

Louisa was lost behind the bed, both feet poking out of

the end. 'It's seventeen degrees right now, can you imagine? EIGHTEEN DEGREES IN NOVEMBER,' she shouted, making the cat sit up and look around for the noise. Her head appeared suddenly, suspended above the duvet, her body lost behind the bed. 'I can't remember what eighteen degrees feels like; the summer seems forever ago and anyway, that was mostly rain. I want sun, sun on my face, on my arms, neck, back, I want my feet to burn on sand and I want to step into the sea and say, "Oh what a relief, it's cool" because it's just so HOT.' She dived down again, her head disappearing, 'Don't mean to DEPRESS, but I'm sure you understand.'

Clara had moved across to a bar stool, perching herself on top of it. 'Hmm, I've never been used to too much heat. In Denmark it's currently about three degrees.'

'THREE?' Louisa's head appeared over the duvet, curly hair wild. 'Good God, how does anyone get anything done?' She looked horrified. 'Surely you should all just hibernate like bears.'

'Well, actually' – Clara smiled, thinking of winters at home: the months of slow-cooked stews, steaming cups of *gløgg* and roaring fires – 'they sort of do.'

As she pulled off her purple hat so that her hair fell around her shoulders, her smile faded a fraction. There would be no more winters like those of her childhood, with all of them sitting round their large oak table, bowls of steaming meatballs ready to be eaten. She blinked, not wanting to keep going over the same old thoughts.

29

In the corner, Lady CaCa was looking down her beak at Clara as she ate her cake, flapping her wings aggressively at the bars of the cage every time she glanced over.

Louisa hopped up onto another bar stool, wearing a large hat with enormous sunflowers stitched into the side. 'Oh, ignore her.' She waved a hand at the cage. 'She gets jealous when someone else is here taking my attention, and also carrot cake is her favourite.' She cut the edge off her slice and delivered it on the flat of the knife into the cage. The parrot looked at it furiously, spinning back around to face the wall. Louisa sighed. 'I fear her strop will last till I leave – she knows I'm packing.'

'What will happen to her?' Clara asked, putting another piece of carrot cake in her mouth. 'This is amazing, by the way,' she mumbled.

Louisa nodded. 'I know. I'm an exceptional baker, always have been, it's one of my skills. That and tarot-card reading. Oh, and glass-blowing. I've never tried kite-surfing but I always feel I'd excel there too. What are your skills, Clara?'

Clara looked startled for a moment. 'Well, I suppose … well, I … '

'Come on, come on, everyone has skills. They just don't like to shout about them because of modesty, which is silly. I am absolutely useless at some things and regularly remind people of them – like the time I tried to learn the violin: just horrendous, like someone was dying in the flat every night. And jigsaw puzzles, ugh, I get so cross, I cut all the little arms off the pieces so they fit – just so infuriating. But

30

I do make an excellent lemon drizzle.' She had thrown her arms wide, the sunflowers moving every time she turned her head.

'So what will happen? To your animals?' Clara repeated, diverting attention away from her skills – or lack of them.

Louisa waved a hand. 'One of the things I need to do before I go is drop my keys in to Gavin. He'll look in on them; he did it once before when I went to Thailand for a shaking retreat.'

'I see,' Clara said, too thrown off course to ask what a shaking retreat entailed. She brushed a crumb from her top lip.

Louisa paused, wiping the corner of her own mouth slowly. 'So how can I help?' She leapt up, the hat falling off. 'I've got about two seconds to do a hundred things, so you'll have to help and we'll talk as we work.'

Clara slid off her stool. 'Of course. What can I do?'

Louisa pointed to a roll of bin liners on the counter-top. 'Perishables. Throw out all perishables in the fridge. Last time I forgot and was nearly killed on my return by a Brussels pâté that was so off it had legs.'

Clara's nose wrinkled as she reached for the roll.

'Sooooo . . . ' Louisa returned to the pile of clothes on the bed, throwing some over her shoulder, holding up others and gradually reducing the enormous pile, 'what can I do for you?'

Clara had opened the fridge and was staring at the contents: mostly bottles of pink champagne, mussels and olives. There was a slab of smoked salmon but it seemed desperately sad to just throw it away. She picked up half a lemon and chucked it in the bag. 'Well, I was wondering . . . I heard you were off, last night in the pub. I was there, you see, staying there—'

'Yes, you said.' Louisa paused, holding up a striped swimming costume. 'Goodness, what a palaver that was. Roz of course propping up the bar, typical stirring. I just needed to rage and she makes me so furious . . . I didn't know Gavin rented rooms: how wonderful, he is enterprising . . .'

Clara's mouth was still open from where she'd been cut off.

'Sorry, sorry, you were saying . . .' Louisa waved her on, squeezing the swimming costume into the side pocket of the now bulging suitcase.

'Well, I just wondered whether perhaps you'd consider letting me house-sit for you, look after your animals . . . but it sounds like you've already made plans, of course you have . . .' Clara trailed away.

'Come and help me sit on it,' Louisa called.

'Sorry?'

'The suitcase. Come on, the taxi is bound to appear at any second and I don't want him seeing my smalls. Although if it's Reg, he's actually already seen . . . Sorry, do carry on.'

Clara stepped across the room to the bed, lowering herself down next to Louisa, who was already perched on the suitcase, wearing the sunflower hat again. On the bedside table was a silver photo frame: Louisa and the most jaw-dropping man. Broody grey eyes, dark brown hair, emerging stubble on a tanned face. Louisa had her arm around his waist, head on his shoulder. He must have been more than twenty years younger than her, closer to Clara's age. Clara almost forgot what she had been saying.

'That was it, really. The house-sitting and, well, I did wonder, about the shop. I've run a business before and I thought, to return the favour . . . I can't pay rent, you see, but I could work for free. It seems a shame to close just before Christmas.'

Louisa scoffed. 'You'll be lucky if you get one customer a day.'

'At least let me try. From what I saw from the outside, it's a wonderful shop.'

'It used to be a wonderful shop,' she said. 'It was a lovely place.' She fell silent, lost somewhere in the past as they sat side by side.

'I was going to move on, but I like it here. I just . . . feel it, do you know what I mean?' Clara said, one hand moving to her stomach. 'That feeling inside, that it's right.'

Louisa raised an eyebrow. 'And people say I'm eccentric.'

Clara felt her cheeks fill with colour. She hopped off the now closed suitcase. 'It was silly, a spur-of-the-moment thought. I'll let you finish up,' she said, reaching for her purple hat.

Louisa heaved herself off the edge of the bed, staring around at the flat that wasn't any closer to looking neat. 'I can't leave you here with everything in this state,' she said.

'I haven't tidied since 1973. The spare room is an actual bombsite.'

'No, of course not, I should have realised,' Clara said, stuttering over the words now.

'But if you are insisting,' Louisa sighed, looking at her with an imperious gaze. 'Begging me . . .'

Clara picked up on her changed tone. 'Oh, I am,' she nodded. 'Begging, that is. It's a cosy flat. I love it, and I can take good care of your pets.' She waved at the cage and the rug.

'Someone does need to look after Lady CaCa and Roddy,' Louisa mused.

'Of course, I'd love to. And I can tidy, it will be no trouble,' Clara added. 'It will be lovely to stay in a home-from-home rather than another B and B.'

Louisa had marched across the room to the kitchen and was sifting through a drawer next to the fridge. In alarm, Clara watched as she pulled out an enormous butcher's knife. 'Well,' she called, bracelets jangling menacingly. Diving back into the drawer, she held up a small bunch of keys. 'Spare keys,' she announced. 'Lady CaCa, Roddy,' she turned to the cage and the rug in turn, 'meet your new room-mate, Clara.'

Clara's face, white with shock moments before, broke into an enormous smile. 'Oh, excellent. Really? Brilliant. I can't wait.'

A buzzer sounded.

'NO LIKEY NO LIGHTY,' the parrot called just as Louisa yelped.

'Agh, the taxi,' she cried, thrusting the keys at Clara and racing from handbag to suitcase muttering 'Passport, tickets, passport, money, passport, underwear, passport, clothes, passport, books, passport, hat, passport, swimming costume, passport.'

'So,' Clara stood on the spot, holding the keys in her hand, 'is there anything much I need to know?'

'No time, no time. I'll email you the details – write down your address.' Louisa flung a pen at her and held out the back of her hand.

Clara started to scrawl on it. 'Although I don't really check my e—'

'Good, good.' Louisa nodded, watching her write. 'Well, a few things before I go – COMING, REG!' she shouted in response to a voice through the letter box below. 'You need to feed Roddy and Lady CaCa, obviously, and Lady CaCa refuses to talk to you unless she has a clean cage. She likes the *Daily Mail* for the lining of the cage – she likes to shit on the headlines, it's her thing, she's a very left-wing parrot – and don't ever give her chicken, or any meat, she won't talk to you for a month. I once fed her something with chicken stock and she vomited it all up over a picture of Donald Trump, which I'm not sure was entirely undeliberate. She speaks only in swear words and TV catchphrases. The shop is not too tricky, the till can stick, we close on Sundays and Mondays, and early on Saturdays, but really hardly anyone comes in. I can send instructions. Actually, Lauren knows – she was in the pub last night, do you remember? The blonde, pretty but also impossibly nice. So unfair. She used to work in the shop part-time when we were busy – talk to her, she's fantastic.'

'We've met actually . . .' Clara put the lid back on the pen.

'Have you? Well, that's a bit of luck.' Louisa read the back of her hand. 'That's a four, is it? Right, excellent. Funny address.'

'I'm Danish,' Clara explained.

'How splendid. I once had an affair with a man from Copenhagen who couldn't pronounce the word "sixth". It was hilarious and he was amazing in bed, so creative. I like Danes.'

Clara found her mouth flapping open.

'On the corkboard is the list of local numbers for if the water pipes break or something is set on fire – you never know, I once had to cancel a fondue night because I'd set the living room alight with lighter fuel – and the recycling goes on a Monday, I think, but I can never remember so I just put it out every now and again and hope for the best . . . and, oh, my son, Joe, he'll need to know – he lives in London, I've been calling him every hour since dawn but no luck, which is not surprising because he's always absurdly busy, so if he phones, please tell him I'll be in touch. Or his number's on the corkboard, so if you wanted you could call him. STOP SHOUTING, REG, I'M COMING. Right, darling, must fly. How marvellous, I feel a million times better knowing you'll be here, you have excellent energy.'

She kissed her on each cheek, Clara barely able to stutter

a goodbye as she watched Louisa turn and head down the stairs, suitcase banging, the large sunhat plonked on her head. Staring down at the keys in her hand, she heard the downstairs door slam and wondered just what she'd done.

Chapter 5

The street seemed to have become even gloomier while she'd been in Louisa's flat. Dusty glass fronts now speckled with raindrops, the concrete paving stones, the tarmac of the road, the clouds above her all the same heavy grey as she headed back up the high street to the pub. There were a few people about: a woman up ahead in wellington boots walking a springer spaniel, a man unloading boxes from the back of a minivan, a cyclist sweeping past – a strange flash of neon and then gone. Her footsteps felt heavy as she made her way back to the pub, pushing through the door of the bar to see Gavin scrubbing at the counter with a cloth.

'There you are,' he said, pausing to look at her.

Clara moved towards him, crossing her arms over her

chest, her skin covered in goose bumps, the pub colder this morning with no punters. 'I went for a walk.'

He continued to wipe the surface. 'Did you get across the fields to the line of trees? There's a stream that runs all the way to the next village.'

'Oh no, I was exploring the high street.' She just managed to stop herself adding that she'd been looking for breakfast, worried that she would offend him, picturing the sad banana and box of cereal on the tray beside her single bed. She must make sure she took them with her. 'Actually, I ended up seeing Louisa. I'm going to stay on, house-sit for her while she's away,' she explained.

'She's really going?' Gavin stopped scrubbing.

'She's gone.'

His eyes widened. 'Gone?'

Clara nodded. 'Just now.'

'Did she say anything?' he asked, not meeting her eye but returning to circling the cloth along the bar.

'Say anything?' Clara repeated.

'A message? For me, or someone . . . She often does when she goes away . . .'

Clara couldn't help a small smile as she watched a blush build in his face. 'She was in a huge rush,' she explained. 'She was going to ask you to look after the animals, but obviously I'm there so I'll make sure they're fed and watered . . .'

'I'll message her through Words with Friends; we've just started a new game,' he said, flashing his mobile at her.

'I don't know it,' Clara said, looking at lots of letters on a board.

'Well, it's basically Scrabble online, an app. It's Louisa's turn; I've been waiting all morning for her to see my last word – six letters, DRAPER. I hope she doesn't have an S because it's so near the triple word, but she's obviously been packing. She'll probably leave me a message there, we often do . . . ' He trailed away, his face now puce.

'I'm sure she will, and I'd love some advice about her pets. The parrot in particular sounds tricky . . . '

'Lady CaCa?' Gavin stopped. 'She's more than tricky, she's a potty-mouthed nightmare.'

Clara laughed. 'Sounds terrifying. Oh, also Louisa asked me to call her son. I've written down his number but I couldn't see a phone in her flat.'

'Probably buried,' Gavin snorted. 'No idea how that woman finds anything. You should see what she keeps in her handbag.'

'Well, I was wondering if you had a landline I could use? Or your mobile? I thought it might be nice for me to intro-duce myself.'

Gavin looked confused for a second.

'I don't have one,' Clara shrugged.

'No mobile?' Gavin repeated, his mouth an O. 'I thought everyone under the age of thirty was surgically attached to one.'

Clara felt the usual need to explain. 'I used to, but . . . ' She paused, not really wanting to delve into this topic further, knowing it threw up lots of other questions. 'But now I don't.'

'Well, go ahead any time,' he said, holding out his mobile. 'Or use the landline by the till. Don't expect an answer, though. Louisa always complains that she has a far more intimate relationship with Joe's voicemail than with any man.' He chuckled at that, a warmth filling his eyes as he said her name.

Clara headed to the phone, tapping out the number she'd scribbled on a scrap of paper. As predicted, it went straight to voicemail, a smooth, confident voice filling her ear and asking her to leave a message. She almost missed the beep.

'Hi, my name's Clara, I'm staying ... well, your mother asked me to tell you that I'm staying in her flat. While she's away, in Madrid. I'm going to run the shop. I think she's tried to call y—'

A robotic-sounding woman's voice cut her off: 'You have reached the end of this message. Please press one to re-record.' Clara was so startled she hung up.

'Oh,' she said, backing away from the phone.

'All OK?' Gavin asked, sitting on a stool staring into space, cloth hanging from his hand.

Clara nodded, knowing the message hadn't been a big success but not wanting to leave a second one for fear of sounding like an idiot.

'I'd better go and pack up my things.'

'I'll help you down with that bag,' he said, following her up the narrow staircase, ducking to avoid the beams above his head. 'It looked heavy.'

'It's no problem,' Clara called over her shoulder, realising she hadn't even had a shower that morning, aware that her hair was filthy. Gavin's wide shoulders and bulky frame filled the stairwell. She felt the walls closing in as she fumbled with her room key, the low ceiling and dark beams pressing down. 'So you only have the one room?' she asked, searching for something to say.

'Just the one, no cause for more,' Gavin said, edging closer to a door nearby as he talked.

Clara had a strange feeling that he was nervous. She jerked her head at the long corridor. 'There seem to be a lot more,' she said, catching a flash of something as he pulled the door shut, the click of the old latch loud, a swift turn of a key in the lock.

'No, no, just … private use, you know,' he said, double-checking the lock, shifting his eyes left and right, unable to look at her.

Clara wondered what was behind the door. She felt the atmosphere shift, Gavin's easy nature morphing into something else. The tension was there in the silence that surrounded them.

'Well,' she said, trying to reclaim the previous mood, 'it's a lovely room. I had a very good sleep, great mattress,' she added, diving into the room to remove the banana as fast as she could. She wanted to clean her teeth after the sugary carrot cake, but with Gavin standing outside waiting for her, she was in a rush now to get out of there.

He took her bag, indicating that she should go on ahead,

quickening his pace as they passed the closed door on the way down. Clara suddenly had a terrible image of a previous guest tied up and gagged, waiting for rescue, something to explain his edgy behaviour.

She paid her bill in silence, thanking him as she turned to go.

'Here, take this,' he said, waving a voucher at her, utterly relaxed again now they were back in the bar, the previous atmosphere forgotten. 'It's for steak night. Tuesdays. Steak and a glass of wine for ten pounds. We serve food on Tuesdays and Saturdays.'

'Oh, thanks,' Clara said, accepting it and tucking it into her jeans pocket. 'Sounds good.'

He insisted on shutting the bar and walking back down the high street with her, shouldering her backpack as if it weighed nothing, pointing out old shops, giving her some of the history of the place. His eyes crinkled as he recounted the time he and Louisa had ice-skated in the car park of the village hall, how she'd fallen and he'd almost put his back out catching her. He was chuckling, lost in the past.

'Thank you,' Clara said as he passed her the rucksack outside the front door of the shop. He left with a last wave and she lugged the bag up the stairs to the flat. She wasn't in the mood to unpack, though; could feel her curiosity pulling at her, wanting to get down and see the shop.

She clattered back down the stairs, trying one of the keys in the door that led off the hall, a side door into the shop. Pushing her way in, she searched around for a light switch;

the shutters pulled down on the window meant the shop was in darkness. She wished for her old mobile then, the ability to make it a torch so she could find her way round. 'Ow!' she yelped into the space, her calf hitting something sharp. Finally her fingers found the promising feel of plastic and she flicked down a switch, then another, until various strip lights hummed into life, revealing every corner of the shop.

It was full to bursting with stock, displayed in the most haphazard way. Shelves were crammed full of dolls, jigsaws, cars, oversized wooden letters and numbers, board games. There were wire baskets overflowing with various goodies: neon footballs, large foam hands and soft toys. Clara wandered down the aisles, marvelling at the number of items, some things hidden behind others, boxes that had fallen down at the back, a thin film of dust on some of the shelves that made her wonder when they were last looked at. It was a riot on the senses, almost overwhelming in its garishness. It reminded her of a mismatched aunt, surrounded by a dozen bags crammed with things, multicoloured shawls draped round her neck, large beaded necklaces clashing with diamanté earrings. She switched off one of the lights to dull the effect as she continued her search.

The till was towards the back of the shop, set on a counter that was covered in paper, receipts, key rings, candy bars, pots of pencils, lollipops and more. It made Clara's head ache just looking at it. A calculator poked out from below a pad, doodles on every sheet: parrots, cats, lots of flowers, stars, hearts, eyes and Gs of every size.

She moved past more shelves at the back, frowning as she saw myriad boxes stacked behind each other, all containing different things. She tugged on the handle of a cupboard in a corner of the room, the door sticking. It opened with a groan and she moved into the small space, reaching up to pull down some of the items on the top shelf: beautifully carved wooden pieces, dust dulling their colours. She ran a finger along the back of a stunning rocking horse, his mane falling over one eye, his body painted in exquisite colours.

As she moved around the cupboard, a thought sparked inside her, the idea growing as she looked deeper. She felt her stomach tighten, her fingers itching to get started already. A smile had formed as she closed the cupboard door, ready to make some drawings of her own, pausing only briefly, distracted by another door across the way. She moved towards it, pushing it open and gasping at the enormous space that opened up before her. She was just about to walk inside when she heard the sound of knocking. A hand flew to her mouth. Turning, she saw Lauren, nose pressed against the pane of glass in the side door.

'Sorry, did I frighten you? You left the door open,' she explained, pointing behind her. 'Then I saw the lights on.'

'Did I? Oh that's dreadful. It's my first day as caretaker, I'm hopeless,' Clara said, her heart still racing from the shock.

'Caretaker?' Lauren cocked her head to one side.

'Long story.'

'Well, there's nothing much to take in the corridor, apart from leaflets for pizza delivery, and I suppose if they brought along their own screwdriver they could make off with the coat hooks. Effort, though,' Lauren mused, looking at Clara and grinning. 'Sorry, I was just walking to pick Rory up from nursery – he does a few hours every day now. Am I a terrible person for admitting that sometimes they're the best hours in my day?'

Clara smiled. 'Of course not, I can imagine you'd need the break.'

'I do need the break,' Lauren said, following Clara into the shop. 'That series of *The Crown* isn't going to watch itself!'

Clara laughed. 'I haven't seen it.'

'It's historically very accurate and interesting and you learn lots about the royal family. And also: Matt Smith. Hmm.'

'Do you mostly watch it for Matt Smith?'

Lauren hung her head so her strawberry-blonde hair fell forward. 'Yes.'

'I don't know him. Not sure he's big in Denmark. We're more into Viggo Mortensen.'

'Um . . .'

Clara raised an eyebrow, 'Are you saying you've never watched *Lord of the Rings*? You are missing out. He was Aragorn.'

'Isn't that all about elves?' Lauren's nose crinkled. 'I'm not really into pixie folk.'

'He's not a pix— Look, he's good-looking, take my word for it.'

Lauren was already distracted anyway, had picked up a large foam finger from a basket and was putting it on. 'I wonder if Rory would get the message better if I wore this when I'm telling him off.'

'Not sure it would have the desired effect,' Clara admitted, looking at Lauren and her oversized hand. 'This, however' – she pulled out a plastic policeman's helmet and popped it on her own head – 'this could do it.'

Lauren nodded. 'Definitely. It would give me that extra authority.' She pointed a hand in front of her as if signalling traffic. 'So are you looking after the shop?'

Clara nodded. 'I'm house-sitting for Louisa and running the shop in return.'

'How brilliant. Yay, a friend!' Lauren said, waving the foam finger around.

'I want to open it up.' Clara shrugged. 'But first I need to do something to attract attention. And, well . . . ' She felt heat fill her face, removing the policeman's helmet as she said, 'I think I've got an idea. Want to hear it?'

She felt lighter climbing the stairs back to the flat. She'd spent the rest of the day in the shop after Lauren left, feeling buoyed by her reaction. She'd started sorting through the stock and had only called a halt when her stomach had rumbled so loudly she thought she had set off some vibrating toy. It had got dark already and she pushed open the door to the flat, nudging her rucksack out of the way.

She knew she needed to sort the flat out, but at that moment all she had the energy to do was get ready for bed.

She obviously made a mistake by not acknowledging the parrot, who called out, 'IS IT BECAUSE I IS BLACK? IS IT BECAUSE I IS BLACK?' as she made her way into the bathroom.

She stood in the doorway, smiling at the sight of the large iron claw-foot bath littered with towels. She whisked around the room as quickly as she could, piling up towels, clothes and more into a heap for washing, and scrubbing the enamel. Searching the bathroom cabinet for something suitable, she reached to the back for a glass bottle of rose-scented oil, pouring droplets into the bath and hearing the clank of the pipes as water gushed from the tap. As the bath filled, she unearthed a tea light from a side pocket of her rucksack and, lighting it with the flame from the hob, sat it on the windowsill, turning the bathroom light off so that the room now flickered with shadows.

As she stepped into the bath, she felt the silkiness of the water, the scent rising off the steam, felt comforted by the yellow glow of the walls. Resting her head back, she felt her muscles unwind, giggling as Roddy the ginger cat padded into the room, immediately curling up in the middle of the heap of towels. Clara shut her eyes, enjoying her first bath in over a week. It was the thing she missed most about her old home; many bed and breakfasts or hostels only had showers. This was blissful, she thought as she allowed her brain to slow down, returning to the day's discoveries, the shop, her plans.

Then the fog cleared, and one single idea leapt out at her, so strong that she found herself lurching into a sitting position and fumbling for a towel. Stepping out of the bath, hair dripping onto her shoulders, she left the bathroom and walked across the flat, too focused to think to find her slipper socks, rushing back down the staircase to the shop, practically dropping the key in her excitement to get back in, knowing where she was headed, what she wanted to see.

She passed the till and the cupboard in the corner and then pushed open the door to the back room. It was a large room, with two bay windows, window seat cushions lost underneath piles of paper, looking out over the square of garden outside. Even in winter the lawn looked lush and green, bordered by hedges and pots filled with evidence of flowers and herbs. A large table sat in the middle of the room, chairs scattered around the edges, and Clara walked around it slowly, skirting empty cardboard boxes and broken toys and leaving wet footprints on the floor as the idea that had begun in the bath became fully formed. This was it, the heart of her plan, and she felt a familiar fizz of excitement. She bit her lip, impatient now to get dressed and get to work.

'Louisa. LOUISA.'

Clara froze in the doorway of the room as the voice echoed in the space.

'LOUISA.'

She moved tentatively through the shop, towards the voice. Just as she emerged through the side door and into the corridor, an eye appeared in the blank space of the letter box.

'Louisa, is that you?'

'Um,' Clara said, pulling her towel tighter as the eye swivelled her way.

'You're not Louisa,' the voice said, stating the obvious. The letter box snapped closed again.

'No,' Clara said, feeling stupid talking to the back of the door.

The letter box opened again. 'Who are you and where is Louisa?'

The eyes were outlined in black kohl and were narrowed in suspicion. Clara had a sudden urge to laugh. She stepped across to the door, her bare feet cold on the tiles of the hallway.

'Hold on.' She pulled on the latch and opened the door to find Roz standing up, one arm behind her back, the other hand smoothing her auburn hair.

She pointed at Clara. 'Your hair is wet,' she said, as if Clara wasn't aware.

'I was having a bath,' Clara explained, feeling absurd lingering on the doorstep in a towel. Not wearing knickers was a surefire way of making her feel vulnerable.

'A bath?' Roz arched a thickly pencilled eyebrow.

'Do you want to come in?' Clara said, desperate to get back to the flat and into some clothes. She was already assessing the best way to climb the stairs without flashing her first guest.

'I wanted to speak to Louisa,' Roz said, folding her arms across her chest.

'She's not here.'

'And who are you?'

Clara frowned. 'I'm Clara.'

'Well, Clara, when will she be back?'

'Back?'

'Louisa.' Roz tapped a long nail on her palm in impatience.

'Oh, she's gone,' Clara said. 'Spain, you know, like she said last night.'

Roz's eyebrows lifted. 'She left.' That seemed to unfreeze her, and she marched across the threshold and straight up the stairs, leaving Clara to close the door and run up after her.

Roz was standing in the doorway, her face twisted as she took in the carnage inside the flat. Louisa's belongings on every surface, Clara's rucksack spilling its contents on the carpet, Roddy's orange hairs covering everything else.

'YOU ARE THE WEAKEST LINK, GOODBYE.' Lady CaCa was parading up and down her perch, looking at Roz, head thrown back intermittently to shout the words. Clara stifled a giggle with one hand, the towel slipping just as Roz turned so that she found herself flashing one breast at her.

'Oh dear,' she said, covering her escaped boob, the Anne Robinson impression still on a loop behind her. 'Sorry, um, how can I help?' she asked, not doing very well at disguising her giggles. She hiccoughed.

'You haven't explained what you're doing here. Have you broken in?'

Clara hiccoughed again. 'Broken … No, of course not,' she said, drawing herself up to her not-very-substantial height. 'Louisa asked me to house-sit for her, look after the animals,' she said, pointing at Roddy, who was curled up in the middle of the bed in a nest made of tie-dye clothes, and Lady CaCa, who was now shaking her foot out, ruffling her wings.

'NO LIKEY NO LIGHTY.'

Clara pretended she hadn't heard the parrot, feeling the sides of her mouth twitch again.

'So she's just swanned off and left the shop to fester, has she?'

'No, no actually, I'm going to open it up,' Clara said, her previous excitement bubbling up, her smile wide. She was about to launch into an explanation, her latest big idea. She wanted to share it with someone. She knew it would work.

She was about to start when Roz cut her off. 'What do you mean, open it up? You can't just open it up. How absurd.'

Clara snapped her mouth shut.

'You don't know a thing about it, and I'm sure even Louisa wouldn't just hand over the keys and the till …' She paused, looking at Clara as if she was about to slope off with a massive bag labelled SWAG, 'to a total stranger.'

Clara was too shocked to interrupt. A breeze from the

open door was making her skin break out into goose bumps as she watched Roz park herself on a bar stool at the kitchen counter.

'It's outrageous. Bad enough that she's just LEFT, but handing over the shop to a nobody, someone not from the village, or even England . . .' Roz arched an eyebrow.

Clara wrapped her towel more firmly around herself. Was her Danish accent that obvious? Did others see her as a stranger? She thought of Louisa, whirling around the place; had she really stopped to think? Had Clara bullied her into a rash decision she would live to regret? She felt her previous certainty that she was doing the right thing shaken as Roz continued to talk.

'I wanted to discuss things with her. If she's not going to run the place . . . well, I'm not talking it through with you. When is she back?'

'I'm really not sure,' Clara said, feeling her fists curl as she stood in bare feet watching this rude women stomp about the flat.

'It's so typical of her, no thought at all, just swanning off leaving the rest of us to pick up the pieces . . .'

Clara noticed a red light flashing on a side table behind Roz, as if emphasising her next sentence.

'And now you want to open up the shop without her. It's preposterous. You have no idea what this village needs, no idea at all.'

'I don't think it takes a rocket scientist to work it out,' Clara said, drawing herself up to her full height as she readjusted the towel. She wished she was wearing clothes. She'd be taken a lot more seriously in clothes.

Roz sniffed. 'I'll leave you to it then,' she said. As she passed by the kitchen counter she dropped a slice of carrot cake into a piece of kitchen roll and folded it up. 'She won't be needing it,' she said, not having the decency even to blush. Striding across the flat with one last sharp look at Clara, she headed to the door.

'NICE TO SEE YOU, TO SEE YOU NICE, SHITHEAD,' squawked Lady CaCa.

When Clara heard the door below bang shut, she rushed into the bedroom to quickly towel-dry her hair and find her clothes, pulling on every layer she had to warm herself up. What an unpleasant woman. No wonder she'd fallen out with Louisa; she was utterly vile. Well, Clara wasn't giving up because of this setback.

As she pulled a jumper over her head, she was distracted again by the red flashing light. It was an answerphone on the table, an old-fashioned one attached to a wire that led into a half-closed drawer and to the missing phone. A red number 3 blinked in the small screen. Three messages. They must have arrived while she was in the shop.

She pressed the button, searching quickly for a pen and paper to write down any message for when Louisa returned, stepping back when she heard a booming male voice fill the room: the smooth, confident man from the voicemail earlier, who now seemed a lot louder and angrier.

Lady CaCa had started yelling, 'MASTER OF THE

HOUSE, MASTER OF THE HOUSE, LOVE ISLAND JOE,' so Clara struggled to hear the first few sentences, but there was no mistaking the tone of the message.

'... I don't know who you are, but you can't just leave a message saying you're living in my mother's flat after packing her off to Spain. I haven't even spoken to her yet, and running the shop? We don't *know* you and ...' The offensive message continued, but Clara had heard enough. She sank onto a bar stool, her head dropping onto her chest, her arms heavy. Did no one want her here? She felt gloomy as she let the voice ring around the flat.

Then she thought of Lauren's reaction, Gavin, the toys downstairs, the ideas she had. It wasn't all hopeless. And she'd seen the village: it needed something to change. She wanted to help. She needed to help. She lifted her head and spoke into the silence.

'I'm not going to just give up,' she said.

And a scream from above added, 'DO YOU FEEL LUCKY, PUNK? WELL, DO YA?'

Chapter 6

Joe slammed the mobile down on his desk. No reply and another message left. What had his mother been thinking, just leaving like that, without any kind of warning?

He rubbed the sides of his head with his thumbs, massaging his temples and trying to focus on the screen in front of him. London was lit up in the window opposite, the East End below, people milling in pubs, moving to restaurants, bundled up against the cold. He could make out the outline of his own reflection in the glass, his tie loosened, his jacket over the chair, his sleeves rolled up. The central heating in the office was always set to tropical, and he felt beads of sweat on his hairline as he threw himself down into the chair.

He'd ordered them all dinner. It was being couriered over and the team were due back in any second. They'd have to eat it at their desks, as Joe had lined up a big night ahead, going through the finer details of the deal they needed to pitch first thing. They needed this one, it was big. He pictured his bonus cheque a few weeks away: this would swing it.

A strip light overhead was humming, dead flies collected beneath its glare, their dried-up bodies incongruous in the pristine office. He should call maintenance and get them to remove them. His hand hovered over the internal phone. Well, they should all be here, so why not? He pressed the number for reception and got them to redirect his call. He knew they'd have to come running. An MD called up in this company and it was more than your job was worth to ignore the request. He felt a flicker of satisfaction, purpose.

Pam appeared at his desk. 'I've finished the filing for the Hache merger and have franked all the mail to go out first thing,' she said, looking back at her coat draped over her desk. 'So if that's all ...'

Joe leant back in his chair, pen in his mouth. 'You've done all the filing, and typed up the minutes from the meeting today, you've proofread Mercer's report for Andrew – it'll need triple-checking ...'

She nodded at each sentence, unable to help another glance back at her coat. She'd been here all day, arriving just after Joe. He knew he should let her go, but the anxiety was making him edgy, needing everything to be absolutely right. Pam was a steadying influence, a mother figure. He could rely on her.

'You'll need to be in first thing. We're going to be here all night and there'll be more to proofread. Five o'clock sharp. I can send the car again.'

Pam's face fell, the lines around her eyes deeper than he remembered, the grey at her temples obvious now in the glare of the strip light. The sight jolted him, and he remembered Matt telling him about her new grandchild. He should ask her; he should let her leave early another night to be with her family. They were just so busy.

'The car would be good, thank you, there's no Tube at that time,' she said.

Joe nodded brusquely, glad to see half his team arrive in the lift behind her.

'Mercer, Adams, anything for Pam before she gets off for the night?' He asked it quickly, Pam spinning around, perhaps dreading the next words.

Mercer, a rotund guy with chubby cheeks and a barrelling laugh, looked across. 'Nothing from me; you have a good night on the tiles, girl.'

Adams, wiry, quiet and bespectacled, shook his head. 'Thanks for staying on so late, Pam,' he said, causing colour to edge into her cheeks.

Joe waved a hand. 'The car will take you back,' he said, turning to Mercer and Adams. 'I've ordered from Nobu, but don't think it's going to be all sushi and caviar; we've got work to do.'

Mercer's smile dimmed. 'Never, boss,' he said, removing his jacket.

Adams was already turning on his computer screen. 'I'll bring the numbers I worked up earlier ...'

Joe felt something easing in his stomach as he looked around at the desks. It wasn't that he'd been lonely, he thought. They had to be here; this deal was important, another bank could sneak in and steal it from under their noses. Still, he couldn't help a small smile as he saw the reflection opposite, three heads leaning over computers, more voices in the room.

Chapter 7

She'd needed to get out, had been talking to herself for the past hour, muttering Danish obscenities as she replayed the conversation with Roz, rewound Joe's answerphone message again and again. She had bundled into her coat and walked back along the high street, stamping out her anger as she puffed out cold air.

She noticed the old-fashioned street lamps in the high street for the first time, glowing orange in a sea of grey. The shop receded into the distance and she headed to the only place that was open, windows blazing. Pushing into the pub, she was surprised to see the bar empty. The enormous fireplace was swept but unlit, the tables polished, but there were no coasters on the surface, no glasses, and no customers.

Gavin appeared, humming to himself, from the staircase to the rooms above, stopping quickly when he saw Clara standing in the doorway.

'Where have you been? You're smiling,' she said, feeling lighter on seeing him. He had such an open face, his ruddy cheeks reminding her of her dad's back home. She needed to write to Dad, she thought; he liked her to check in despite having his hands full with her young twin stepsisters.

Gavin's smile froze and he glanced back over his shoulder. 'Nowhere,' he blurted, slamming the door to the staircase shut, a shudder tearing through the bar.

Clara's eyes widened, wondering what it was that she had just said.

'You don't want to stay, do you? It's just I haven't had the room cleaned yet and the other room ...' He trailed away, Clara becoming more and more confused. He had definitely said there was only one bedroom up there.

'The other room?' she said, inching forward.

'No other room, I meant,' he said. She watched a red stain creep up his neck, over the top of a tattoo she couldn't make out.

'It's OK, I'm not staying,' she said, and it seemed to be that comment which reminded Gavin where she'd been all day.

'Hold on, why are you here? Don't you have a house to sit in and a shop to run?'

Clara had propped herself up on a stool and was scratching

at the counter with a nail as he moved behind the bar, watching her.

She nodded her head. 'I do.'

'Well then.'

She paused, took a breath. 'Do you think Louisa really wants me there?' The sentence was out in a rush.

Gavin frowned. 'What do you mean? Of course she does, she gave you the keys, didn't she?'

'She did,' Clara said, scratching the counter again, the earlier doubts starting to subside. Gavin was right, she hadn't misread things. 'I was just worried that maybe I'd bullied her into it.'

He snorted. 'Have you met Louisa? Woman couldn't be bullied into anything. She once chased a UKIP councillor down the street with an umbrella.'

Clara found herself smiling.

'What's happened? Earlier you were so sure about it, and now all this.'

Clara bit her lip, not wanting to tell him about Roz, about the voicemail from Joe. 'Nothing. Just being silly.'

Gavin reached underneath the counter and pulled out a glass, shovelling some ice into the bottom and reaching to spray lemonade into it. 'Here,' he said, pushing it towards her. 'On the house.'

The kind gesture almost made her well up; she hadn't realised that she needed reminding that people cared. 'Thanks.' She took a sip, watching him tie an apron behind his back and bend to start stocking one of the small fridges, the glass beer bottles clinking as they butted up against each other. She could feel her muscles easing, the sugar from the lemonade racing around her veins and renewing her energy.

She was just about to ask about the argument the previous night, the history between Roz and Louisa, when the door opened and a blast of freezing air swirled around the bar. Clara longed for the huge fireplace to be lit, or even the radiator to actually radiate heat. Then she heard the voice and felt a cold hand grip her insides.

'You again.'

She snatched a look over her shoulder, hoping that it was just her imagination. But no, there she was again, same suspicious expression, lips stained a deeper red, a long black winter coat making her look like Death itself. 'I was just going,' Clara said, stumbling off the stool and hitting her knee on the bar. 'Ow, *lort*!'

'What did you call me?' Roz said, still standing in the doorway with her coat buttoned to her neck.

'I didn't, it was Danish for ... um, it's a swear word, but it wasn't at you, it was at my knee, see ... '

'I don't know what minee is; is that Danish for something obscene too?'

'Roz, let it go,' Gavin called.

'No, *my knee*, not minee ... ' Clara repeated slowly.

'I thought she would have gone by now.' Roz spoke as though Clara wasn't there.

Gavin's mouth puckered. 'Oh, I see. So you've had a few words, have you?'

Clara found her eyes darting around the carpet, at the threadbare patches, coloured swirls, the legs of chairs and stools. 'I'll just be off.' She wasn't in the mood to get another dressing-down from Roz.

'Finish your lemonade,' Gavin growled. This menacing edge was new and Clara found herself slipping back onto the stool. She hadn't been too keen on the idea of walking past Roz in the doorway anyway. 'Now, Roz. Coming or going?' he asked.

'I'm not thirsty,' she said, sniffing and turning on her heel. The sound of the wind picked up as she moved back outside, Gavin's mutterings lost as the door finally closed on her.

The room seemed to hold its breath until Clara bit her lip and looked back at Gavin. 'So, to answer your earlier question, someone might have had a word.'

She found herself telling him everything – Roz's visit, Joe's message – as he topped up her lemonade and then added vodka. 'I think she wants to talk to Louisa about something, but she wouldn't tell me what.'

Gavin sighed, taking out a stack of coasters and littering them along the bar. 'She's been after the shop for years; she put in an offer ages ago, but Louisa pipped her. Roz has always been desperate to get rid of her, and as you saw, they're not exactly bosom pals ...'

'No, I, um, picked up on that,' Clara said, a small smile escaping. 'And the fete? What happened at the fete?'

'Oh, that.' Gavin stopped what he was doing. 'Yes, that

was unfortunate. There was a disagreement over the judging of the Most Moist Cake and somehow Roz's entry fell. She had it out with Louisa, who had been judging, by the coconut shy, and a few of the coconuts were just within their reach . . .'

'Gosh.'

'Yes, it was quite spectacular. For a thin woman, she has an excellent arm. But it wasn't just the cake; Roz and Louisa have been on and off with each other for years. Planning permissions rejected, some row over a shared fence, a gentleman I think they both rather liked . . .' He coughed at that part. 'It just sort of exploded that day. Literally.' He leaned over the counter towards her. 'Come on, Clara, you were so excited earlier; don't let her stop you. She's all right really, Roz. Bark a lot worse than her bite. She just likes things as she likes them.'

'She doesn't like me,' Clara pouted.

'That's her loss,' he grinned. 'And look, I got this earlier.' He wiped his hands on his apron and reached for his phone by the till, holding it out to show her a text from Louisa: *Found fabulously pretty house-sitter for Lady CaCa and Roddy. She's going to run the shop, poor lamb, so be sure to visit her lots as she'll get lonely. But if anyone can do it she can.* The message made Clara smile, heat rushing into her cheeks at the compliment.

'Oh, and she did have an S and she hit the triple word with SUNG, forty-two points!' Gavin smiled fondly at the phone. 'So you can't go,' he said, coughing and tapping the screen off, placing the phone back by the till. 'She's relying on you, you promised.'

'But what about Joe? His message was s—'

Gavin put a hand up. 'No, no, no, it's not anyone else's decision. It's Louisa's and she wants you and that's the end of it.'

Clara's mouth was still open.

'Now do you want to live there for a bit?' Gavin asked her.

Clara nodded.

'And do you want to run the shop?'

She paused, thinking of her earlier plans, her head nodding quickly.

'So that's settled,' Gavin said, clinking her glass with his. 'You're staying.'

A woman appeared from the staircase behind, hair tied back with a knotted headscarf. 'All done, Gavin, I've put it back like you said I—'

'That's GREAT,' Gavin said, lurching towards her, blatantly cutting off the rest of her sentence. 'I'm sure you have,' he added.

The woman looked at him in surprise. 'Well, I'll be seeing you next week, same time,' she said, moving past him.

Gavin nodded quickly. 'Same time, yes, same time.'

Clara watched this bizarre exchange in silence. The vodka had gone straight to her head; food seemed like forever ago. Who was this woman? What had she been doing upstairs?

Gavin was puce when he returned to the bar after

ushering the woman out into the street. They'd stood under the porch for a while, Gavin handing her something, and then she'd left. Clara was about to ask what it was all about, but found the question freezing in her throat as she looked at his expression.

'Well,' she said, stepping off the stool and pushing her empty glass across the bar. 'I'd better get going then.'

Gavin couldn't meet her eye, was scrubbing at the spotless countertop.

'Thanks for everything, for everything you've said,' Clara said, hoping he'd look up and smile at her.

He flicked his eyes over her face. 'Not at all,' he said, his voice low. 'My pleasure, you come back in here soon.' At last he looked up properly, meeting her eye.

Clara wiped the puzzled expression from her face and gave him a small wave. 'Shall do. And I'll see you in the shop. Two days, OK? Come along in two days' time. I've got a surprise.'

The thought made the walk back a lot quicker. She let herself in and rushed straight through to the shop, where she pulled out one of the oversized wooden numbers, a large number 2, which she placed in the window to the side of the shutters, grinning as she did so.

Tomorrow was where it was all going to begin, she thought as she climbed the stairs. Tomorrow she'd unpack, deal with the carnage of the flat and everything else. She wouldn't think about Roz or anyone else who didn't want her here. She was going to make a difference. She didn't notice the answerphone this time; she didn't see the red 4 blinking into the darkness.

She was just dropping off into the deepest sleep when out of the silence she heard 'MY PRECIOUS, SHITHEAD.' At least Lady CaCa was pleased to see her.

ZE is not a real word, Gavin, and why do you ALWAYS have the Zs, Xs, Qs and Js when I'm left with six vowels and absolutely no hope of using them?

I'm sorry I left in such a hurry but I really couldn't wait around. I knew you'd talk me out of it and I needed to escape. I'm so glad Clara is taking on the flat. Lady CaCa does enjoy company; perhaps she will pick up some Danish? Roddy of course won't notice that anything has changed. Do be sure to remind Clara that he adores salmon fillets with sweet chilli sauce and there are lots in the freezer.

Madrid is a hoot. I'm right in the centre of things so there are dozens of shops and squares and outdoor cafés serving tapas. I have eaten so much paella in 24 hours I feel like I am now half woman, half prawn.

I've been walking everywhere and starting to get my bearings. The galleries are something else. I adore all the art and have convinced myself that I should now retrain as a surrealist painter. I feel that style might suit my personality. You know how

I like to experiment in the kitchen? This seems the painting equivalent. No one thought bacon, syrup and chocolate sprinkles would work until I pulled out my fabulous Chocolate Surprise. I had to look at lots of Goya, as he is a local lad so to speak, but his pictures are all rather dark and terrifying. I think I'll stick with telephone lobsters and men with apples for faces.

I'm writing to you from the café outside my hotel as I smoke from a shisha pipe! It's only raspberry tobacco, so don't have heart failure; this is no Amsterdam. Later I'm planning to drag myself back up to my room. I have a small stone balcony that I can sit out on as gorgeous Spaniards, a lot of swarthy Heathcliff types, walk by with beautiful women draped on their arms. Then I'll get dolled up and head out into the city for a night on the tiles.

Chapter 8

She'd changed Louisa's sheets, the new cream duvet cover smelling of lavender washing powder, the duck-feather pillows impossibly soft. She had unearthed the softest grey cashmere rug from the top of the wardrobe and had draped it over the duvet. She lit a candle by the side of the bed, pulled out a dog-eared novel from her rucksack and nestled down under the covers. Despite the haven she'd created, however, she barely slept, woken by the ideas tugging at her, Roz's disgruntled expression, Gavin's kind words, everything batting back and forward.

She yawned as the sunlight leaked through the edges of the curtains and the blind above her head. Lady CaCa looked at her in disgust; she quickly covered her mouth. Bleary-eyed, she stood in her woollen slipper socks, hands wrapped around her mug of coffee, and started planning the day ahead. With lilting country music playing out of Louisa's record player, she set about tidying the flat: packing away clothes, piling up ironing, scrubbing at the bathroom and kitchen, dusting and polishing until the whole place sparkled. When she eventually stopped, her stomach was growling, her arms were aching and she was in desperate need of a shower.

When she emerged from the bathroom, she felt lifted, the flat already seeming bigger, a smell of bleach underpinning everything else. Later she would give the place a few personal touches, but for now she popped the last of the carrot cake in her mouth and made a mental note to go food shopping.

Lady CaCa raised one eye at her as she approached, growing increasingly fretful as Clara grabbed the handle on the top of the cage.

'Come on, girl,' Clara soothed. She'd decided to take the parrot downstairs so that she had company in the shop.

'I'LL BE BACK.'

She descended the stairs, surprised at the weight of the cage, hearing Lady CaCa's wings as they hit the bars.

'THERE'S NO PLACE LIKE HOME,' the parrot called out repeatedly.

'And I'm not taking you away from it,' Clara puffed, putting the cage down outside the door to the shop and turning back towards the stairs.

'NO LIKEY NO LIGHTY! NO LIKEY NO LIGHTY!'

'We're going to have fun,' Clara called over her shoulder as she returned to the flat to tempt Roddy down with a fresh bowl of food.

The cat had moved from bed to rug and back again but had barely shown a flicker of interest in doing anything else. Food wasn't working, so Clara produced a piece of wool and dangled it in front of him. He stared at her as if to say, 'Do you think I'm an imbecile? It's wool – you need to get a life,' then rolled over onto his other side to stare at the empty woodburner instead. Clara had to pick him up and carry him down the stairs, grappling with the key to get the door open. On seeing the cage, he panicked – Lady CaCa was about the only thing that got him moving – and shot out of Clara's arms into the shop, scratching her in his haste to get away. Alarmed at seeing her following him inside carrying the cage , he made a beeline for the opposite end of the shop, parking himself in the middle of a pile of princess dresses and nestling down for another nap.

'Right.' Clara clapped her hands together and smiled at them both. 'Big day,' she announced.

'IT'S GOODNIGHT FROM ME AND IT'S GOODNIGHT FROM HIM.'

'Not quite the attitude,' she said, disappearing into the cupboard to unearth a hoover and a cloth.

The next few hours were spent finishing sorting the stock and then cleaning and tidying. She stacked any mismatched stock neatly away in the cupboard and lined the shelves with toys, prices displayed on colourful labels. Dragging a stool across the room, she strung up bright polka-dot bunting, then hung some pictures she'd found leaning against the wall in the back room: an enormous framed clown with a bunch of coloured balloons in his hand, a juggling duo, a ringmaster and an elephant. A mirror on the wall behind the till made the whole place feel bigger, and she grinned at her own reflection.

She mopped the floor until the black and white squares were spotless. Moving across to the counter, she piled all the stray pieces of paper into one bundle, which she placed underneath the till. She wiped the counter down and propped a couple of toy trolls next to the till, their neon hair sticking out at every angle, then looped the bunting along the counter, smiling as she stood back and admired her work. Looking up at the large clock hanging over the door, she started at the time, her stomach grumbling as if it had just worked out that she'd skipped lunch.

With no car, she realised with a sinking heart that there was only one place to go for supplies if she wanted them now. She shrugged on her coat, wrapped a scarf around her neck and huddled into its warmth as she walked the few paces to Roz's post office next door.

The shop was crammed full, the only light coming from the smeared window and a flickering bare bulb. Magazines were displayed in a rack on the wall, newspapers were stacked in piles on the floor. Shelves rammed with various essentials lined the opposite wall and an island in the middle was stuffed full too. Clara quickly grabbed a few things, holding out the edges of her coat to act as a make-shift basket.

She could sense Roz watching her from a stool behind the counter, the occasional sigh making Clara cringe. Were they going to have another row? Perhaps she should just starve instead? She felt the scrutiny as she piled the items up next to the till, Roz's thin mouth practically disappearing as she scanned each one.

'So you're staying,' she said pointedly, looking at the spread in front of her: a loaf of bread, a pint of milk, a jar of marmalade, a cucumber and a packet of sliced ham.

'Yes,' squeaked Clara, determined not to be bullied. 'Staying,' she repeated, paying with her card.

'Where's your bag?' Roz raised a pencilled eyebrow. 'Five pence if not.'

'Oh, I forgot,' Clara stammered. What was it about this woman that made her nervous? 'Right,' she said, spilling change out of her purse as she searched for one of the tiny coins. Roz looked disappointed when she produced one and slid it across the counter.

Clara scurried out, the bag bulging, cutting into her hands, feeling Roz's eyes burn into her back through the glass shopfront.

'Clara!' Lauren waved.

Clara stopped, heart still pumping from her shopping excursion, vowing to make a large online order that night on Louisa's ancient-looking desktop computer.

'How are you?' Lauren asked, huffing to a stop in front

of her, cheeks pink from the cold and with a large faux-fur hat on her head.

'I'm fine. I'm great, actually, just in the middle of sorting the shop.' Clara gestured, feeling the tension drain away.

'That's great. Look, I'm rushing to pick Rory up from nursery, but I'll pop in later and we can have a play date. Oh God, I mean a coffee. Sorry, too much mum chat. NOT a play date. I won't make you get the Lego out or anything. Well, maybe Operation, as I actually really like that game, though it is bloody hard – I always kill him off when I go to take out his Adam's apple. So disgusting.'

'Right,' Clara said, unsure what she was talking about. 'I'm not sure we have that game in Denmark. Lego, though. We love Lego.'

'Oh,' Lauren said, waving a gloved hand, 'of course. Look, I really must dash. Mrs Stevens always gets pissy with me when I turn up late, like she might be about to call social services, so I'd better g—'

'Run,' Clara giggled. 'I'm in the shop whenever, just pop by. I'd love to have a coffee.'

'And is your plan going smoothly?' Lauren asked.

'Yes, it's coming together,' Clara said.

'How fab. Yay. I can't wait to see it. And so glad you're staying on in the village,' she called as she half walked, half jogged away.

Clara watched her leave, her straight glossy hair streaming out as she turned down a side street. She smiled, feeling a glow from the promise of a new friendship and a renewed flicker of excitement at the project awaiting her.

She turned to head back inside, but just before she did, she paused outside the shop, looking at the white shutters still pulled down over the windows, the burgundy sign above. She knew what she had to do next.

Chapter 9

Clara fell into bed that night utterly drained. The sheets were cold, but she was too tired to jump out of bed to get her socks. She wrapped the duvet around her, waiting to warm up, her back aching, her hands red-raw from cleaning and polishing and assembling things. The woodburner in the flat needed wood and kindling and she made a mental note to add that to her online order. She had barely been able to lift Lady CaCa's cage back up the stairs to the flat. Roddy followed moments later but only because Clara had opened another tin of cat food.

What would people say? She could barely sleep with excitement, as if she were a child again and tomorrow was Christmas Day. What would they say when they saw it? What would Gavin and Lauren and Roz think? She pictured the children in the village, their faces aglow under woollen hats. She bit her lip, feeling a sense of focus fill her. She had been wandering for a few months now with no real purpose; it seemed like fate to find herself in this village, knowing she might make a difference. She squeezed her eyes shut, willing sleep to come so that she'd be bright and perky tomorrow for the big day.

It seemed like only moments later that the alarm clock was ringing next to her and she was stepping out of bed, hopping from one bare foot to the other as she located her slipper socks and Louisa's dressing gown and fuchsia fleece. Sticking the kettle on, she raced to get ready, even finding a moment to put some mascara on, her blue eyes glittering back at her in the small bathroom mirror.

It was time. Downstairs, she had positioned herself on a chair near the counter, and was finishing her second coffee as she watched the clock above the counter move to nine o'clock. Then, with great pomp and ceremony, she pulled up the shutters so that winter sunlight flooded into the shop, shining on her new window display. It seemed to look even better in this light.

She had brought out the old wooden toys that she had found in an unloved heap in the cupboard, cleaning them, scrubbing at the coloured wheels, the brightly painted wood in purples, greens, vivid reds. She had found jigsaws depicting countryside landscapes and had glued these up to create a patchwork of fields and sky. In front of this backdrop she had placed wooden train tracks, curving around and above each other, wooden puppets resting in groups watching the tracks, wooden animals by their side. Now, with her breath held, she picked up one of the train carriages and placed it at the top of the track. Letting go, she watched in delight as it set off, triggering a chain of events so that the display was a moving feast for the eyes.

She returned to her chair, unable to sit still as she waited for people to stop outside, watching curiously, the children wanting to come in and have a go themselves. She hopped to her feet once more, hovering by the counter, her heart lifting with every movement. With the burgundy façade, the jigsaw-puzzle backdrop, she knew the front of the shop looked enticing. The clock's hands moved round; a man in a suit passed the shop on his phone, but his eyes didn't flicker from the ground in front of him. An elderly woman pushed a tartan-covered trolley past on the other side of the street. A pigeon pecked at the pavement just outside, not interested in the wooden attraction above him. Clara sank into the chair. No one. No one had stepped inside the shop in an hour.

By eleven o'clock she felt bereft, returning to the flat to make another cup of coffee. Not even Lady CaCa calling, 'I'M KING OF THE WORLD' could raise a smile. She picked up Roddy, pushing her face into his soft fur, the cat purring in contentment. She had been sure people would come. She walked half-heartedly back down to the shop, feeling all her plans slither away.

No one came into the shop. She ate her ham and cucumber sandwich on her stool, her mouth dry, the time moving hideously slowly. She moved the trolls on the counter. She moved them back. Pacing quietly to the back room, leaning against the door frame, she felt the lack of sleep catch up with her. She had planned to work on this room tonight, knowing that her ideas for it might transform the shop into something wonderful. Now she wondered if she should spend the evening in the bath, reading a book, a candle flickering, blocking out all the hopeless feelings.

She was so deep in misery that she didn't hear the bell above the shop door tinkle, suddenly becoming aware of a babbling from somewhere behind her. She spun round, seeing Lauren standing in the centre of the shop, turning with her mouth open. Rory was clutching her hand, tugging on her arm.

'Look, Mumma, Mumma, look.'

'Clara,' Lauren breathed. 'It looks great, you've transformed the place.'

Clara felt heat in her cheeks as she moved towards her. 'I haven't even started yet,' she said. 'I had all these plans, but' – she felt the disappointment of the morning wash over her – 'no one came. No one cares. Louisa was right.'

Even as she spoke, however, she could make out figures on the pavement outside, small groups huddled, one face pressed against the glass, her little mouth a rounded O.

'Nursery's just finished,' Lauren explained. 'Rory dragged me in here; he adores trains and the display is amazing.'

'Train, train, train,' Rory babbled, toddling to the front of the shop.

'I can show you if you like, Rory,' Clara called, following him. The shop bell rang out again as she rushed forward to get the carriage started. Rory watched in delight as she pushed it down the track so that it whirled around, the bright reds and greens a blur. Rory clapped his hands together. ''Gain, 'gain.'

A small group of children pushed in from outside, diving behind the legs of their mothers and one lone father, who seemed a little lost in the commotion as Clara beckoned them forward to show them all again. The shop was suddenly filled with giggles and voices and people moving in between the aisles, and she felt her whole body loosen, her feet light as she slipped behind the counter.

One boy, missing both front teeth, was craning his neck to see the selection of toys on a top shelf.

'Do you want me to get anything down for you?' Clara asked, which made the boy stare at the floor before biting his lip and then nodding furiously. He pointed to a large box just above Clara's head, and she lifted it down.

'What do you say, Chris?' A woman whom Clara assumed to be the boy's mother appeared behind him.

'Thanks,' the boy said, staring through the plastic window of the box at the remote-controlled car inside.

'Is that what you want then?' the woman asked him.

The boy nodded at her, air whistling through his teeth as he said, 'We could make a track in the office.' He turned to Clara. 'My dad moved out, so he doesn't need it any more,' he explained. 'They have to get a divorce now.'

'Oh,' Clara said, taken aback at this information.

'Chris!' The woman went pink. 'God, sorry, he's telling everyone at the moment; it's like Divorce Tourette's.'

The boy was still gazing at the box. 'This is so cool,' he breathed.

'It's his birthday,' the woman added. 'His dad's sent an e-card,' she rolled her eyes, 'so I thought I'd better make up for it.'

'I can wrap it up for you if you want? I've got paper and bows and things.'

'Thanks, you are sweet,' the woman said, handing over money and smiling at her. 'But it will be totally wasted on him. It will stay in the box for about two seconds.'

'My dad moved out when I was about your age,' Clara said to the boy, who looked at her with large solemn eyes. 'He still loves you, though.'

The boy took a breath. 'That's what he said.' He didn't look sure.

The mother smiled at Clara over his head, mouthing a thank-you before steering him towards the door. 'Come on, Chris, we'll be back another day.'

Lauren dashed across the shop. 'Well done, Clara, seriously, it's ace. Can you come over on Monday afternoon? Patrick takes Rory swimming and it's my opportunity to exercise and stuff.' She smiled. 'I could do with some company. I'll leave my address. Three p.m.?'

Clara nodded over the blip of another till entry. 'I will, thank you, I will definitely.'

'And I'll be telling everyone to get down here,' Lauren said, fetching Rory from where he and two other boys had started to build a fort out of beanbags and boxes. Clara smiled, watching her pick him up, his little legs kicking as she removed him from the shop. 'More, Mumma, more.'

Then the next customer distracted her and she went back to the till, tapping in the amount to be paid, looking up moments later to see the ominously still presence of Roz staring into the shop from the pavement, her mouth puckered in disapproval as her eyes roved over the display in the window. Clara had a sudden urge to laugh. 'Oh *lort*,' she muttered.

'What's that?' the lone father asked. His green eyes behind thick designer glasses seemed to sparkle with amusement.

'Ah.' Clara blushed, looking at the little girl in his arms. 'It means, um, "have a nice day" in Danish,' she said, feeling her toes curl with the lie.

'*Lort, lort*,' the little girl repeated.

Clara grimaced, hoping her dad wouldn't google the word when he got home.

The man didn't notice her expression, giving her a grin as he paid for a train carriage. 'Great display. You've got a real eye for detail.'

Clara found herself strangely shy as she caught his gaze. 'Thanks,' she mumbled, forgetting all about Roz.

'Amber loves it. Don't you, Amber?' he asked. Amber was already holding out her hand for the carriage, wriggling and bucking to get down.

The man deposited her on the ground and ruffled her hair, the same light brown as his own. 'Totally overexcited. If only her mum could see her . . . ' He tailed off, sighing out loud, so that Clara found herself tilting her head to one side in sympathy. 'Still,' he said, clapping his hands together, 'this has cheered us up.' He grinned, light reflecting off his glasses.

'I'm glad,' Clara said, wanting to talk more but aware of another customer standing behind him.

The man gave her a sloping smile and waved a hand. 'Well, see you round,' he said.

'You too,' Clara replied, watching him take his daughter's hand and lead her out of the shop. Was it her imagination or did he pause at the door to look back at her?

The next customer cut across her musings. 'Excuse me, what does the large wooden number four mean in the corner of the window?'

'The four . . . ?' Clara blinked, still thinking back to the lone father and child. 'The four,' she repeated. 'It means four days to go.'

'To go till what?' the woman asked. Her son was staring up at Clara, waiting for her response.

Clara pulled herself together, bending down to his eye level. 'Until the next display. Four days, and then overnight it will transform into something else.'

'Like magic,' the boy said, his eyes bulging.

'Exactly. When I wake up and come downstairs, I find it is completely different.'

'Elves,' the boy whispered.

Clara nodded solemnly. 'Very likely,' she agreed.

The mother broke into a smile. 'Well, Lucas, we'll have to come back and see that, won't we?'

'In four days,' Lucas repeated, as if his mother were an imbecile.

'Exactly. Four comes after . . . ?' she asked him.

'Two,' he replied solemnly.

The woman looked at Clara and grimaced. 'He's not entirely wrong.' She lowered her voice. 'But I might have a word with the nursery. Right,' she said more loudly, 'we'll see this nice lady in four days then. Say thank you.'

The boy was too busy staring at the box he was carrying.

'Nankoo.'

'That'll do.'

What do you mean, you hated my Chocolate Surprise? You told me at the time that it was a ground-breaking dessert. I shall never believe another word that passes your lips. Is *Sense and Sensibility* really your favourite Emma Thompson film, and do you really find Noel Edmonds loathsome too? You see, I am now second-guessing everything you've ever told me.

It rained for two days on the trot in Madrid so I took a coach to Valencia. The journey itself was utterly hideous but it's lovely to be on the coast and looking out on the Mediterranean. The sun has decided to welcome me here and I've been out exploring. It's a strange place; some parts look like the set of a sci-fi movie, all large white buildings and shallow turquoise pools. I keep expecting chaps in white helmets to appear on the horizon.

I've cycled just about everywhere today. The old river has dried up so they've transformed it into green parks and cycle paths; it's all rather lovely. My shins ache now though so I've retired to the rooftop of the hotel which has a hot tub looking out over the beach. It is terribly hard, Gavin, being such an intrepid explorer. I have had to drink a great deal of sangria to ensure that I'm really soaking up the Spanish culture. Maybe you should do a Spanish-themed evening in the pub? Serve paella and sangria and hire someone to do flamenco. I watched a woman in a small bar in the city doing it, she was just incredible. Stamping her feet so fast they were a blur, body twisting impossibly, ruffled skirts flying – it was breathtaking. I think back to my energetic efforts when the Macarena comes on the jukebox and feel horribly inept. Do think about it, it would be such fun. Although I'm not sure where one finds an authentic flamenco dancer in Suffolk.

There's a quarter-final of something tennis-related on tomorrow at L'Àgora, an enormous strange-looking building that looks like a monster mussel coming out of the ground, and Andy Murray is playing so I've booked tickets to watch him. I'm going to go dressed in a Union Jack flag and paint my face like one of those fanatical types at Wimbledon and see if I get on television. If the tennis is on Sky, be sure to check in; I imagine they're bound to feature me. My sign will say 'GO ANDY' because everyone uses tennis players' first names. Do you remember when we all called Henman 'Tim' as if he was a favourite son? It's very strange. I wouldn't dream of calling Rooney 'Wayne'.

How are Man U getting on? I do miss watching *Match of the Day* with you, I learnt such a lot. I still shake my fist when I see Ronaldo on the back pages of the papers here because I remember you don't like him.

Will you send Roddy and Lady CaCa my very biggest kisses and tell Clara she is an absolute saint? I did like her face, so it's nice to know I was right about her – she has the most fabulous skin, doesn't she? As if she'll never see a line in her life. I imagine in Denmark she just eats raw eggs and red cabbage; do you mind asking her for any tips? I keep forgetting to use my night cream so it's no wonder I look like something that was dragged up from the ocean.

I've been avoiding Joe's calls all week, is that terrible? He just sounds so cross with me on the answerphone and I do hate it when he's cross with me.

Oh, and I did like the way you attached all your letters to my word. TO and AT were acceptable but don't think I didn't notice JE, and the J on the double letter, which seems incredibly unfair when you can't possibly tell me what it means. If you talked in your Words with Friends language no one would understand a word you say. Still, I will soon catch up. I have a couple of rather fabulous letters up my sleeve.

Chapter 10

'Mum, MUM?' He hung up again, crossing the lobby of his building, his shoes clacking on the marble surface, the sound echoing round the cavernous space. He pushed through the revolving doors, pressing her name again.

The Mercedes was waiting, engine running, in the bay outside. Joe didn't recognise the driver, but he wasn't one for chatting with the chauffeurs the firm used, often working in the back of the car. He had already told the man the destination when he'd booked it, so there was no need to do anything but try his mother for the tenth time that hour.

She'd been running around a harbour in Valencia looking for a boat when she'd suddenly disappeared.

'DARLING, thank goodness. Do you keep going through tunnels?'

'No, I think it's you. I'm just in the car, heading home.'

'But it's so early.'

'I stayed all night.' Joe rubbed at his face with one hand, the conversation already making him weary.

'Gosh, you are so diligent. Is the job going well? Everyone keeps asking me all about you and I always struggle to pin down exactly what you do. Isn't that awful? After so many years. But I just say M and As in a very knowledgeable sort of way, as I know that means mergers and acquisitions, and darling, they are ALWAYS impressed, always. Then I get a bit bogged down in the details. What are you again? Your title? I know it's something presidential; it always makes me giddy with how important you sound . . .'

'Mum . . .' Joe's head had been aching on and off since midnight, and now with this whirlwind of chatter he found he just couldn't think. He needed to talk to her, seriously, about just what she was up to.

' . . . senior vice president or deputy president or something. I know it's American . . .'

'MUM,' he said, making the driver look at him with wide eyes in the rear-view mirror. Joe thought of cupping a hand over the phone and explaining, but what would he say? He ignored the look.

'Did you want to speak for long, as I really need to find Pedro. He's on one of these boats, but there seem to be dozens of them. And they all look the same to me . . .'

'I want to discuss you leaving Yulethorpe, the shop an—' Joe said, trying to cut across her.

'. . . I'm booking a jet ski for this afternoon. I met Pedro in a bar last night and he's organised a fabulous deal for me. Two hours for twenty euros, an absolute bargain, don't you think, darling? And I've never jet-skied before. It looks thrilling. I was completely put off water-skiing in my twenties when your father made me do it in choppy water off the Isle of Wight. I swallowed half the sea and got smacked in the face by one of the skis. I still think I might have fractured my nose. The bottom half of it has always been angled slightly to the left since then.'

The rare mention of his father had stopped Joe from responding. He was suddenly a young boy again, desperate for more stories about his dad, not wanting to ask his mum, who always seemed to get angry or tearful when he did. He imagined his father teaching his stepsister and brother how to water-ski. Joe had never tried. Why did it still sting?

'I think jet-skiing will be just my cup of tea. I'm going to have to wear a wetsuit, though, can you imagine? Me squeezing into neoprene? Horrific. I'm so worried Pedro will laugh. Not that he'd be interested in someone ancient like me. He's very young. I think he might be homosexual. Not sure . . .'

'Mum. Can you just sit still for five minutes while we talk about you upping and leaving.'

'. . . it was just a fleeting thought I had. And you can't really ask, can you?'

Joe had started to suspect his mother was avoiding things. He let her continue for a few moments, leaning his head back against the seat and closing his eyes. There was something wonderful about her voice that transported him back through the years, nestled in the crook of her arm on a sofa or bed as she made up fantastical stories for him. She had always been a great story-teller and now she was in her element, embellishing details of her night in the bar, Pedro's clothing, his accent. Joe felt his head tip to the side, the driver pulling up outside his block.

He jerked upright, realising he was drifting off, the night's work catching up on him. His mouth was dry as he waited for the driver to open the door. He stepped out onto the pavement, thanked the man and placed the mobile back to his ear, his mother not noticing anything had changed.

'... Everyone wears leather trousers. I'm thinking of buying some. But do you think it's a bit mutton dressed as? I remember Gavin saying he'd always had a crush on Olivia Newton-John, and she looked sensational in them at the end of *Grease*, do you remember? But then she was about fifty years younger than me and much, much thinner ...'

Joe had made it up to the top floor of the block, the lift opening out into his penthouse suite. The floor-to-ceiling windows opposite were spotless, every surface wiped down, his belongings tidied away, hung up or shut inside cupboards. He'd never been one for hoarding, but for a second even he was shocked by how stark it all looked. He should contact that interior designer again, see what she could do.

'Mum,' he said, falling onto the beige leather sofa, resting his head back. 'Focus. What happened?'

The direct question ended her soliloquy. There was silence from the other end of the line. Joe could make out a seagull's caw, some distant shouts. He pictured the harbour: bronzed Spaniards moving from boat to boat, hauling up buckets of glistening fish, his mother standing, skirt billowing, as she stared at her mobile.

'Mum,' he repeated, his voice softer. 'Come on, what happened? You just left.'

He didn't want to say 'again'. He wondered if she realised he was thinking back to those years when they'd travelled around the country together, never settling, staying in some places only for a matter of weeks. Joe had lost track of the number of schools he was enrolled in and then removed from partway through the year. He'd stopped making friends in the last few, knowing they'd be off again, searching for what, he'd never been sure. Was Mum doing the same now? He'd thought she was happy, settled, and this scared him, as if the years had fallen away and she was back to the same broken woman she'd been after his dad had walked out on them, leaving overnight, a letter propped up on her dressing table. He'd never even said goodbye to Joe.

They'd moved out of their house and she'd talked about an exciting new start by the sea. Joe had loved the idea – what eight-year-old wouldn't want to spend their days on the beach, chasing waves, exploring rock pools, making sandcastles with moats, digging holes? The village by the sea had lasted less than eight weeks. They'd left that for the city, a new city, Manchester, to be closer to Granny, who always smelled of pipe smoke and mustard. He'd been teased for his posh voice in that school, learnt to keep quiet in the playground to stop them from standing there exaggerating all their vowels, making him want to be swallowed up by a hole in the ground. They'd moved around like that for over four years before finally settling in Yulethorpe.

Was she doing the same out in Spain? Running from another hurt? Had something happened? Was it more than the shop? He wished he could ask her directly. She had always shared things with him, but in recent years he'd struggled to ask her questions, talk properly about things. He'd assumed she was happy. Suddenly he was full of the same worry that had gnawed away at the insides of his eight-year-old self. When he'd sat at the top of the stairs waiting for her to come back from nights out, waiting for the click of the door, her heels on the tiled hallway floor. The relief that she hadn't left him too.

'It was so depressing, darling,' she started, her voice barely louder than a whisper. 'People had just stopped coming in.'

'To the shop?'

'To *our* shop,' she corrected. 'I was thinking back all those years to when we first opened. People would drive for miles to visit us. Do you remember?'

Joe found himself nodding, unable to speak.

'It was a wonderful place, the pulsing heart of the village, but recently it's just felt like someone has come along and pulled the plug on the whole place. It's a ghost town. If it wasn't for G— friends, I would have left years ago.'

'So what do you want to do now, Mum?'

'I'm not sure,' she said in a small voice. 'I just couldn't stay any longer.'

'Do you want to travel for a while? Do you want me to handle the shop?'

Her tone changed and Joe could tell he was losing her again. 'Oh darling, I don't know what I want. This is all very serious and I'm in a spin still. Ooh, I think I see Pedro ... no, no, it's just a man with very snaky hips ... Honestly, I've been wandering around here for hours ...'

'Mum, really, let me help,' Joe said, desperately trying to get back to the conversation, to help her. 'I could get you quotes. I could put it on the market if you want to release the capital from it. I want you to be comfortable, not to have to worry in your retirement.'

'I know you do, darling – you're so good. Now let's not talk about depressing things any more, I really can't face it. Tell me about London. Do you have a girlfriend? Not that I'm pressuring you. I'm not desperate for grandchildren. I'm a dreadful knitter anyway, so I'd make a questionable grandma ...'

She was off again. He knew the conversation had come to a close, that she didn't want to talk any more about serious things. He needed to go to sleep – he had to be back in the office in a few hours – but it was great to hear her on the other end of the phone. He let her carry on, her voice washing over and through him as he closed his eyes on the leather sofa and drifted off to sleep.

Chapter 11

By the end of the week, Clara felt exhausted. She needed a *søndagshygge*, a lazy Sunday, so she spent the day taking long walks, cooking a stew, a bolognese and more treats for the freezer from the enormous online order that had arrived, lighting the woodburner with the new logs.

On Monday morning she got everything ready in the shop, putting a new wooden number in the corner of the window to count down to the next display. She couldn't help squeezing herself in excitement. She'd be unveiling it tomorrow and she couldn't wait; she'd loved putting this one together. Just before three o'clock, she went upstairs to change into something she could exercise in: leggings pulled out of her bag, and a big enough top to cover any bulges. It might be good to go for a jog, she told herself, blocking out the whistle of cold wind as she turned off the high street and into a side street, heading to the end where a pair of cottages were set back from the road.

Lauren's cottage was painted white, with a thatched roof, tubs of lavender outside the front door, a flaking wrought-iron bench underneath the window and a large knocker on the door that Clara reached for, laughing as Lauren appeared almost immediately, dressed in black leggings, a short-sleeved T-shirt and a neon-pink headband.

'Was that a bit keen?' she asked, standing in the door-way. 'They've been gone about ten minutes and I'm totally overexcited about you coming... Oh my God.' She stopped, wrapping her arms around herself. 'It is frickin' freezing, get inside now,' she said, pulling on Clara's arm.

Clara had twisted round to look back over her shoulder. 'It's all so lovely, so English.'

'It is, isn't it? Although the cottage is listed, which is bad because I can never have a kitchen extension.' She pouted. 'And Patrick nearly sold it when he found out we weren't allowed to put up a Sky dish.'

Clara looked back at her, brow creasing.

'For Sky TV,' Lauren explained, seeing her incomprehension.

'Oh, of course,' Clara said. 'We have that in Denmark, and the in-ter-net,' she added slowly, pretending to be clueless.

'You're weird. Now come in,' Lauren said cheerfully, standing to one side to let Clara squeeze past. 'Sorry about the world's smallest corridor. Go into the room on the left;

I've lit the fire, hence the absurdly thin T-shirt when it's minus twenty outside.'

Clara ducked into the front room. 'It gets that cold at home,' she said, picturing the thick layer of snow that would be covering the park near their old family house in Denmark. 'This is magical,' she said, forgetting everything and just looking around the front room with its low cream ceiling and thick wooden beams, the yellow-and-grey-striped cushioned window seat, plastic toys loaded into a large box in the corner of the room, a few stray pieces of Lego scattered on the floor.

A woodburner crackled opposite, the inside pulsing as if it had an orange heart. 'How gorgeous,' she said, feeling instantly relaxed as she stood in front of it, holding out the palms of her hands as a sort of automatic response to any heat source.

'It's so nice to light it,' Lauren said, following her into the room. 'I hardly ever do, as a toddler is essentially a flammable hazard and I don't trust him not to scale the wire mesh, open the door and cover himself in ashes or worse.' She shivered at the thought. 'It's like he tries to head straight to danger no matter what you do. The other day he was convinced he could fly after seeing an aeroplane, followed by my dreadful explanation of the power of flight, which somehow meant he thought he could throw himself from his bed because he, quote, had a large wingspan too. I practically died hearing the thud – totally relieved to see him crying and then running away from me as I tried to check him for injury.'

'Oh God, I can imagine,' Clara said, for a moment wondering what she herself would be like as a mother. Would she be safety-conscious, or would she let them roam wild and free? 'It's lovely seeing children in the shop,' she went on. 'I'm not used to being around them, and they're so mad and joyful. I love it.'

'They're certainly mad,' Lauren confirmed. 'So, are you just over here for a while, from Denmark, that is? You sound so ... English. How have you ended up in Suffolk?'

'Part of my travels. I've lived over here for a few years. I left my job a while back.' Not wanting to expand, she continued, 'I originally came out this way because I wanted to see a village like the ones in *Midsomer Murders* – it's really big in Denmark,' she explained with a laugh, keen to ensure the mood stayed light.

'Really?'

Clara nodded. 'Huge. DCI Barnaby is a pretty big deal.'

'Weird,' Lauren said, throwing another log into the woodburner.

'I worked in London for a few years, but all that is in the past now,' Clara said hurriedly, picking at a loose thread on her sleeve.

Fortunately Lauren was distracted by a loud pop from the logs in the woodburner and didn't ask any more. 'Now, given that you've turned up in sports kit but it's arctic out there, why don't we do an exercise DVD? I have this one from America that is for different abilities, so we could do the first level and maybe next week go up to the next one.'

'OK,' Clara said, pleased to be off the topic but alarmed to be diving into the exercise part of the meeting.

'Let me set it up then. First, though, tea? Coffee?'

She moved through to the kitchen as Clara called out 'Coffee,' returning moments later with a tray piled high with mugs, biscuits and even a small bowl of popcorn.

'Maybe we should watch a few minutes to see what we're letting ourselves in for,' she suggested, opening the DVD wrapping with her teeth.

'Oh, it's a new one,' Clara said.

Lauren grimaced. 'Sort of. Last Christmas, in fact. Don't tell Patrick, he thinks I'm up to Level 3 doing AbsTastic.' She patted her stomach. 'Men are idiots,' she said. She reached to put the DVD into the machine, then sat back on the sofa and pointed at the tray. 'Help yourself to milk or cream, it's in the small jug – and there's sugar if you want it.' She grabbed a small handful of popcorn as the DVD introduction music kicked in.

Ten minutes later, the coffee had been drunk and they'd both kicked off their trainers and were curled up watching the three perspiring women on the screen lying on the floor and crunching into balls.

Lauren popped a second chocolate digestive into her mouth. 'That looks hard,' she commented, a crumb escaping from her mouth, which made Clara giggle. 'Do you think they are actually robots?'

'I wonder if they exercise all day every day to look like that,' Clara mused.

'I wonder if they are Photoshopped.'

'I think that's only in photos,' Clara said, reaching for another biscuit.

'Gah, it's sickening,' Lauren said, pointing at the screen. 'I bet they have high-flying jobs, keep their toned bodies in perfect shape *and* perform sex acts on their partners every night.'

'*Hold da kaeft*,' Clara said, admiring one of the women's leotards.

'What does that mean?' Lauren asked.

'I'm not sure of the exact translation. It's rude. Your equivalent is bloody hell, I think.'

'Ooh.' Lauren's eyes widened. 'Great,' she said, twisting round to look at Clara. 'I keep using really stupid alternatives to swear words because I don't want Rory to pick up any. And Patrick says I'm not allowed to say frickin' any more, which is totally not a swear word, but anyway.' She reached out and put a piece of popcorn in her mouth. 'Teach me some Danish ones. Most of my English ones don't even make sense. Yesterday I actually said, "Oh for actual fudge sake", which made me want to cry. It has to stop.'

'OK, well . . . the rudest is probably *rend kusse* or *fuck dig*,' Clara said as Lauren practically spat out her tea.

'Not sure that'll cut it,' she said, wiping her mouth with the back of her hand.

'*Rend dig* means the same and is pretty bad,' Clara admitted. 'There's *kælling*, which means bitch, but I like that one when I'm really cross and need to just let it out.

Go to hell is *ga ad*, or you could try *lort*, which is sort of like poo or shit.'

'I like that, it sounds a lot more aggressive than it is,' Lauren said, practising it. '*Lort!*' She pointed at the wood-burner before picking up a nearby Action Man and shouting, '*Ga ad!*' in his face.

'Very good,' Clara said, giggling. 'Oh look, they're doing burpees,' she said, pointing at the screen.

Lauren snuggled deeper into the sofa. 'What a woman – I feel like I'm getting thinner just being in the same room as her.'

Clara rested her head back on the soft leather of the sofa, the crackling logs and the smell of popcorn making her feel woozy. For a second she closed her eyes, enjoying the warmth, thinking of home: drinking *gløgg* around the family fireplace, playing endless rounds of cards, safe from the cold outside. She had an intense craving for a *romkugle*, a rum-flavoured chocolate treat, alarmed at the sudden lump in her throat as she remembered whose favourite they were. 'This is so *hygge*,' she said, exhaling slowly.

'Is that bad too?' Lauren's forehead creased in worry.

'No,' Clara smiled. '*Hygge* is great. It means … well, there's not an exact English word for it, but it sort of means things are very cosy. With the fire, the drinks, the company, the low lighting … it's all *hygge*.'

'*Hygge*,' Lauren repeated. 'That's nice: I like it.'

Outside, a car's headlights moved across the darkening room and Lauren squeaked, breaking the vibe by diving off the sofa onto the floor and yelling, 'Quickly, Clara, quickly,' as she did so.

In a rush, Clara followed her lead, unsure of what was happening. Lauren was lying flat on her back, knees bent as if she was about to give birth. Clara did the same, about to ask why when she heard the front door open and voices outside the room.

'*Lort*,' whispered Lauren, doing a sit-up.

Clara started giggling as she copied her, noticing biscuit crumbs on her chest as she lifted herself up.

As Patrick and Rory appeared in the doorway, both women turned to look at them, puffing in their exertions. Patrick peered at them lying at haphazard angles on the floor, then glanced at the tray of empty wrappers, popcorn kernels and coffee remnants, one eyebrow lifted. 'Good workout?' he asked.

'Hmm,' Lauren said, manoeuvring herself into a sitting position and raising one arm to put it behind her head in some kind of stretch. 'Really motivating,' she replied, without a pause.

Clara, a terrible liar, merely nodded from her prostrate position in front of the fire. Fortunately the room was so warm it had given them both pink cheeks, and she thought they might get away with it.

'Mumma, is that nopcorn?'

'Oh *lort* . . .'

Chapter 12

She'd stayed on for dinner with Lauren and Patrick, eating steaming bowls of risotto from trays in the living room and watching a scary movie about a writer living in a wood. Patrick had walked her back to the shop and she was grateful for the company, still replaying moments from the film in her head, jumping at the shadows.

She wasn't sure what time it was when she heard the noise, her eyes snapping open, staring into black nothingness. The alarm clock's digits were saying it was just past 2 a.m. Had Roddy got up? Had Lady CaCa moved in her cage? She thought of the film; the man stalking the writer in the wood. There was the noise again: a voice, a low voice. Lying in bed, she felt fear freeze her to the sheets, her body taut, every muscle strained, listening for the next whisper of sound. There it was again: a man's groan, something bumping into something else. Oh my God, she definitely wasn't imagining this. Someone was down there. She could hear them lumbering around by the door to the shop. They were here to burgle it, to steal Saturday's takings. Why had she left the money in the till?

Perhaps it was picturing herself ringing Louisa to tell her she'd allowed her to be robbed that got her moving. She placed both feet on the floor and straightened up slowly, reaching for the dressing gown she had thrown over a chair. Her mind was racing ten moves ahead as she pulled on her slipper socks as quietly as she could. The sounds had stopped and she paused, hoping whoever it was had changed their mind, had looked at the lock and left. Panic gripped her as she racked her brains. Had she locked the internal door? Had she remembered?

She knew she had to stop them. Creeping out of bed, she scoured the flat for anything that might help her. She reached for the wooden hobby horse she had brought up to the flat earlier that day. She'd been braiding its mane, planning a cowboy window display for some time in the future. She picked it up by its head, feeling the satisfyingly heavy weight of the wood in her hands. Looping a string of fairy lights around her arm like a lasso, she felt more prepared, a surge of anger coursing through her now at the audacity of this burglar. How dare he sneak in like this and scare her? How dare he rob a toyshop? She needed to tell him he was a *braendt*.

She decided that speed was of the essence, so she flung open the door from the flat and bounded down the stairs, shouting out a string of offensive words, a mixture of Danish and English. A bulky figure wearing a long dark overcoat turned towards her, his eyes widening in alarm. Her shock tactics had worked, she thought as she raised the hobby horse above her head and hit him with the pole.

'Fuck,' he said, doubling over immediately, hands raised to protect his head as she knocked him to the floor, wrapping the fairy-light wire round him as quickly as she could.

'What the f— What the hell are you ...' His words became muffled as the wire pressed into his face, cutting across his cheeks and mouth.

He hadn't got a weapon, she noticed with relief, just a nasty bunch of keys in his hand that she quickly reached out and snatched from him.

He roared out, making her leap backwards. 'Gimme 'ose 'ack ... mine.'

She turned quickly, racing back upstairs to the flat to plug in the landline she'd disconnected earlier after a window company representative had rung four times in half an hour and she had told him he was a *svin* and to stick his triple-glazed PVC windows up his *røu*.

She had done it, she had tied up a burglar. Now she needed the police to get here and she could relax. He hadn't made it into the shop, she thought with some relief.

'Don't move, they're on their way! Don't try anything stupid!' she found herself yelling, suddenly picturing the horror movie and fully expecting him to start crawling towards her up the stairs, groaning, clawed hand reaching for the next step and the inevitable weapon that would be lying around (pitchfork/kitchen knife/axe).

He was shouting things at varying intervals but the words were still muffled as she scoured the kitchen counter and the sofa cushions for the phone. Finally she located it in the drawer she'd tidied it into, underneath a tea towel. Staring at the handset, however, she realised that in her panic she couldn't remember the number for the police in England. She tried the Danish one, punching the numbers in, her breath coming fast.

'*This call cannot be connected.*'

'*Lort!*' He mustn't know. 'They're coming right now,' she yelled over her shoulder, almost cringing as she imagined his face peering around the bottom of the door, limbs free of their shackles, crawling across the space to kill her.

She kept her eyes on the door as she punched in one of the numbers on the corkboard. There was the sound of glass and chatter at the other end and then a familiar voice. 'Hello, the Fox and Hounds, how can I help?'

'Gavin,' she hissed, 'it's me, it's Clara. Can you hear me?' She pressed the phone into her ear, desperate to be in that pub, surrounded by people not about to stab her.

'Who's me? Louisa, is that you? Are you calling from Spain? We're having a lock-in, it's like old times, but we miss you ...'

Clara didn't have time to ponder the fact that his voice

sounded different, softer. 'No, it's me,' she repeated, 'Clara. Someone's broken in. I'm calling from the flat. He's downstairs right now.'

Gavin had obviously heard enough to realise it was serious. 'Clara? OK. Stay there,' he said in a louder voice. She felt instant relief that he was going to help her. 'I'll be over in two seconds.' She heard him yell across the room. 'Clive, I've got to go out for a few minutes. Man the bar and don't let anyone take the tip jar. It wasn't funny last time and it won't be funny now.'

This added piece of normality made Clara feel reassured. She gripped the phone even tighter, knuckles strained white.

Gavin's voice came back on the line. 'You get yourself somewhere safe. I'm going to hang up now, OK, but I'm coming straight to you. Got that, Clara? It's OK, just get somewhere safe.'

'Thank you,' Clara whispered, feeling her throat thicken with emotion.

She hung up and stood straining her ears for noise. Aside from her own breathing and the clashing chords of ominous imaginary music pounding in her head, she couldn't hear anything else. It had gone quiet downstairs and she inched her way over to the door and glanced out.

She sagged in relief. He was still tied up, still where she'd left him, though he was bucking back and forth, trying to free himself from the wire. She had a momentary flicker of pride in her tying-up-burglar skills. Maybe she should barricade herself into the bathroom? Gavin wouldn't be long; he had sounded really worried. He'd be here soon. She should definitely hide.

The man stopped bucking, perhaps seeing her silhouetted in the doorway. 'I'm her son,' he shouted from the foetal position. 'I'm Louisa's son,' he repeated.

Clara froze. How did he know Louisa's name? A lucky guess? Had he seen post in the corridor?

'That's what a burglar would say,' she called out uncertainly, taking a step back towards the flat door.

Lady CaCa suddenly woke up, shaking out her wings, craning her neck. 'JOE JOE MASTER JOE, LOVE ISLAND JOE.' Her squawking drowned out the start of what the burglar was now yelling at Clara.

'. . . the son of the woman who has let you house-sit, who has allowed you to reopen the toyshop she was planning to close, who has left you to care for a fucking nightmare of a parrot and the world's most laid-back cat? A burglar would know all that, would they?' he panted.

Clara had started to feel dread build during his speech, and by the end she had rushed out of the flat, clattered down the stairs and was bent over him. 'You're Louisa's son. You're Joe.'

He looked up at her through a faceful of wire, one eyelid clamped shut by a fairy-light bulb. 'I am. And you must be our house-sitter.'

Clara swallowed. 'Clara,' she said in a small voice. Tentatively she started to attempt to unravel him. 'So

110

sorry ... here, let me ... sorry, there's a bulb under your ... in your, um, thigh bit.'

He was muttering, sweat along his hairline, red-cheeked, hair askew.

Clara felt the heat flood her own face as she tried to detangle the bulbs, pulling her hand away as she accidentally brushed the crotch of his suit. 'Sorry, there was ... there's a couple of tricky wires,' she said, watching him slowly shake them off him.

When he stood up he seemed to fill the entire corridor, blocking out the bare bulb above him, smoothing his hair as he looked down his nose at her.

'STAY RIGHT THERE. GET AWAY, CLARA!' came a shout from the doorway, and Gavin barrelled into the corridor, flicking the switch so that they were flooded with light. Clara blinked at the sudden change.

Gavin marched down the corridor in wellington boots, a tea towel still slung over one shoulder. The burglar – Louisa's son Joe – was standing in a pool of plastic wire, a red mark on the side of his face where she'd hit him with the pole, the hobby horse lying ominously on the floor. His brown hair was sticking up and his grey eyes were glaring at her. She thought back to the photo she'd seen in the flat. Aside from the fact that the man in that had been smiling, it was definitely the same person. He was thinner in the face than she had imagined, paler. And a lot better dressed; that woollen overcoat looked designer, as did the suit underneath.

'Get away from her,' Gavin called, stepping forward

111

before Clara could warn him and twisting Joe's arm behind his back.

'Agh.' Joe doubled over. 'Fuck.'

'I've got him, Clara, don't panic.' Gavin twisted Joe's arm harder.

'Gah.'

'Don't squirm,' Gavin shouted. 'It's all right, Clara, you're safe n—'

Clara was holding both hands up, waving them, cutting him off. 'Gavin, it's OK, it's Joe. I was wrong, it's OK.' She watched Gavin's face register the words.

'Joe?' he repeated, letting go of his arm and spinning him around to look him in the face. 'Joe as in ... Louisa's Joe?' Gavin seemed flustered, leaping away from him. 'What the hell are you doing creeping in here at two in the morning?'

'I drove up from London. I was handling a deal in New York,' Joe was saying, his mouth turned down. He bent to pull the wire from his feet. 'God forbid I get attacked entering my own home,' he growled, looking at Clara with such disgust she couldn't help flinching.

'Thought he was a burglar,' she mumbled, almost to convince herself she had done the right thing. The horse on the floor stared back at her with its glass eye.

'Well, why don't we get upstairs and warm up, eh?' Gavin said, sensing that the atmosphere was about to turn even frostier.

'Good idea.' Clara felt a rush of gratitude. 'I'll put the kettle on. The English like tea, yes, tea fixes everything.'

She padded back up the stairs in her slipper socks, aware of Louisa's lurid dressing gown, her pyjamas underneath. She moved to the counter, smoothing her hair. She never felt in control when not wearing a bra. She hadn't failed to notice that Joe, even puce with anger, was a bit gorgeous.

Clicking on the kettle, she held her breath as Gavin and Joe moved into the flat. Joe was removing his overcoat, a smart navy suit and crisp white tie below. He looked absurdly overdressed in the eclectic space.

Lady CaCa seemed the only one delighted to see him, marching up and down her pole, head flung back, repeating, 'NICE TO SEE YOU, TO SEE YOU NICE, JOE,' and not calling him a shithead once. Roddy merely opened one eye, noted that there were more people in the flat than normal and rolled over again, his paws up around his face as if telling them all to shut the hell up and let him sleep.

'You've really done wonders,' Gavin said, moving into the room, taking in the wiped-down surfaces, the clothes tidied away, the touches she'd added.

Clara nodded, grateful that he'd noticed the difference. The aching arms and red-raw hands were a fine pay-off if she had improved the place.

'You can see the floor for a start,' Gavin laughed. 'I never knew it was this big. Louisa just always seemed to have so much ... stuff. It looks so ... so different.' He moved through the room taking in the changes. Clara had discovered a stack of boxes and had put away a hundred and one things, draping throws and blankets over sofas and chairs and adding lamps to every nook and cranny.

Joe looked up from his iPhone, eyes scanning the room before dropping back down to the message he was tapping out. Clara felt her shoulders droop as the kettle clicked off, steam rising in a cloud.

'Tea?' she asked.

'I'm not staying,' Joe said, not looking up.

'Oh.' Clara found herself shifting from one foot to the other. Something about Joe made her nervous. She was trying really hard not to keep apologising. The livid red mark on his face didn't help relax her.

'You've got so many candles,' Gavin said, bending down to look at a cluster on either side of the woodburner. There were more all along the mantelpiece, on the nest of tables, lined up on the windowsills, all different heights and sizes. 'Bet they look brilliant when they're all lit.'

'Probably burn the place down,' muttered Joe, just loud enough for Clara to hear. She felt herself stiffen.

'This rug might be the softest thing I've ever felt,' Gavin said, moving across to reach a hand out, stroking the blanket that was folded up on the back of the rocking chair. 'It's so cosy in here,' he added.

'I have some more things planned.' Clara smiled over at him, glad of the distraction.

'Going to get an architect in and bash down some walls, are you?' Joe snapped, slipping his mobile into his inside pocket.

'I . . .' Clara's mouth hung open. She was too surprised to

think of anything to say. She folded her arms in front of her defensively.

Joe was rubbing at the red mark on his face.

'Would you like some ice for that?' she asked, turning to the freezer.

'What, for the massive bump *you* made?' he said, eyes narrowed.

She bit her lip. 'I really am sorry.' She paused. 'At least I was protecting your property,' she added, giving him a small smile, an attempt to charm.

He looked back at her in stony silence. Too soon.

'Maybe I should get you to come into the pub, take a look around, give me some ideas,' Gavin mused. He was in his own world now, oblivious to the frosty exchange in front of him.

'I'd love that, Gavin,' Clara said, desperately rootling in the freezer for the ice cube tray. Locating it, she stood up, pressing some pieces out onto a tea towel and offering it to Joe. He shook his head. 'So where will you go?' she blurted, watching him move around the flat, his lip curling as he took in the unmade bed, an abandoned bra on the floor. She felt heat creep into her face as he turned back to her.

'I'll stay at the pub. You got a room, Gavin?'

'I've got a room, no need to pay,' Gavin said, waving a hand in the air dismissively.

'I'll pay,' Joe growled.

'But really, that's silly, you can't stay there. Please stay here, it's your home, your mum's.'

'I'd rather not,' he said, pulling out the phone from his pocket for what seemed like the seven billionth time.

Clara felt as if he had dropped the bag of ice on her. 'No need to be a *svin*.'

'A what?'

'Nothing,' she mumbled, trying to remember that she had smashed this guy in the face and was sleeping in his home; she shouldn't be rude. But he was making her angrier and angrier with his narrowed eyes and his slick suits and his stupid tappity-tapping on the phone that never seemed to stop vibrating. She felt cold water drip onto her leg and quickly deposited the ice in the sink behind her.

Joe had moved across to get his coat. Lady CaCa, clearly sensing that he might be leaving again, started squawking as he shrugged it on. 'I AM YOUR FATHER!'

Gavin frowned. 'Well, as fun as it is standing around here, I think I'd better get back. Long day tomorrow and all that.' He turned to Clara. 'You've got the new unveiling, haven't you?'

'Unveiling?' Joe lifted an eyebrow in question.

'Whole village is talking about it, Joe. She's had a countdown going in the window,' he explained.

Clara smiled weakly. The shop plans seemed a million years ago.

'Something exciting?' Gavin asked with a broad smile. Clara went to answer but he held up a hand. 'Don't ruin it for me. I'm curious too, you know. Right, Joe, shall we get off, leave Clara to get some sleep?'

'I can stay at the pub instead, let Joe . . . ' Clara began, guilt making her trip over her words.

Joe had already walked across to the door. 'No, please, I insist.' He voice dripped with sarcasm.

'But . . . ' Clara bit her lip as Gavin walked past, resting a hand on her arm. 'I've got it,' he said under his breath.

She swallowed her feelings, nodding at him as he turned away. Joe had already left the flat, his footsteps loud on the stairs below.

Chapter 13

Joe trudged along in silence next to Gavin, who, he noticed, had a tea towel slung over one shoulder. He drew up the collar of his winter overcoat, his temple still smarting from the blow from the pole. What had the bloody woman been thinking? Any harder and she might have killed him. He felt his head throb, the mild headache he always seemed to have now overwhelming him, so he barely paid attention to what Gavin was saying.

'All changed a bit since you were last here, I imagine?' Gavin indicated the shops opposite. Joe hadn't been looking, only now seeing the empty glass fronts, the FINAL CLEARANCE signs in a couple of the windows.

He grunted, not trusting himself to speak through the headache.

'Louisa packing up seems to have made it all real,' Gavin went on. 'I always thought we were just going through a bit of a bad patch. Like Gigglesworth, a few miles away, when the old pub on the corner closed and all the business went elsewhere. I thought we'd get through it, sit out the winter and start up again. Yulethorpe was voted Best-Kept Village only four years ago. It's a great place ...' He tailed off, his head bowed.

'Bit of a backwater,' Joe said.

'Not to those of us who live here.' Gavin's voice sounded gruff.

Joe shrugged. 'No need for a raft of shops when people can get everything online. Seventy-eight per cent of the population buy things that way. The supermarkets deliver to the back of beyond.'

'How depressing,' Gavin said.

Joe paused. He'd never thought of it like that; he liked the convenience. He bristled at the implicit suggestion that he was doing things wrong.

'I'm not too depressed when I'm eating wasabi prawn rolls delivered within the hour from the finest restaurant in London, and the internet means you can get things cheaper – not that that's my concern,' he couldn't help adding.

Did he imagine it, or did Gavin roll his eyes?

'I suppose you like interacting every time you buy a sandwich,' Joe said, a defensive edge to his voice. He could hardly think through the throbbing in his head.

119

Gavin shrugged. 'I'm old-fashioned, I guess.'

They'd reached the pub. Gavin led him in through the glass-panelled door, the room flooded with light that made them both blink. There was a bald man behind the bar stacking glasses on the edge of the counter. 'All OK, Gavin. Everyone left. The tip jar hasn't been touched.'

Gavin was thanking him as Joe looked around. It really did look bleak. Joe had never been inside the place before, though he'd heard all about it from his mother – the steak night, the Monday pub quiz, her games of darts with this Gavin character. Joe looked at him. He was enormous, round, meaty head resting on massive shoulders, a tattoo mostly hidden by his sleeve; Joe imagined a mermaid or a heart with an arrow. He knew he was being an arsehole but he couldn't seem to snap out of it. He just wanted to crawl into bed and sleep. He pressed lightly at the throbbing mark on his cheek.

'I'll show you the room.' Gavin indicated a door to the left of the bar.

'So what's she like?' Joe blurted out.

Gavin gave him a blank stare; the clock on the wall reminded them both that it was now nearly 3 a.m. 'Clara?'

Joe nodded, resisting the urge to add, 'Of course Clara, who do you think I meant, Mother Teresa?' His head was pounding now; it had been a long night, after a long day.

Gavin had a think. 'She's one of those people who gets pleasure from the simpler things, you know.'

'Simpler things?' repeated Joe.

'You know, she stops to really drink things in, live in the moment. She's just . . . well, she's peaceful.'

Joe looked up at him in amazement, wanting to point at the livid bruise on his face. Peaceful she was not.

Gavin rested a hand on the door handle. 'She's done amazing things already with the shop. People were flocking in the day she made that first display.'

'Display?' Joe raised an eyebrow.

'She'd found all these old wooden toys, vintage pieces. I doubt Louisa even knew she had them in stock – you know what she's like, hoarding things, picking things up from all over the place . . . it was her passion.'

Joe hadn't known that. It was years since he'd spent a decent amount of time at home. Louisa had started the shop when they'd moved to Yulethorpe over twenty years ago. Joe had been twelve years old and had thought a toyshop was the coolest thing. He'd always wanted to be in the shop with her, serving customers, showing off the toys, helping her to order new ones. They'd visited suppliers together. He'd felt like the luckiest boy ever. Then he became a teenager, discovered girls, joined the football team, wanted to get straight As. When he moved to London to go to university and got his first job in the City, the shop had become just a quaint reminder of his childhood. He realised that in the last few years he'd stopped even really asking about it.

'Well, she must have spent hours on it. The wooden tracks looping all over the window, the carriages looking spick and span, the backdrop all these different jigsaws made up to look like one big landscape – it was really very striking. She's creative, definitely; Louisa would have loved it.' Gavin looked off into the distance, a small, sad smile on his face.

'What's in it for her?' Joe asked.

'In it?' Gavin frowned at the question, brought back to reality. 'I think she just thought she could help,' he said.

'Hmm.' Joe didn't believe it for a second. No one just appeared in a village and started overhauling a shop and flat if they didn't have a motive.

'Where's she come from?'

'Denmark, I think,' Gavin said. 'Or Norway. One of the Scandinavian countries definitely. Which one is IKEA?'

'If she's from Scandinavia, how has she found herself in rural Suffolk?' Joe asked.

'Never asked,' Gavin said. 'She's a bit quiet about her reasons. She's travelling around, I know that – has a big rucksack with her life piled up into it. Her English is good, though, as if she's lived here for years.'

'Quiet about her reasons. Maybe something to hide?' Joe said, seizing on the idea.

'If she has, I doubt it's anything sinister. She's a great girl, Joe, you need to give her a chance. If it hadn't been for her ... ' Gavin tailed away, perhaps seeing Joe's expression. Had he been about to say that Louisa had had no one else to help her? That thought made Joe even pricklier.

'We'll see.' His father had always told him never to take people at face value. He could see how his mother might have been fooled: all that blonde hair, the rosy cheeks, the dimples in her cheeks. He would have to be on his guard; everyone else seemed to have been hoodwinked by her.

He followed Gavin up the stairs, deep in these thoughts, and turned to a door on his right.

'Not that one,' Gavin called out in a high-pitched voice.

Joe snatched his hand back from the latch; he certainly didn't want to burst in on a couple sleeping or another guest roaming around their room naked.

Gavin looked positively wide-eyed. 'It's this one. This is yours,' he said, pointing him into the room ahead, where a small single bed nestled under the eaves. Joe tried not to let his face show too much distaste, used as he was to the firm paying for penthouse apartments and a lot of square footage. He could probably touch all four walls if he lay down on the carpet.

'Thanks,' he said, moving past Gavin.

'You haven't got any luggage,' Gavin said, and Joe realised he'd left his bag in the corridor next to the shop. He was damned if he was going to go back now and get whacked over the head again.

'Bollocks,' he breathed.

'I'll get you a toothbrush.'

Joe wrinkled his nose, imagining something left behind by a previous guest.

'I think I've got one still in its pack,' Gavin added, as if reading his mind.

Joe was used to hotel bathrooms packed with Molton Brown toiletries, the softest high-thread-count Egyptian cotton towels, marble surfaces. He sniffed as he noticed the minuscule shower, the loo in lurid avocado green, the tiny square of mirror. Gavin returned with the toothbrush and he managed to look grateful, accepting a towel and some toothpaste too.

'OK, good night then, hope it's comfortable,' Gavin said, his voice hushed as he turned to leave.

Joe nodded and closed the door, instantly regretting his bad mood. He'd just wanted to fall into his own bed after a manic day in the office. He'd apologise in the morning; Gavin didn't seem like a man to hold a grudge.

Standing in the room, the ceiling a couple of inches from the top of his head, he stared at the tiny bed under the eaves, the open curtains, the window showing nothing but the navy sky spattered with stars, no other lights for miles. How different it was to London. He found the quiet disconcerting.

He glanced at his watch: 3.10 a.m. He would quickly check his emails, fire a few over to his team; good to remind them he was still working too.

He pulled the flowered curtains across and rested his head against the velvet headboard of the bed. But as he tried to focus on the emails he'd received, his mind wandered back over the evening's events. His team sounded like they were ready to close this latest deal soon. There'd be another company to target, of course, but he could project-manage things from here for a few days; he'd get Pam to block out his diary. They had a couple of clients not too far away; he could say he was scouting for the next deal. He wanted to stay close, find out what this woman was up to. He tried not to worry what Tom, the other MD, would say if he knew.

Getting up to clean his teeth, he stared at his face in the mirror. It was the lighting that made him look so grey, his eyes so bloodshot. He took out a silver packet from the inside pocket of his jacket and hoped that one of the pills would ease his headache. Then he went back to the bed, kicked off his shoes and lay down under the thin duvet, shutting his eyes, his head throbbing, Clara's face behind his eyelids as he fell into an uneasy sleep.

Mainland Spain was just too chilly so I've headed south to the Canaries. I'm in El Cotillo now, on the west coast of Fuerteventura, and it's much hotter. Although it's so windy here I have lost both my sunhats. I've signed up to do yoga on the beach – tell Clara I'm in a group with a man from Denmark who can do the most brilliant sirsa padasana. I think he has double-jointed everything, it's unnatural the way he bends.

I can't believe she knocked out Joe. The poor darlings, I should have warned her he might appear. Is it a big bump? Oh, he will be cross. Do give him a kiss from me, how gorgeous that he's come up to visit. I hope they get on. She could melt anyone and Joe needs to slow down. We were always thick as thieves when he was little and his father left. Do you remember I told you he used to stand on the table in our flat and recite poetry for me when I was sad because he knew I loved poetry? He is a lovely boy at heart – I miss laughing with him, he can be impossibly serious now.

Fuerteventura is marvellous. Everyone is nude

here, it's wonderful, we all just frolic about in the sea, everything on display. One of the men in a bunker near me (they have these wonderful little stone bunkers to keep the breeze at bay, like posh windbreaks) only wears a neon-yellow cock ring. I'm very excited to see if he changes it for another colour later in the week so will be returning to the same beach for the next few days. I'll send you one of the carved wooden penis bottle openers they sell here so you can feel part of the fun too. You can put it behind the bar, it will be such a talking point!

I'm glad the shop is doing well, that display sounded wonderful, but what of my animals? Is Lady CaCa being an absolute pest? Does she still spit her water when Phillip Schofield's on TV? Poor Phil, I've no idea what she has against him, he seems SUCH a lovely man. You know the vet told me to put her cage on the floor because that will sort out her 'personality disorder'. Apparently if parrots are placed in cages above humans they think they're superior to them and play up. Nasty little man, I'm going to start using the vet in Gigglesworth. I told him firmly that it was nothing to do with Lady CaCa's cage placement; she has always behaved as if she is superior to humans and frankly her ability to concisely comment on the news of the day does seem to prove that she has every right to do so. Imagine if I'd followed his advice.

Can you imagine a subdued and meek Lady CaCa saying GIVE US A CRACKER? Horrific.

Has Roddy finally decided to do something with his life or is he still wafting around in his smoking jacket, daydreaming? I long for the day when he brings a dead mouse home. Maybe living with a Danish girl will help him become a bit more of a warrior; she'll have good strong Viking blood in her.

I've used the double letter tile but frustratingly it barely helps me. I am limping to a heavy loss. I fear that only using up all my tiles will save me. If you have the Q, I will scream; I have been hoarding Us in preparation for it.

Chapter 14

Clara replaced the wooden number 1 with zero and rolled open the shutters, gasping when she saw three children and their parents already staring at the shopfront. Giving them a shy wave, she smiled as they stepped forward, taking in all her hard work. A young girl started clapping, tugging at her mother to look closer, pointing to one of the robots in the display.

Clara was really pleased with this latest effort. She had spent hours cleaning and finding batteries for all the robots, managing to stick a few in place so that their arms whirred up and down but they remained frozen to the floor. She had made the bottom of the window look like a cratered planet, with various alien soft toys piled up around the robots, which beeped and whirred and moved. The backdrop was painted navy blue – she still had paint underneath her nails – and she had scattered different-sized glow stars in clusters all over it, completing the scene with large flashing fairy lights, the bulbs painted red. A futuristic moving display.

She heard the tinkle of the shop door before she had returned to the counter, the hum of voices in the shop making her heart skip.

'Clara, this is brilliant,' Lauren gushed, arriving in a whirlwind, Rory held in her arms, jabbering and pointing as he twisted to be free. 'Rory loves the robot with the scary eyelashes and spanners for hands. I can't stay long but well done you, it's fantastic. I'll tell all the nursery teachers about it, although you can see the flashing lights from a hundred yards away – the shop looks like this wonderful beacon amongst all the grey.'

'I'm glad, I've been excited about this one.'

Lauren bent forward, frowning. 'I can see – you look like you've had absolutely no sleep,' she said.

'Funny you should say that.' Clara stifled a yawn. 'I had a visitor late last night.'

'A visitor?' Lauren lifted one eyebrow. 'That sounds very mysterious and exciting.'

A customer approached before Clara could explain.

'Look,' Lauren said, moving Rory to her other hip, 'I've got to run anyway. Pop over later, once the shop's closed, and tell me all about it.' She was already backing away. 'I know, darling, we're late, but we're always late so they expect it,' she was saying to Rory as she headed out the door.

Clara was at the till for the next hour or so, packaging up toys. She was running low on the remote-controlled robots she had used in the display; the aliens with eight eyes also nearly sold out. In just one morning, she thought, wanting to rush and tell Gavin to call Louisa. She took a quick photo of the shop crammed with customers. It was wonderful to hear noise and giggling and laughter.

Just as she was putting her camera away, she noticed Clive moving into the shop, brushing at his sideburns, biting his lip. She gave him a smile and a wave, wondering what he was doing there. His cheeks and the bald spot on the top of his head blushed pink.

He approached the counter. 'I was wondering if I could buy some glow stars. Wanted to put them on the ceiling of the spare room as a surprise for when my nephew visits,' he said, his voice low, stuttering over the words. He was looking over his shoulder, not at all comfortable.

'Of course,' beamed Clara. 'What a gorgeous thing to do.' He turned an even darker shade of pink.

Just as she was popping a bag of the stars across the counter towards him, she felt a sudden chill, a draught blowing through the shop. Standing in the doorway glaring at them was the spindly frame of Roz. Clive had practically dived behind the counter.

'Roz,' he spluttered.

'Clive,' she said, approaching, staring pointedly at the bag. 'Buying something?'

Clive looked wretched, wringing his hands as if he might

deny all knowledge of the bag and the receipt lying next to it.

Before Clara could help him out, she noticed that the father with the piercing green eyes was back, no daughter in tow but more stubble on his chin, loitering by the One Direction figurines. He gave her a lopsided smile, his hand raised in a wave.

'Hey . . .'

She knew she was staring at him as he pulled out a large camera and approached the counter. 'Hey.' He gave her a dazzling smile, white teeth on display, a thin gap between the front two. 'I'm Sam.' He reached out a hand to shake hers, his grip strong, a wave of peppermint as he spoke. 'We met briefly before.'

'I remember,' Clara said, nearly adding, 'you're the good-looking widower with the penetrating gaze' but just holding back. 'I'm Clara.'

'Hi, Clara.' He did something sexy with the 'l' in her name. She was too busy staring at him to pay much attention to the next sentence. 'I'm a journalist for the local paper and your displays would make a great little news story. Do you mind?' he asked, holding up his camera.

Clara paused. 'Oh,' she said, as the words finally filtered through. 'I'm not sure actually.' She was about to explain that it wasn't her shop, that she would have to check with the owner, when Joe appeared in the doorway, taking in the excited children, the window display, the man pointing his camera at Clara behind the counter as if she was posing for a photo. She knew what it looked like: that she had invited local press to cover it all. He must think she had an ego the size of the room.

'Joe, this is Sa—'

Joe's mouth curled into a sneer as he cut her off. 'I'm just here to pick up my bag,' he said, moving across to the side door. 'I'll be one minute,' he added. 'Wouldn't want to disturb your photo shoot,' he said pointedly, disappearing into the corridor beyond.

Clara felt herself getting hot, wanting to explain that she had been approached for her photo, that she would have asked him.

Roz was looking delighted at the turn of events, rushing over to the door calling Joe's name. He returned with his bag, greeting her with a stiff smile as she launched in for a double kiss. Clive stepped backwards, as if hoping to blend into a toy display behind him and be forgotten. Clara was distracted by another customer at the counter.

'That's twelve pounds,' she said, straining to listen to Roz and Joe. She had a queue in front of her now, and Sam was snapping away from the corner of the room, her eyes drawn to him as he passed her.

Roz and Joe stood out of the way scrutinising her every move, and as the children and parents gradually thinned, Clara felt her fists clenching and unclenching as Roz's various criticisms reached her ears. The shop was 'tacky', the display just a 'gimmick'; Roz couldn't see what all the fuss was about.

'The glow stars aren't even glowing, it's the daytime,' she added, with a nasty little laugh tacked onto the end that finally made Clara spin round.

'They look amazing at night. I was going to leave the shutters open so the children can visit just before closing and see them. It gets dark so early now.'

'Sounds like a blatant security hazard, leaving shutters open at night,' Roz said, turning to Joe, who hadn't been listening to Clara's explanation.

'You can't leave the shutters open overnight,' he spluttered, his suspicions about her laissez-faire attitude clearly solidifying.

'I know that,' Clara hissed from the corner of her mouth, smiling as a freckled boy reached up and deposited an alien soft toy on the counter, his mother, one hand on his ginger hair, reaching for her purse.

'It would be completely reckless. Then you really would get a break-in.' Joe continued to lecture her, looking preposterous in his smart suit surrounded by Barbie boxes and bright yellow trucks.

Clive had taken that moment to sneak away. Roz, seeing him leaving, scurried after him, hissing at him in a low voice. Poor Clive, Clara thought, he looked like he was paying for his visit to the shop. She would be sure to say hello to him more.

Joe had just approached when Sam reappeared with his camera. As the flash went off to her left, Clara took a breath before skirting round the counter to link arms with Joe.

She must try to win him over, let him see all the wonderful things she wanted to do for the place.

'This is the son of the owner,' she announced to Sam with a smile. 'Smile, Joe, it's great press for the shop.'

Joe lifted one hand to shield his face as if he were an A-list celebrity trying to avoid the paparazzi. Something about the action made her want to tease him; he looked so serious, as if he couldn't remember how to relax. She thought of the photo upstairs, a younger version, a carefree stance, an untroubled look. Where had that man gone?

'Oh come on, Joe, you want the readers to see that strong jaw, that steely gaze,' she said, preening and smiling as the camera went off. 'And we want them all in here for the big event.'

'What big event?' Joe asked her. 'News to me.'

'Our new venture,' Clara said, looking solemnly at him then turning to Sam. 'It's going to be huge. A real departure for us. I'll give you an exclusive. Do put it in your piece, we want everyone to know about it, and do come along. It's in four days' time.'

'But ... what the ... ' Joe's mouth was opening and shutting as Clara continued to smile for the camera.

Sam looked up at them both. 'Now just Clara on her own, please,' he said, his eyes burning into her.

'Would you like me in the back or out here?' Clara asked sweetly as Joe stalked off. She watched him go, a bubble of laughter rising up in her. She wasn't normally so provocative, but there was something about Joe that made her want to annoy him. His desire to take life way too seriously reminded her of someone, and the thought made her uncomfortable. She knew exactly what it was like to be that person and she knew how amazing it was to let go.

Chapter 15

He'd return when the shop was closing; he couldn't believe she'd suggest keeping the shutters open. What next? Leave the till open and watch as the entire neighbourhood walked off with his mother's money? She really was a completely reckless hippy. Fine, the shop had been full, but Roz was probably right: it was no doubt a flash in the pan, a curiosity, and the novelty would soon wear off.

He was right to stick around; she would be far too busy draping herself over that photographer to run the shop. He bristled as he thought back to the way she'd looked at him. Why was she having her photograph taken anyway? And she'd tried to drag him into a picture. What would his bosses say if they saw? His diary said he'd spent the morning in a client meeting in Norwich; he didn't want some local news article to bust him in a lie.

He spent the day on his phone, a constant yo-yoing of emails and calls with his team in London as they sorted through the final details of this latest merger. One of the associates had gone AWOL the day before, not answering his phone. Tom wanted him fired. Joe spent twenty minutes saving the guy, who'd been practically living in the office, sending emailed replies at dawn.

The headache was back, at the front of his head behind his eyes, and he massaged his temples. He'd forgotten the lack of a café in the village – not that he'd frequented the restaurant, Bertie's, which had always been heaving and the service way too slow, the owner constantly stopping to ask about everyone's day. He got in his car, continuing to make calls, and headed to the nearest town and the nearest Starbucks. Semi-civilisation, he thought, as he paid for the public car park and walked past a woman reading a newspaper and a couple snogging on a bench.

God, he had to get in touch with Gemma. He'd met her last week after they'd messaged each other on Tinder. She'd been all right, good-looking, and they'd made plans to see each other for drinks after work tonight. He tapped out a message and sent it, knowing he wouldn't be seeing her again. He checked his profile: six new matches, briefly passing over their faces. As he swiped along, they all seemed to merge into one professionally dressed, clear-skinned thirty-something woman. There were so many women in

London, so many dates to go on. He wasn't even sure what he was looking for any more; when did you stop, decide I'll see how this one works out? He swiped again.

He got back to the pub, showered, neck craned at an uncomfortable angle as he shampooed his hair, and pulled on a fresh shirt and trousers. He left off the suit jacket and tie, selecting a Ralph Lauren cashmere jumper and Grenson suede brogues. Feeling marginally better, and popping the second pill that day into his mouth, he headed out, pulling his scarf around him, surprised at the chill in the air.

She had shut the shop but the shutters were still up and the space-themed display could be seen flashing a mile away. Like a big neon arrow for potential burglars. He noticed a girl with a long plait holding her father's hand as she gazed at the backdrop of stars. He tried to look at it as if he were that small child; he had to admit the effect was quite something. But irresponsible . . . He shook his head, ready to talk to Clara about the shutters again when suddenly they were whirring shut.

He let himself into the corridor as she was locking the door from the shop. 'Oh, it's you,' she said, hand on her chest.

'Should I be relieved you're not holding a horse's head?' he said, surprising himself as the words spilled out.

She only showed a tiny flicker of surprise before smiling at him, and he felt something in him thaw. She sat on the bottom step and started pulling on walking boots.

'I wanted to talk to you,' he said.

She looked up and said, a defensive edge to her voice,

'Look, I've closed the shutters. It was only for a bit, just so the children could see the effect on their way back from school.'

'It's not about the shutters – I'm sorry, you were right, it looked good. It's about—'

'It's been a long day,' Clara stood up and shrugged on her coat, 'and I need a walk before it gets really dark, and cold. So if you want to talk, that's where I'll be.'

He wasn't used to being cut off in the middle of a sentence; he wasn't used to walking. 'Can't you . . . ' but she was already clicking her tongue with impatience so he relented. 'Fine.'

He went to the cupboard underneath the stairs, pulling out a winter coat. 'I keep a few things here for when I'm back. Old clothes.' The coat was last season's Canada Goose parka. He took his phone and keys out of his pocket, resting them on a stair to transfer them to the coat.

'Are you coming then?' She was wearing a purple knitted hat, her long blonde hair falling down her back beneath it. She walked out, leaving him in the semi-darkness of the corridor.

He followed, pushing one arm through a sleeve. 'Bloody hell,' he muttered, watching her turn down a side street. What was she in such a hurry to see? He set off after her.

She was standing, her back to him, leaning against a wooden five-bar gate, looking out over a churned-up field, the furrows straight, pools of murky rainwater collected in between the lines of soil.

'So the shop,' he began, about to launch into a speech he had prepared, and practised, on the way up from London.

'Isn't it amazing, you forget there are any houses at all,' she said, gazing out at the unbroken view, the countryside stretching for miles.

He joined her at the gate, stamping his feet to warm up, the wind lifting his hair. He'd forgotten how quickly the village became fields, with the woods beyond. He had spent hours exploring the area as a boy, playing in the woods with school friends, building wigwams, damming rivers, cycling down leafy slopes making skids in the mud with his BMX. Then it had all stopped. As a teenager he'd been busy working on his exams or seeing his father in London at the weekends. He'd often resented returning to the back of beyond, had been far too busy then for the bracing walks his mother always gushed about. You'd think she'd discovered the eighth wonder of the world the way she spoke about the woods.

'Yes, you do,' he agreed, wanting to get her back on track. 'So, the shop. It's all very well you walking in and taking over like this, but ... Are you listening?'

'Sorry.' Clara turned, the fading sun turning her skin a shade of pink. 'It's just a perfect evening to be out. I am listening,' she added in the most vague voice, which suggested she really wasn't. 'Shall we walk?' She set off down a track that skirted the field.

Joe felt his confidence leaking away as he continued to walk alongside her, dodging a puddle, his suede brogues nearly getting covered. 'I'll be needing to come in and start taking stock of things, you see.'

He wiped at a mark on his sleeve as Clara stopped again to look at another view. What was this woman doing? How could anyone amble in this way? Who had time to faff about, smell flowers and sigh as they stepped over stiles?

'I'm going to be staying on, get the accounts in order, see what the situation is in terms of income and outgoings.' He stared at her then, wanting to see her reaction. Had that foiled her plans? 'Then find a buyer.'

He left a momentary pause; when she didn't respond, he opened his mouth to continue.

'Is that what your mum would want? To sell?' Her voice was low and quiet.

He bristled. Something about the way she said it felt as if she was telling him he didn't know his own mother. 'Well, she left, wanted to close it. I'd say she'd be pretty grateful if I could salvage some money from it all.' He stepped in a puddle, cold water shooting over his foot, dampening his socks, splattering mud all over his brogues and the bottom of his trousers.

'All OK?' Clara said in the same irritatingly dreamy voice, as if she couldn't see what he'd just done.

'Fine,' he snapped.

Clara shrugged. 'Your mum didn't seem that preoccupied with the money side of things, more the fact that no one came in any more, and that's changed,' she said.

He knew it. She was trying to put him off finding a buyer; she had her own plans for the shop.

'And if they keep coming in, she will make money again.'

He scoffed. 'What, as judged by your profit from all of about a week being there?'

Clara lifted her shoulders again and dropped them. What was she playing at? Was this nonchalant approach some kind of tactic?

'So I'll come in, start going over things. I'll base myself in the flat in the day, I need somewhere where's there's Wi-Fi anyway so . . .'

Clara had stopped again, arms folded on top of a fence. She looked around at him and he trailed away. 'I know you want to talk, but can you be quiet for a few moments? Just unwind, take it all in,' she said, moving her arm across in front of her in an arc.

He nodded, wondering quite what she was up to. Was this a power play? Was she really just interested in the view or was she buying time? He watched her through narrowed eyes as she returned to resting on the fence, chin on top of her folded arms, eyes shut as the sun sank beneath the line of trees beyond. She had the longest eyelashes he'd ever seen, like a porcelain doll's, and luminous skin, the evening light softening her features. He almost forgot who she was, why he was right to keep up his guard.

'If we're not going to talk about it, shall we head back?' he said. 'Now that it's getting dark.'

She let out a small sigh, as if he had somehow broken her mood. He didn't care, wanted to have things wrapped up. The woman walked at about half his pace; Jesus, by the time they'd navigated their way back, it would be nightfall.

He had things to do. He didn't want to just leave her here, though.

'What an amazing sunset,' she said, indicating the fields stretching into the horizon.

It was his turn to sigh, and he did it loudly. She was treating him as if he'd had his eyes shut the entire walk. 'Yep. Great,' he said. He stared where her finger was pointing, realising for a moment that she was right: it was quite beautiful. The churned-up mud in sentry lines reaching for miles, a patchwork of fields beyond and then the enormous dusty-pink sky, leaking into blues. He didn't see sunsets like this in London, the houses and apartments often blocking out the horizon, and anyway he was always in the office when the sun set, just a reminder of the work left to do that day.

Thoughts of the office increased his heart rate, and his mind instantly turned to the things he'd left in motion that day. He wondered if the company they were negotiating with had got back to his team. Their last offer hadn't been high enough; they wanted three bar at least. He knew he might have to step in and put the pressure on at some point. His hand reached automatically for his jacket pocket. He would get an update from Pam. He wanted to know if Tom had noticed his absence; he didn't want him stirring things up. The last thing he needed was anyone in the team running to Karen.

He patted at the pocket: empty.

Clara had turned away from the fence and walked past him as he was pulling the pockets inside out, as if his phone would materialise in the lining. He stepped backwards, not looking, a cowpat squelching over the brogue that wasn't wet. He was too distracted by the loss of his phone to even notice the marks on the suede.

'Where the . . . ' he was muttering. The headache that he hadn't noticed on the walk had returned now, his temples throbbing. He patted pointlessly at the pockets again.

Clara was a few feet away, the village a backdrop behind her as she called to him, 'Looking for something?' Her expression was strange, a small smile on her face as she tucked her hands into the pockets of her own coat and waited for him to reply.

'My phone, I thought I'd put it in this coat, but . . . ' He was patting at his trouser pockets now, his heart racing faster with each failed attempt. God, if he couldn't find it, he'd have to head back to the office. His whole life was on that phone. He needed to be on a conference call in a couple of hours and he had all the contacts in the handset. Why hadn't he written them down?

'It's back in the shop corridor,' she said cheerfully. 'On the stairs. You left it there with your keys.'

'What?' He looked up, Clara's words only just reaching him through the fog of his thoughts. He clenched his jaw. 'Why didn't you tell me?'

'I thought it might be nice for you not to have it on you. You seem to be quite attached to it.' She turned back towards the village, her stupid swishy blonde hair flicking behind her.

He followed her, stumbling a little on the uneven ground, his feet now sodden, his trousers probably ruined. 'You have no idea what you might have done. I need to be contactable at all times. We've got billions riding on this deal, billions.'

She had stopped walking, but didn't turn round.

'Of course it's fine for you with your frolicking about the countryside looking at sunsets and animals. "Ooh, it's a deer, it's a flower, it's a sunset",' he called out in an attempt at a high girl's voice, the accent decidedly German. 'When some of us have jobs to go to, work to do. And it's probably just an act anyway; I know it's all part of some kind of long game you're playing.'

She turned to face him, her nose wrinkling at the phrase. 'Long game?' she repeated. 'We're not in Canary Wharf now, Joe.'

'Yes, a long game,' he said, stepping towards her. 'You've somehow decided that my mother is vulnerable. She takes off for Spain, leaving her shop and flat conveniently empty, just as you appear, *voilà*, out of the blue, with your good intentions' – he made speech marks in the air – 'and your oh-let-me-just-stick-a-glow-star-on-it attitude, as if somehow it's all one big, happy coincidence ...' He knew he was sounding paranoid, but he couldn't seem to stop himself, his heart still racing, palms sweating.

Clara was opening and closing her mouth.

'It *was* a coincidence,' she stressed. 'Why would I want her gone? It's not exactly Harrods,' she said, growing more confident with each sentence, her cheeks reddening as she spoke.

'Oh, great, insult the place, it *is* my mother's livelihood after all,' he cut in, not wanting to hear her pathetic excuses.

'I know it is, and I'm just trying to help, to do something nice,' she said, lingering over the last word. A strand of hair had escaped from her purple hat and whipped across her face, and she pushed it back with a swipe of her hand.

'And there's nothing in it for you, oh no,' Joe said, his voice dripping with sarcasm. 'Just being nice to someone you've never met and don't know the first thing about.'

'I liked her,' Clara said, her voice growing quiet, her fists unclenching. For a second Joe thought she might start crying. She didn't seem the type but he couldn't be absolutely sure. His voice softened a fraction.

'I like her too,' he said slowly. 'Which is why I want to know why you're here, what exactly you're up to.'

'Look, Joe, I don't know what has happened in your life to make you quite so suspicious, but where I come from, we actually trust each other.'

He cut her off again, his hand on his chest, his voice getting louder. 'In the land of pixies and elves, is it? Where you all prance about singing to the wind and unicorns float past rainbows in the sky?'

She couldn't speak for a moment, watching him hop from foot to foot. 'Denmark, actually.'

Feeling foolish, he stood stock still and took a breath. 'Well, I don't know why you're not off being fabulously NICE to someone over there.' He thought that was as good a place as any to leave things and with a nod set off past her, trying not to slip in his mud-soaked brogues. He picked up the pace, surprised by the beads of sweat breaking out on his hairline. Was he really this unfit? Fortunately she was such an ambler he would be able to get back to the shop in good time, find his phone, send an email and be out of her way before she had even left the field.

Nice, he scoffed to himself. He thought back to the expression on her face as he accused her: the sad eyes, the slightly wistful expression. For a brief moment he wondered whether she was telling the truth. Then he put his shoulders back and pushed on. No, his instinct must be right: no one was that nice.

Chapter 16

'Yay, you came,' Lauren said, opening the door. 'And Rory is in bed and Patrick is working late, so . . . ' She waved the bottle of wine she had dangling by her side.

Clara was barely over the threshold when she began. 'He's a *rend kusse*,' she announced, pulling off her purple hat and reaching down to unlace her boots. 'A total and utter *rend kusse*.'

'Whoa, whoa, whoa, who is a what? Isn't that the really bad word? The one we only ever use in emergencies? Doesn't it mean . . .' Lauren whispered the translation, doing a pretty obscene mime at the same time.

Clara nodded. 'It is an emergency; he is a complete *kusse* who thinks I'm out to steal his mother's shop and take her flat and plunder it for jewellery and gold and' – she followed

Lauren into the kitchen, accepting a glass of wine that she instantly started waving around – 'probably kidnap her animals and, and ...'

'And breathe,' Lauren laughed. 'Look, let's not wake Rory with your deranged Danish outburst; let's go into the conservatory.' She pointed over her shoulder and grabbed a couple of blankets on her way past.

Lauren settled herself on a threadbare sofa, throwing a blanket over her legs and inviting Clara to join her. They huddled under the tartan blankets, Clara's wine wobbling as she began.

'He thinks I'm just this, what's the word, con, con, you know, a con *kunstner*.'

'Jeez, woman, your language.' Lauren had started giggling, lightly shaking to Clara's left.

'No, you know, a con ...' Clara was waving her wine around, 'CON ARTIST,' she practically screamed as she remembered the English translation. 'And that I'm here with some devious motive when in fact I just thought it would be a nice thing to do.' She stressed the last few words, sinking deeper into the sofa as she finished, collapsing into the cushions, all the anger out now, spent.

'Well,' Lauren said, taking a slow sip of her own wine, 'I'm glad we cleared that up.' She looked sideways at Clara. 'So who are we talking about and what has happened exactly?' Her mouth was twitching as if she was trying to stop a smile. It made Clara relax for the first time in a while.

Clara rested her head back on the cushions. 'Let's just

drink wine and sit here and look at the night sky,' she said, realising that through the conservatory glass the whole sky was filled with clusters of stars. 'Beautiful,' she breathed, feeling the wine warm her insides and her body relax as she gazed. A star shot across the sky, as if personally sent to cheer her up.

'Right.' Lauren clapped, reaching to fill up Clara's glass. 'That's enough astronomical appreciation. I need the quick version and I need it now.'

'Fine,' Clara said, taking a sip. 'So Joe came to the shop at the end of the day and essentially accused me of wanting to stay in the village to rob his mother of her livelihood.'

'He said that?' Lauren said, mouth falling open.

Clara thought for a moment about their exchange. 'Basically, yes.'

'Wow.' Lauren took a gulp of wine. 'That's terrible.'

Clara nodded miserably.

'What are you going to do?' Lauren asked.

'I suppose I should leave,' Clara sighed. 'That's what he wants.'

'Do *you* want that?'

Clara thought about her plans for the shop and shook her head. 'No, I want to stay. Not forever, but long enough that I can make a difference.'

'Then you *should* stay – you can't let him bully you out of there. Louisa trusted you to look after things and that's what you're doing. And wonderfully, I might add,' Lauren said, putting a hand on Clara's arm.

Clara couldn't help a small smile. 'So what am I going to do about him?' She drank more wine; just picturing his face caused her to knock it back quicker.

'Well, you've already hit him round the head and knocked him out.'

Clara shot a look at her.

Lauren shrugged. 'It's a small village; word gets around.'

'Gavin told you,' Clara accused her.

Lauren took another sip of wine. 'Yup, Gavin totally told me. I liked the bit about the fairy lights, by the way. So your next move could be ... um ... to hospitalise him?'

'Lauren,' Clara whined, 'I'm serious: I need your help.'

Lauren nodded, a solemn expression on her face. 'You're right, I'm sorry. I'm going to help. OK,' she said, after a momentary pause, 'you could have it out with him right now. In the flat?'

'He's not in the flat. He's staying in the pub.'

Lauren's forehead creased. 'In the pub, while you're staying in his mum's place, which has two bedrooms. Weird.'

'He refused to stay,' Clara admitted. 'I had just whacked him in the face with a horse's head.'

'Fair point. OK, scrap that idea, we need to be cleverer anyway.' Seconds later, Lauren sat up poker straight, spilling drops of wine on the blanket. 'Ooh, I've got it.'

'You have?' Clara said, dabbing at the wine.

Lauren looked at her, nodding furiously. 'You should play it the other way. Don't have it out with him at all. Get him on your side. Make him see first-hand that you're not there for any deep, dark reason. Charm him! Woooooo him,' she said, accentuating the word.

'Woo?'

'Court! Seduce!'

'How can I? He is completely convinced I am about to make off with the takings.'

'Invite him to move in and make him see you're a force for good not evil.'

'I could, I suppose ...' Clara turned the stem of the wine glass around. 'I'm just not sure he would want to, and I'm definitely not sure he has it in him to be nice and understanding.'

Lauren nodded. 'Louisa told me he is a bit hard. Always working, always on the move, never just chills.' Her eyes lit up as she spoke. 'Oh that's BETTER,' she said, warming to her theme. 'Look. You need him to see that life isn't all City deals and stress and profit and money. You're all about this *hygge* stuff, right?' She pronounced it *huegaaaaaah*. 'You've transformed the shop and the flat; Gavin told me it looks like a centrepiece in a home improvement magazine ...'

She paused to look at Clara encouragingly, and Clara nodded slowly, not sure where she was headed with all this.

'Well, you should transform *him*! *Hygge* him! You've done wonders with the shop and the flat already, so just think what you might achieve with an actual live person!'

Clara had already started shaking her head. 'No, no, that's impossible. You can't *hygge* someone who doesn't want to be *hygged*.' She knew this wasn't a word, but Lauren wouldn't have a clue.

'You don't tell him!' Lauren practically smacked her forehead with her palm. 'You just set about changing him, chilling him out, softening him, showing him the *hygge* life,' she said, her eyes sparkling, the wine now mostly on the blanket rather than in her glass.

Clara paused, about to protest again, but then she thought about it. He was certainly very stressed. She knew what that was like. She thought back to a time in her past when she had needed to make a change. When she had been dressed in designer suits and sky-high heels, blisters on her feet as she clacked over marble floors. Another meeting to attend, a conference call to get to, another client to call. The anxiety as she pushed the button for her floor in the lift, feeling the steel box closing in on her; fears that she wasn't good enough, despite the work, despite the hours. But wasn't Joe right in the middle of all that, unable to embrace a change? Could she really show him there was another way?

'Right, let's open another bottle and draw up more specific plans,' Lauren said, weaving out of the room, glass in hand. 'I'll fetch Rory's easel; this shit just got serious.'

A couple of hours later and Clara was floating back to the flat, various thoughts coming together in her wine-addled mind. Before she went to see Joe, she knew she had some work to do. She let herself into the flat, ignoring Lady CaCa's call of 'NICE TO SEE YOU, TO SEE YOU NICE, SHITHEAD,' and started sourcing what she needed from various cupboards. Phase One: Operation Make Joe's Room Look Super-Hygge.

She set about transforming the place, tidying and cleaning his room into a Zen-like haven. She smoothed out the fresh linen on the double bed, plumped his cushions, draped a large faux-fur blanket over the duvet and snuck a hot-water bottle in between the sheets. She stopped for another drink but she knew she wasn't finished. She placed a sheepskin rug in front of the old Victorian fireplace and swept the hearth, placing different-sized candles in the space. After a few more sips of wine she set about polishing every surface, the smell of beeswax lingering in the air. Veering unevenly across the room, she drew the charcoal-grey curtains, then fetched a couple of the lamps from her own room, placing one next to a battered cherry-red leather armchair in the corner by the window and the other beside the bed. She piled up a selection of books on the side table, poetry mostly, and stepped back to admire her work. It was ready. Operation How to Get Your Hygge On was a go. Now she just needed her specimen.

The wine fuzz was still helping as she made her way straight to the pub, arriving in a whirl of energy at the door of the bar. With her purple hat and her mismatched coat she was transported back for a moment to that first night, when she had seen Louisa arrive in such pomp. She felt as if she was channelling her.

'Clara!' Gavin called from behind the bar, his smile wide as he pulled a pint.

She made an unsteady line for him, bashing into a low stool and a customer on the way.

'Oof, ow, sorry.'

'Here to celebrate?'

Clara gave him a quizzical look.

'The display,' he laughed, 'A triumph. The children are already trying to guess what you're going to do next.'

Today's display felt like many moons ago, and Clara blinked. 'Of course. Display,' she said.

Gavin stopped pulling on the lever and leaned over to her. 'Everything all right?'

Clara nodded, her eyesight marginally blurry. 'All's OK,' she said, wondering if she was slurring, 'Jusht here to see Joe.'

'Wait,' Gavin said, moving down the bar towards her. 'I forgot. I sent a picture of the window to Louisa. She loved it. She said, "All I can see is children smiling and it's made me whoop. Also KE is not a word" – oh, that last bit's for me,' he said, coughing over his embarrassment.

Louisa's message was the nudge that Clara needed, her resolve hardening as she stepped around the bar and headed up the narrow stairs. She wanted to stay in the village and she needed things to be OK with Joe. She passed the forbidden door – a pause as she hovered outside. She could pop in, just briefly, before she saw Joe. There was a noise behind her and Gavin's head suddenly appeared at the bottom of the stairs. 'He's straight ahead,' he said in a loud voice. 'Where you were. The only room,' he added, watching as she moved on by.

'Yes, yes, of course,' Clara said, hopping as if she'd been prodded with a hot stick.

Her hand wavered in a fist over the door. She couldn't get out of it now. She could hear Joe's voice inside. Was he with someone? Silence. Perhaps she was a bit drunker than she'd thought.

She knocked. No reply. She knocked again, knowing that if she didn't get this over with, she wouldn't have the nerve.

The door opened wide in one swift movement, and Clara, who had been leaning heavily on it, stumbled into the room.

'You,' he said, stepping back as she careered in, no doubt fearing she was here to hit him with something wooden. She straightened up, holding both hands aloft in mock surrender as if to prove she hadn't brought along any particular sharp or heavy toys to brain him with.

She was huffing as she spoke. 'Needed to see you. Say sorry.'

'What's that?'

'I came,' she said, catching her breath, 'to say I'm sorry.'

He had opened his mouth, looking ready to pounce. As the words left her, she saw his mouth snap shut, and then open again. 'Oh.' He raked a hand through his hair. He looked bizarre, she suddenly noticed. His shirt was ironed, collar stiff, tie poker straight but his trousers were rolled up to the knee as if he were about to go paddling, socks and mud-covered brogues abandoned by the bed. 'Clara, that's nice of you, but I'm right in the mi—'

She wasn't listening, didn't follow where his arm was pointing, just wanted to get the words out.

'I came to ask if you'd consider starting over, if you would come and stay in the flat. I don't like the thought of you being here while I'm there, and maybe we can decide what to do next.'

She watched Joe look back at the tiny bed under the eaves, and imagined him bent almost double when he lay down to sleep. He seemed to be talking to the bed. It was odd. 'I'm sorry about this. I won't be long.'

'Please,' she added. 'Why have you hung a sheet on the wall?' She stepped across to it. He had secured a white sheet to the ceiling so it dropped to the floor like the backdrop in a photographer's studio. Was he doing a photo shoot?

Now he was talking again, but in what sounded like Chinese. She must be hammered. She leaned round him to catch his eye. That was when she saw it, the open laptop on the chest of drawers next to the bed, the screen split into four. Four men staring at her from various offices round the world. A conference call. They all had bemused expressions on their faces.

'Oh! Hi!' She waved at the screen; two of the four men lifted a hand in greeting, the other two stared at her stonily. 'Eek,' she added to Joe, who had gone completely white, frantically trying to scoot her out of shot.

'Clara, I'll just be a moment . . . ' He leaned down to the screen, 'Sorry, it's just, um . . . housekeeping, in the hotel I'm staying in.'

'Oh.' Clara slowly realised he meant her. 'Housekeeping.' For some reason she then chose to adopt an accent, picking up a water glass from a side table behind Joe. 'Oh aye, Mr Alden, sir, och.' She'd gone for Scottish, she didn't know why. 'I'll be going, och.' She then bowed at him and walked away.

Joe looked at her aghast as she shrugged at him from near the doorway, hoping she was now out of shot. He turned and said something in Chinese to the screen and one of the men nodded, leaning forward to switch off his monitor. Two of the others soon went dark too, until there was just one man left, a man with a very small head, and shoulders so wide they filled the screen.

'Tom, I'll catch up with you in the morning. Sounds like it's all in hand.' She could hear the slight tremor in Joe's voice. Had she messed things up for him? Tom didn't look that impressed.

'Where are you staying?'

'Just outside Norwich. You know what it's like in the sticks. No Hilton here.' Joe laughed, a short, sharp bark. Clara hadn't heard the sound before. His shoulders were completely tense beneath his shirt, his neck muscles throbbing as he smiled at the screen.

Finally Tom left and Joe reached across and closed the laptop, sitting with his head in his hands on the bed. Clara didn't say anything, biting her lip until he looked up at her.

'Oops,' she said as he finally caught her eye. 'So you speak Chinese. That's very um ... impressive.'

'And you speak . . . Irish?'

'Scottish,' she mumbled.

To her relief, he laughed, a real laugh this time, low and smooth. Maybe all this would be OK.

'Oh God.' He rubbed at his eyes, stiffening once more as he looked back at her, perhaps remembering their last exchange earlier that evening. 'So . . . '

Clara needed to get the words out, the reason she came, 'Please come and stay in the flat. I'm sorry about earlier.' She stared at him as he looked at her, loosening his tie with one hand. Then, nodding stiffly, he moved to put some things in his leather holdall. Reaching behind her into the wardrobe, he pulled out a row of suit bags, folding them over one arm. He nodded at her. 'OK, I'll come.'

Clara nodded, a small smile that the first part of the plan had gone seamlessly. Well, sort of seamlessly. She turned to go before he could change his mind, moving down the corridor and heading for the stairs.

They didn't talk much on the way back, Clara careful to watch the paving stones, walk in a straight line, Joe clearly stumped by this new turn of events. He got out his phone halfway along the road, covering the mouthpiece. 'Work,' he announced, turning a little away from her. 'Need to debrief the team.' She nodded, looking forward to getting in and downing a large glass of water.

She waited on the edge of the sofa as he finished his call in the corridor downstairs. She had had time to light all the candles in his room and the living room and turn on the lamps, and was feeling woozy and relaxed as she settled back into the sofa. She was excited to see his reaction.

Joe appeared in the flat doorway and immediately turned the overhead light on.

'Oh.' Clara blinked, almost falling off the sofa. Lady CaCa started marching up and down her pole, squawking 'GOOOOOD MORNING VIETNAM' as if it were 8 a.m. and even Roddy had been roused from his snooze on top of the laundry basket. 'Could you turn it off again?' Clara said.

She heard a sigh and a low mutter, but the room was returned to its calm pools of light and flickering shadows on the walls.

'Quite dark in here,' Joe mumbled, moving across to his room and disappearing through the door.

Clara watched, held her breath.

He reappeared in the doorway. 'You lit candles. Lots of them,' he said, unable to keep the surprise from his voice. Was it good surprise? Bad?

'I thought it would help make it more homely, relaxing,' she said.

He looked back over his shoulder. 'It's nice,' he said, clearly not one to embellish.

She smiled. She would settle for nice.

'That's good,' she said. 'Sorry about earlier, but I'm glad you're here now. I'm off to bed,' she added, standing up and yawning.

'I'm going to stay up, emails and things, you know,' he

said, not quite meeting her eye. 'But yes, um, thanks. I'm glad too.'

'All right then.' She moved across to her own room. 'Well, goodnight,' she said. 'Welcome home.'

She scurried into her room, not waiting for his response, and leaned back against the door. This was definitely going to be harder than it looked.

How wonderful to hear that everyone's talking about the shop. It's like Clara's taken it back to all those years ago when people made detours to the village to visit us. I'm so pleased, and you are being an angel looking out for her. Thank you for the gorgeous photos, do keep them coming. I feel I'm there too.

Fuerteventura is proving to be my ideal home and I've just rented a room overlooking the harbour. You can sit on the balcony and watch the sunset on the horizon. There's been a storm out in the Atlantic and the waves rolling in are enormous. It's thrilling to watch them rise up and then come crashing down so spectacularly on the line of rocks at the mouth of the bay. The noise is something else.

The rocks protect the bay from the worst of the waves and there's a ladder rather like in a swimming pool leading down into the sea, so on calm days at high tide I just climb down the rungs and dip into the ocean. It's gloriously refreshing. I might live here forever, eating bream and pretending I'm a painter/writer/lady of the night. Every restaurant seems to serve the most mouth-watering fish dishes, a large glass counter outside to show off the many catches. I always choose the fish with the saddest expression and hope by eating him he might feel more at peace.

What of the pub? Did you go ahead and arrange another quiz night? You shouldn't be put off by what happened last time: you were quite right to eject her, she had drunk far too much and was entirely wrong. Everyone knows Mary I was the first queen of England. Matilda sounds like an entirely made-up person. Arrange it for a night when Roz won't come and ruin the whole quiz by questioning your trivia. If you like, I will send you some questions. Firstly, ask people what Simon Cowell's son is called. It's Eric. Isn't that marvellous? He's so brave. And did you know that Gran Canaria wasn't named after the canary bird but is from the Latin word for dog? That will sort her out.

Chapter 17

The next few days went by in a blur; Clara would head into the shop looking over at Joe's bedroom, the door shut, with no idea if he was in there or not. Spotting his car outside as she served customers, looking up and seeing him duck into it, mobile to his ear. In the evenings she baked, storing up treats in tins for when he appeared, leaving him notes, gifts, frustrated to always miss him, just hearing a door edge closed, an electric toothbrush, low muttering as he made yet another phone call in the middle of the night. How could she possibly *hygge* a man if he was nowhere to be seen?

This morning, though, her mind was full of the shop. The moment was nearly here, her big idea, in the flesh. She had changed the countdown in the window that morning to a large number 1 and waved at a little boy and his father passing outside. Over the course of the morning she was gratified to see a trickle of people in the shop, and familiar faces passing in the high street beyond. It made her feel more like a part of the village, as opposed to a visitor.

It was the last day working on her surprise and she spent much of it running from the back room to the shop every time she heard the bell on the door, which was happening a lot more often than before. She couldn't wait to have things up and running the next day, she thought, as she carefully worked on the new sign. The coloured chalk lettering on the board announced her idea in bold, and knowing that it would be placed outside the shop first thing really made it real for her.

The day swept by, and with no one else in the shop to help her, her whole body ached by the time she closed for the day. Still, the room at the back was ready for the big unveil the next day, and she had enlisted Lauren's help to ensure that all ran smoothly. She felt tired but happy as she stirred some wine into the sauce she had made for dinner. Twisting the peppermill over the bubbling saucepan, she closed her eyes, enjoying the rich smell, the light steam on her face. Joe had returned an hour or so before, moving like a zombie to his room, where she could see him crashed out, shoes still on, face down on the bed. Perhaps it was the smell, but suddenly he was in the doorway, one hand flattening the the hair on the back of his head, the bags under his eyes even more pronounced.

'Dinner,' she trilled, knowing that Operation Hygge needed a win.

He looked at the table set with place mats and napkins, a glass filled with spidery branches and curling leaves in the middle, candles dotted around. 'I don't normally ...' He really did look grey.

'What, eat?' she laughed, placing a large plate on one of the mats.

'I don't really have a set dinner time; mostly takeaways or snacks at my desk.'

'Oh,' she said, hoping the pity didn't show too obviously. 'Well, I made loads,' she said, careful to be casual.

He hovered over the plate. 'It does look good,' he said, slowly lowering himself into a chair.

'Drink?' she offered, and he stood bolt upright again. She jumped; he really was the most unrelaxing person.

'I'll get them. You sit down. You cooked. What would you like?' he asked, walking over to the kitchen and staring, rather lost, at the cupboards in front of him.

'There's an open bottle of wine in the fridge,' she said, sitting in the other chair, swallowing the giggle that threatened to bubble over.

He returned with the bottle and poured her a glass. She noticed his hand shaking a little, a splash of wine missing the glass.

It felt good to be sitting opposite someone at the large table. She had always been used to family and friends clustered round for meals. Dinner in Denmark often went on well into the night. Hostessing was what she did best. She loved preparing a meal, laying the table, making the surroundings really beautiful, perhaps with a centrepiece; she missed her Kubus candleholder, but they had yet to design a travel version. She was pleased with the branches and leaves she'd collected on her walk.

'Pork?' asked Joe between mouthfuls.

Clara nodded. 'I slow-cooked it to make it really tender,' she explained. 'It was on a low heat throughout the day. It's a real winter warmer, my m— we used to have it at home,' she finished, feeling a small stab of pain.

Joe apparently hadn't heard her, too busy wolfing it down. She had never seen anyone eat that quickly. She supposed she should see it as a compliment to her cooking. She looked down at her own almost-full plate.

Joe was wiping his with a piece of bread as she waited for a word from him, maybe a thank-you. His phone lit up where he'd left it on the table and he scraped back his chair as the buzzing began. 'Got to take this,' he said. She felt herself bristle with annoyance as he stood up, meal abandoned, moving back through to his bedroom talking at full volume.

'I told you to tell me when they called. Don't tell me you've only just heard back from ...'

She sat and ate the rest of her dinner listening to him through the thin walls.

'... so tell Clarke he can't keep dicking us about if he expects us to be able to go to them with a decent offer. You know the drill ...'

She realised he probably wouldn't return and stood up with a sigh, clearing the table automatically. Plates clashed together so that she had to check them for chips. She washed up quickly with fast circular scrubbing, her hands hot and pink in the suds. She could still hear him talking next door, his voice raised at intervals. She wondered who was on the other end of the phone.

He emerged when she was back in the living room, curled up in the large suede armchair, the lamp on next to her, tea lights lit, deep in the middle of her book, lost in a story set in a coastal village in Devon in the 1950s.

'Sorry, work call; a deal is about to collapse.' He rubbed at his temples.

Something about the action and his haggard face made her relent. 'I made *risalamande*,' she said, 'and there's hot chocolate in the saucepan.'

'Thanks,' he said, looking back at the wiped-down table, the washing-up drying on the side. 'And for— oh.' The phone had gone again and Clara was left to smile tightly as he answered it.

'It's fine,' she muttered under her breath. 'My pleasure.' He looked across at her, but she didn't think he'd heard her.

This call was quick, Joe turning his back to hiss some pretty blunt messages down the phone. 'Well, get him back in. Was I wrong to trust you with this? . . . No? Then sort it.' He hung up with a huff.

'YOU'RE FIRED!' Lady CaCa screamed from her perch, which seemed pretty appropriate.

Clara was about to get up and head to her room, keen to keep reading and drink her hot chocolate in peace, but

Lauren's words returned to her, the plan to force this man to relax. 'Hold on, sit there,' she said, hopping up and pointing to the sofa, which she'd covered in blankets. He walked over to it uncertainly and sat down, feet flat on the floor, back rigid, as if he were waiting in a doctor's surgery.

Moments later, she carried through a tray holding a steaming hot chocolate and a bowl of the *risalamande*, a sort of rice pudding topped with cherry sauce. 'Why don't you have it here, unwind a bit?' she said. She noticed with a small flicker of triumph that his eyes had widened as she set the tray down on the table in front of him. She moved across the room and put on one of Louisa's classical LPs. With the lamps and the flickering candlelight, she knew she had created the perfect *hygge* home.

She watched him from her spot in the armchair, forgetting to even pretend to turn the pages of her book. He had tasted the chocolate, closing his eyes as the warm liquid went down his throat, and exclaimed over the first mouthful of the pudding. He visibly relaxed, his body sinking backwards onto the blankets, his head resting against the cushions. The music wound around them both, the gentle sound of a flute and the soft chorus of woodwind. She felt her own body unfurl, muscles ease, the food and music lulling her into a sleepy happiness. And then, just as her eyes began to close, the insistent, piercing whine of an alarm shattered the calm.

Roddy shot off the sheepskin rug in front of her to cower under her armchair, Lady CaCa started calling out 'OH MY

GOD, THEY KILLED KENNY!' on repeat and Joe jumped to his feet, slamming down his empty mug as he did so.

'What the . . . ' Clara had spilt chocolate down her front.

'It's an alarm,' Joe said, as if she'd thought it was something else entirely. She was Danish, not stupid.

'I get that, but why?' she demanded, dabbing pointlessly at her ruined top.

Joe already had his phone in his hands, brow creased, not looking at her as he replied: 'It's to remind me that the New York markets have shut, so I'll need to call in for an update.'

'But it's nine p.m. and we're eating *risalamande*,' she said.

He looked up at her then, as if she'd spoken entirely in Danish. 'But the New York markets have closed,' he repeated, as if she hadn't heard the first time. 'It might impact our deal.'

'Fine,' she said, closing her book, unable to pretend any more tonight. 'Have the room to yourself, ring *all* the markets, for all I care.' She knew she sounded petulant, but she was tired from her day and just wanted to relax and enjoy the evening. There was no way this experiment was going to come off.

There was no response from Joe; he was still staring at the phone in his hand and didn't seem to have heard her. Nor did he notice her getting up to leave.

She blew out the tea lights on the mantelpiece and snapped off the lamp by the chair. He was tapping on the mini keyboard on his phone and the noise of the buttons made her clench her teeth as she pulled the arm off the record player so that the music came to a screeching stop. Not only was he nowhere near being *hygge*, she wondered if he was stealing her ability to relax too.

She moved across the room, past the table towards her bedroom.

'Clara,' he called out, hand over the phone as he looked over at her.

She exhaled quickly and turned around. 'Yes,' she replied in a tight voice.

'Thanks for dinner.'

She was too cross to do anything but acknowledge him with a half-wave of her hand as she spun back round, pushed into her bedroom and closed the door behind her with a slam.

Chapter 18

Waking with bubbles in her stomach, Clara lay in bed excited for the day ahead. She couldn't wait to see the reaction to her new venture and had completely forgotten why she had tossed and turned before falling asleep the night before. So distracted was she by thoughts of what the day held, she couldn't even be cross with Joe when he emerged, and found herself pouring him a coffee and sharing a croissant with him as he read the news on his tablet and she sat in tense anticipation, barely able to concentrate on her breakfast, watching the hands of the clock move round.

'Have a lovely day,' she called, clattering down the stairs to the shop.

She couldn't hear any response over Lady CaCa's call of 'SUITS YOU SIR, SHITHEAD.' Had she imagined his hand reaching into his pocket and popping a pill from a strip as she'd rushed past? The thought disappeared almost as soon as it had arrived as she dragged the blackboard outside. She felt a thrill as she positioned it on the pavement, the words standing out in primary colours, the letters bold and cartoon-like. Would people be intrigued by its announcement?

It was a crisp day: a clear blue sky, sunlight hitting the other side of the high street, slicing the houses in half with its golden glow. The wind had dropped to a gentle breeze. She turned back into the shop, fetching the large wooden zero for the window. This was it. Would people still be interested?

Lauren arrived moments later, puffing and pulling off scarves and gloves. 'I've dressed for deep winter but it's boiling out there,' she said, her cheeks flushed. 'Well, boiling is probably going too far – it is November after all – but still ...'

Clara felt doubts building as she looked around the empty shop. What if no one came and she'd asked Lauren to be here for nothing?

'Soooo?' Lauren said, smiling. 'Can I see it?'

Clara found she couldn't speak, a lump now in her throat as she moved silently through the shop, leading Lauren to the room in the back. The space had been transformed, and Clara watched Lauren's face as she stared around.

'It's huge,' she said. 'Wasn't this just a stockroom?'

Clara enjoyed her confused expression, a reminder of how

far the room had come from the dusty space she'd first laid eyes on, home to broken toys and empty cardboard boxes.

The table had been wiped down and covered with newspaper, and stools had been placed all around it. In the middle of the table were tubes of paint and PVA glue, jugs of water, pots of sequins, buttons and beads, and paintbrushes. A large red bin stood in one corner. On the other side of the room were clusters of comfortable-looking chairs around low tables. There were lamps on in every corner, candles in brackets on the walls and a small table to one side covered with a gingham cloth, kettle and mugs, and a selection of home-made cookies and cakes on plates under cling film.

'It's perfect,' Lauren said, moving through the room as if in a daze. 'It looks so cosy and inviting. I can just picture it filled with people.' She turned back to Clara, her eyes sparkling. 'It must have taken you hours. It's fantastic. Just what we all need: a place to bring our children, somewhere to spend some time with friends.'

'But will anyone come?' Clara bit her lip, the nerves making her stomach leap about.

'Of course. The sign outside is great, and did you see the local paper this morning? There's a fab piece in it all about today, with a gorgeous photo of you. You'll be on the website too.'

'Really?' Clara felt her earlier excitement build and they both turned towards the sound of the bell above the door.

'All right,' Lauren said, heading out into the shop, 'let's get this show on the road.'

Clara followed her, pleased to see a few children already browsing the counters, where a choice of wooden toys was out on display.

'It's a Paint Your Own Toy workshop, shall I show you?' Lauren was already bustling people through. She bent down to a young girl with a long brunette plait who was clutching a wooden dinosaur. 'Is that what you want to paint?' The girl nodded quickly, her mother peeking through to the workshop, moving towards one of the armchairs. 'Clara, she wants to paint a T rex,' and with that, Clara had her first customer.

The morning was filled with noise, questions, the smell of coffee, parents laughing and swapping stories. The cakes had all but disappeared and Lauren had barely strayed from the counter, tapping up things on the till and sending customers through to Clara.

Clara felt a lurch of joy as she looked at the large table crammed with children on stools, tongues out, concentrating their hardest on painting their toys, some parents leaning over to help, others sitting in the armchairs watching them enjoy themselves over their coffee.

Only once did they come close to disaster. One of the boys was so excited to finish the wheels on his wooden car in fire-engine red that he bounded over to show his father. At which point Joe appeared in the doorway and tripped over said excited child, causing Joe to yelp and the child to cry. Other children then looked up from what they were doing, hands and faces smeared with paint, as if the room was filled with little savages. Clara swallowed as Joe made his way over to her, frantically dabbing at his trouser leg.

'Here,' she said, reaching for a sponge. 'It's water-soluble, so it'll wash out,' she added.

He looked at her, then at the sponge. He didn't take it. 'What's going on? Have you opened a crèche? Have you invited half the village round to smash up the place?'

Clara took a breath, desperate for him to see what she was trying to do. 'I've turned this room into a workshop and café,' she said. 'There's nowhere in the village for anyone to go in the day. I wanted to create a warm, cosy place where people could bring their children. The room was just being wasted; now it's full of life.'

'Full of mess,' he corrected.

'That too,' she nodded, trying to stay upbeat. The frown on his face was making her nervous. 'But it will all be tidy in the end, and look at the fun they're having.'

Joe gave the table a cursory glance and grunted. At the sound, the little boy who had told Clara about his parents' divorce the other day looked up from the table and gave him a gap-toothed grin. Joe met his eyes, his expression changing in the face of such happiness.

'Can you draw ducks?' the boy called out.

Joe took a step forward, and then looked over his shoulder as if the boy was talking to someone else.

'Can you draw ducks?' the boy repeated, head tipped to one side.

'Ducks?' Joe said, looking impossibly awkward leaning

177

down in his sharp suit to address the small boy on the stool.

'Yeah. I can't draw them. My dad could draw but he doesn't live with us any more. Can you try?'

'I ... Oh, well, I ...' The boy thrust a pencil into Joe's hand. 'Um ... I'm not sure ...' Joe turned to Clara, holding out the pencil as if it was a contaminated item. 'He wants me to draw him a duck.'

'An excellent idea.' Clara beamed at the little boy. 'I often think there should be more ducks on trains.' She stifled a giggle as Joe turned back round, an uncertain look on his face as he hovered over the wooden toy.

Then he leaned down and started to draw: a careful rounded eye, a beak, wings, spindly legs. As he worked, the boy was growing more and more excited, sitting on his hands and calling out 'That's it. That's really cool.'

It took an age, but Clara watched Joe slowly create a cartoon duck, reaching for a rubber when he thought the tail could be improved. He was all concentration, a methodical worker, a small smile tugging at his mouth. 'I've done webbed feet,' he pointed out to the boy.

The boy craned his neck to see better. 'Awesome.'

'Do you think the wings look right?' Joe asked him, pressing the pencil up to his mouth as if he was studying a portrait.

'The wings are the best bit,' the boy said solemnly.

'Thanks, mate,' Joe said, and Clara had to hide a laugh in her hand.

He flushed red as he stood up, giving the pencil back to the boy, who was already turning towards the tubes of paint. 'Gonna paint him blue.'

'Good plan,' Joe said, placing a hand briefly on the boy's shoulder before snatching it away as Clara looked up at him.

'He likes you.' Clara smiled as the little boy gave Joe a double thumbs-up before slapping blue paint all over his duck.

'Nice boy,' Joe mumbled to his shoes.

Lauren's head appeared in the doorway. 'Clara, you're needed,' she called, giving Joe a cursory nod.

Joe's eyes widened as he turned in the direction of her voice, all thoughts of the previous few moments seemingly forgotten as he asked in a businesslike tone, 'Are you paying staff?'

Lauren's eyes widened in surprise. 'I offered to help Clara, actually. And you are?'

Joe sniffed and mumbled something about being the proprietor.

Lauren breathed out slowly. 'Of course you are.'

Clara cringed. 'Tell them I'll be along in a minute.'

'Shall do,' Lauren said cheerily, before turning to Joe. 'A pleasure to meet you,' she said with a small huff, then turned back into the shop.

Clara laughed, trying to lighten the mood, but Joe hadn't noticed anything amiss, back to looking harried, smoothing at his suit.

'Look, I need to get to a meeting; in fact I'm already late. I'm not sure if I'll be back this evening.'

'Oh, OK,' Clara said, eyes darting past him, hoping he wouldn't notice that one of the children had left a massive purple hand print on the freshly painted cream wall behind him.

He pulled out his phone. 'What's your mobile number, in case I need to get hold of you?'

'Ah . . . ' The purple-handed child was coming their way. 'Um . . . I don't have one.' The child passed with no paint-based drama and she breathed out.

'What do you mean?' he said, lowering his own phone, unable to conceal his surprise. 'Everyone has a mobile.'

She shrugged and looked up at him. 'I don't.'

'But . . . that's just archaic. How does anyone get hold of you? Smoke signals? Telegram? Jesus Christ, no phone,' he said, as if she had just announced that she had no vital organs.

A mother looked at him sharply from one of the armchairs.

'I have email!' Clara said, wanting to cheer him up a bit, bring back the Joe she had just glimpsed. 'Though actually,' she had to add, 'I rarely check it.'

Joe rolled his eyes.

Clara bit her lip, restraining herself from making a joke about carrier pigeons. Joe suddenly didn't seem to be in that kind of mood, and she didn't want to ruin the small progress she'd made over the last twenty-four hours.

'Right, I really do have to go.' He rubbed his jaw. 'I'll call the landline in the flat when I'm heading back and let you know my ETA.'

'Good idea,' she said, punching him lightly on the arm. He took a step back. 'Hope it goes well!'

He looked at her through narrowed eyes.

'Your meeting,' she said super-slowly, wondering why he looked so strange. Where was he going? Did he really have a meeting?

'Yes, that,' he mumbled, not quite meeting her eye. He turned to pick his way back through the room the way he had come, only just avoiding having his feet stuck to the floor by the purple-handed child, who was back holding a whole tube of glue.

'Let's find your mum, shall we?' Clara said brightly, steering the child quickly away.

By the time she looked up again, Joe had disappeared.

Chapter 19

Joe had finally shut the laptop in the early hours and was considering taking a shower. He'd snuck in late, around midnight, and Clara had been in bed. He'd been tempted to wake her up, apologise, tell her the workshop had been a good idea. After he'd left that morning, he'd had more time to think about it. His reaction had been a confusing mixture of tiredness, nostalgia and guilt. The atmosphere had been buzzing. It had reminded him of those early days in the shop with his mother, children racing around in excitement, new toy deliveries, giggles and chatter. He had loved the place then. Why had he been so unpleasant?

He drew his arms over his head, cracked his knuckles. His back muscles ached from leaning over the computer, his eyes were strained from the light and he just wanted to wash the day away.

As he padded to the bathroom, towel looped around his neck, he paused in front of her bedroom door. The shower was ancient, pipes clanging into life the moment you twisted the hot water on; it would wake her, and although a few days ago he probably wouldn't have cared, now he found himself wavering. She had obviously spent hours preparing the workshop; she must be exhausted too.

Ever since the row by the field when he'd ruined a £230 pair of brogues, she'd been nothing but nice to him. He hadn't been expecting it, had only agreed to stay in the flat because another night on that single bed in the pub and he'd be seeing a chiropractor for a year. Yet all week she'd been leaving him thoughtful dishes, little notes, and his initial suspicions had started to melt. Perhaps it was just her way of getting him on side, but he wasn't sure any more. He had been short with her earlier; he couldn't keep taking her niceness for granted. He felt a surge of relief that she didn't know what he'd been up to that day.

He turned to head back to his room, the living room empty, the dark squares of familiar photographs along one wall. He found himself drifting towards them, his hands clammy as he stood in front of them.

His proud mother had displayed numerous photos of him at different ages: his graduation day, when he'd had the most horrific hair in straight curtains; in a too-big suit as a pre-teen at an older cousin's wedding; his mum and him, mouths wide open, arms in the air as they hurtled down a ride at Alton Towers; standing by his first car, a battered Ford Fiesta that he'd paid for out of his first pay cheque. He looked impossibly young, a different person, and yet it had only been just over ten years ago.

He'd been avoiding it. The last photo, older, faded: him blowing out candles at his eighth birthday party, his dad in a heavy cable-knit jumper, one arm resting on Joe's shoulders, his mother, wild curls tied back, on the other side, so proud as he puffed them all out. He examined the photograph as he always did, felt the same pain. His father had left the week after, telling his mother he'd be living with Rachel, the PA who used to accompany him on his overseas business trips. Such a stereotype.

There were no other pictures of his father, and Joe had been too proud to ask his mum if he could have that one, drawn to it every time he stayed. He traced the man's face in the photo, other memories rising up unbidden. The day his mum had told him after school that Dad had moved out, she'd made chocolate cornflake cake and it had turned to stodge in his mouth as she spoke. He hadn't known much about divorce; Jenny in his class was always crying about it, but he didn't like Jenny so he'd never learnt what it was.

Seeing his father at weekends, watching Rachel get bigger and bigger until one day he was introduced to Harry, his stepbrother, a tiny bundle with eyes squeezed shut and an upturned nose. Waiting on the driveway for his dad to pick him up, hands clutching his school report, wanting to show him the A in maths, the A that he knew would bring a flash of pride to Dad's eyes. It had started to rain, and he had tucked the report under his jumper, his mother assuming he'd been picked up long ago. Standing under a tree as the rain got heavier, trickled down his back, the card damp, the blue biro splodging, the A indistinguishable from the rest of the grades. Knowing his dad wasn't coming. Going in when it got dark, being wrapped in a towel by his mother, whose tears on the top of his head felt just like the rain.

The sneers from Pete in his class, who always asked where his dad was, making the rest of the football team look at their shoes. Joe feeling his fists curl tight, the answer frozen somewhere inside him, scanning his eyes along the sideline, waiting for the day he'd be able to turn and wipe the smirk from Pete's face, only ever seeing wild curls, his mum's face-splitting grin, always dressed differently to the other mums. Hitting Pete in the jaw; the way his knuckles throbbed for days; getting suspended from school.

He moved through to his bedroom, sat on the bed, chest bare, unbelievably tired but all at the same time not tired. His brain whirring with the day's events: Clara, his visit, the work calls, the unsent emails, Tom's snide message asking if he'd disappeared. He knew he should probably be driving back to London right now. He'd get a couple of hours' sleep, then he'd leave. He reached automatically for the suit jacket he'd flung over the bedstead, the inside pocket. A couple of pills would be enough to knock him out, shift the headache at least.

He felt disorientated when he woke, staring at the light-shade in the middle of the ceiling, hearing the clatter of pans outside the door. He was on his feet and moving out of the room before he'd really woken properly. The kitchen and living room were flooded with light. Clara was standing at the oven in his mother's cartoon apron, a spatula in one hand.

'Oh good, you're back, I didn't hear you come in, and I didn't want to burst into your bedroom in case ... well, that would be inappropriate ...' She tailed off, the hiss of a frying pan behind her. 'Pancake?'

'What time is it?' he asked, rubbing at his face, still bare-chested, hopping as he stubbed a toe. 'Fuck,' he said, sinking into one of the chairs.

'Nearly nine.'

'I should have left hours ago,' he said, his toe throbbing.

'You look better for having got some sleep,' she said, placing a plate in front of him. 'There's cinnamon and nutmeg in the pancakes, it's a Danish thing.'

Her hair was glossy in the sunlight; she looked absurdly fresh-faced and raring to go. 'No time,' he said, almost putting a hand over the glass as she poured him an orange juice.

'Everyone has time for pancakes. They are one of life's essentials. Like oxygen, dogs, children and chocolate. And WINE,' she added with a yelp that made him jump. 'I can't believe I almost left out wine,' she said, shaking her head and returning to the pan.

Was she always this chipper in the morning? He'd never known anyone so full of *joie de vivre* before at least two coffees. He absent-mindedly reached for the knife and fork, the air warm with steam, the smell conjuring up images of fresh bread.

'IS IT RAINING I HADN'T NOTICED.'

Joe stared at Lady CaCa, wondering what kinds of films his mother watched.

The pancake was still warm and he hadn't realised how hungry he was until he stared down at the empty plate seconds later.

'Fast work,' Clara said, scooting across and depositing another pancake in front of him.

'Thanks. These are good,' he added, smiling and then worrying he had pancake in his teeth. 'So ...' He took another mouthful, chewing quickly, not wanting to talk with his mouth full. It seemed to be an age until he could swallow it. She was still looking at him expectantly. 'Big day planned?'

She shook her head. 'No, not really. The first few people are returning to pick up their painted toys, and we've got a new display to plan.'

'We?'

'Not Lauren,' Clara said quickly. 'Gavin's offered to help out. For free. Well, for dinner actually, tonight. He's getting Clive to run the pub for him.'

'You've invited Gavin for dinner?' Joe looked at her in surprise, imagining the bulky Gavin next to her, her peach complexion and blonde hair a stark contrast to his tattoos and massive forearms. An unlikely couple, and that was ignoring the twenty-year age gap.

'I've invited Lauren and Patrick, her husband, too. Would you like to join us? I'm going to make a Danish beer fondue, I adore it. I've ordered all the ingredients online.'

Joe found himself nodding in agreement, moments later wondering just what he was thinking. He really must be tired. He was used to sushi with colleagues or clients, or meals eaten in haste at his desk, not long-drawn-out dinners struggling to make endless conversation with strangers. He never had anything to say. Unless they wanted to discuss the stock market. Invariably, though, he was asked what book he was reading or what his hobbies were. Maybe he could get out of it now, remember a vital weekend engagement? He went to open his mouth, to fabricate some excuse, but Clara was smiling widely at him, a row of straight pearly teeth, her eyes sparkling as she clapped her hands together.

'Wonderful, I can't wait to host something. At home we have so many dinners. I've missed them . . .' Did he imagine the slight fade in her eyes? Her mouth shutting into a thin line? He wanted to see her face light up again.

She scraped her chair back from the table. 'Right, lots to do.' She avoided his eyes as she took his plate over to the sink.

'Yep,' he said, 'me too. Leave them,' he called as she started stacking the plates. 'I'll wash up.'

'YOU COMPLETE ME.'

He ignored Lady CaCa and went to stand just as his phone started to vibrate. Looking down, he saw it was a local number and felt a stirring of unease. That had been quick.

He tapped a button and the call was cut off. Was he doing the right thing?

'You didn't answer,' Clara said with a raised eyebrow.

He shifted in his chair. 'It wasn't urgent,' he said, suddenly not wanting to explain what he'd arranged, which was ridiculous. It was his decision, his mother's shop and future.

Clara was looking at him, her head cocked to one side. He stood up quickly, aware of his mussed-up appearance. 'Right, well. I'll finish up here and then head into London.'

'But it's the weekend,' she said.

Joe shrugged. 'We're about to close a massive deal.'

'But . . . ' He could see her swallowing down her next sentence. 'Sounds good,' she trilled, heading to her bedroom.

He bit his lip and watched her go before heading to the sink. Should he tell her? He ran the hot water and started to wash up. Coward, he thought as he plunged a plate into the water.

He couldn't remember the last time he'd washed dishes, and moments later he was completely absorbed in the task, other things forgotten as he scrubbed and dried. He wished he could stand there all day, lost in thoughts of nothing; put off the moment he had to get back to work. He paused, a plate dripping onto the floor, surprised by this revelation. He loved his job, he reminded himself; it was all he knew how to do.

She was already back in the shop when he headed out into the high street, straightening his tie. He could see her standing behind the counter, laughing at a small girl who was holding up a box to show her. She was wearing a flowered dress, her blonde hair loose. He remembered what Gavin had said, that she was peaceful. Aside from a flicker of something else earlier in the flat, he'd noticed the same. She seemed so relaxed in herself, at ease. He was twitchy, unable to settle, moving from task to phone to activity to sleep, never remaining in one place for very long. She seemed to move at a more languid pace. He thought back to the walk across the fields, her constant stopping to take in the view, to comment on the landscape. She had really taken it in; she was present in the moment and, seemingly, happy.

He thought of the money he'd spent trying to capture that feeling: the physio he'd booked for the office to help with his back and neck trouble, the acupuncturist he didn't tell anyone about, the pills he took, the online searches for something more powerful than Rescue Remedy, a million corporate stress balls, away days, new cars, new clothes, new girlfriends. What was Clara's secret, he wondered.

He realised he was loitering on the pavement and she had caught him staring into the shop at her. She waved one hand, frowning slightly, and he started and spun round, pressing on his car key, hearing the familiar bleep as the rear lights flashed as red as he imagined his face to be.

As he started the car, he went to plug his phone into the in-car system but, gripped by a sudden feeling he couldn't explain, he found his finger reaching for the off button. He turned the radio on and set it to Classic FM, letting the gentle noise fill the car as he pulled away from the kerb, heading back to the capital.

The calm mood that had brought him here seemed to vanish the moment he stepped through the revolving glass doors of his office block. He was met by the grey faces of his team, cartons of empty Chinese food from an excellent restaurant in the City littering the desks, in amongst heaps of paper and trade magazines. It looked like chaos: phones ringing next to scrawled Post-it notes and half-drunk mugs of coffee. The sight seemed to bring on the first headache of the day, his heart racing that little bit faster as he got them to bring him up to speed. No one dared mention the time, but knowing that they would have discussed it made his insides tighter, his voice emerge as more of a bark, needing to reassert authority, show them he was still the boss. He hoped they hadn't said anything to anyone upstairs. But he knew that if he'd been them, he would have.

A few hours later and he was on the phone to the client, the pitch book open in front of him and the figures rolling off his tongue as he tried to keep the sale on track. He got up to pee and realised that at this rate he wouldn't be going back to Suffolk before midnight, if at all. At that moment, the sleepy village felt completely removed from this world. On his way back to his desk, he went to fetch his fifth coffee of the day and ran through the latest details he needed to be on top of as he stood by the machine, his mind full of clients and mergers and dollar signs.

A workshop! How heavenly, what a wonderful idea. It's an enormous room, so how clever to make it useful. She's being so enterprising there'll never be a need for me to come home.

To be honest, at the moment I'm not sure I'll ever want to. I've discovered a French patisserie (in Spain! I know!) around the corner from my new flat and am now living almost entirely on chocolate eclairs. They are melt-in-the-mouth delicious. I've become best friends with one of the women behind the counter after giving her a collection of my books. She's learning English and was delighted to be given Lee Child and Jilly Cooper to read.

I'm heading to Corralejo soon, on the other side of the island. There's a fancy hotel where we are going to play tennis and have spa treatments. I'm planning to be entirely wrapped in seaweed. I'll lose so much weight, despite the eclair consumption, you won't recognise me. I'll come back into the pub and you'll ask Clive, who is that GORGEOUSLY THIN woman and I will say TA-DA and reveal that it is me, but after seaweed.

Right, you must send me some photos of the workshop and do tell Clara she's doing a fabulous job, what a revelation. I'm so pleased it's bringing some joy back to the place. And what do you mean, Joe is staying there? He never stays at home; last time he did, the Rachel cut was in fashion, do you remember? Those layers never suited me, although Paula the mobile hairdresser admitted afterwards that she'd never even watched *Friends*. Goodness knows who she modelled me on. And imagine not watching *Friends*. It's like admitting you've never masturbated. Still, I am pleased if he's there to help with things. I just assumed we'd lost him to his London life forever.

Chapter 20

Gavin was sitting in the corner of the workshop, serving coffees and chatting with customers. He'd insisted he'd wanted to and Clara beamed at him as she moved back through to the shop and the counter. He'd given her a thumbs-up, his sleeves rolled up today so that Clara could make out the seagull on his forearm.

There'd been a steady trickle of people shopping for Christmas presents. Clara was helping them choose gifts, pointing out some of the games she'd put on display, asking them questions about their children's interests, laughing at anecdotes. She felt a familiar fondness for the shop wash over her; you couldn't be miserable in a toyshop. It was wonderful to be surrounded by children, faces lit up as they roamed the aisles or chose wooden toys to accessorise in the workshop.

She felt a frisson of excitement as she looked across at the locked cupboard, where the pieces for her next display sat in boxes on the shelves. The countdown was back and lots of children were trying to guess what might be featured next.

'GIANTS!'

'NOT GIANTS, FAIRIES.'

'PIRATES.'

Clara grinned at them all, refusing to be drawn.

A man with gelled hair and a paunch was standing at the counter as she turned around. He was clutching a thick folder and held out his hand as she walked over.

'Mrs Alden, I presume. Your husband came in to see us earlier this week with a view to us heading down here to take some photos, measurements and the rest.'

Clara looked at him, lost at the word husband and not understanding the rest. 'Sorry, I'm not ... Louisa Alden is away at the moment, abroad.'

The man with the gelled hair looked down at his folder, a frown on his face. 'Ah, the owner. No, we spoke with a Mr Joseph Alden.'

'Joe ...'

'Yes, Mr Alden was keen for us to get things moving as quickly as possible, Mrs ...?'

'I'm Miss ... I'm ... I'm no one,' Clara said, realising she had no right to do anything, say anything, a nasty feeling creeping over her.

'Well, we're here from Strutt and Sons to see if we can't get this place valued and on the market as soon as possible.'

He smiled, one front tooth overlapping the other. Clara found herself staring at it. 'We called Mr Alden this morning but he didn't answer. We were booked for later in the week but an opening came up and he seemed in a hurry to have it valued, so here I am. I thought I'd get ahead of the curve.'

'Valued . . .' she said, suddenly realising what he meant. That Joe really was thinking of selling the shop. She looked around, a coldness sweeping through her. All this. Everything Louisa had started, worked on for years, would be gone.

The man started to look a bit unsure, shuffling some pieces of paper in his folder as he spoke. 'He did say number fourteen, the high street. Alden Toys.' He produced a single sheet with the words confirmed in scrawled pen.

'I'm sure,' Clara said in a quiet voice. What could she do? Send him away? Refuse to let him in, with his nasty tape measure and the camera looped around his neck?

'There's a flat above?' he said, eyebrows shooting up as he jerked his head.

Clara nodded, not trusting herself to speak.

'Two bedrooms, bathroom, large kitchen/diner?' he read from his sheet of paper. 'Perhaps if I start in here, you can show me up there afterwards?'

Clara looked helplessly around her, a small boy clutching a large rubber snake and a girl kissing a fluffy penguin proving no help to her. 'Right . . .'

The man was taking photos now, every now and again

talking into a slim silver Dictaphone he had pulled from his top pocket. 'Turn-of-the-century building converted into shop with flat upstairs. Very few original features left in the shop below but a good-sized window, excellent space to suit many needs, current use: toyshop . . .'

'In there?' he said, indicating the locked door of the cupboard.

'Storage,' she whispered.

He nodded and bustled on past, scrutinising the counter, the till. Clara thought she saw hunger in his eyes as they roved across each surface. Should she put a stop to this? It didn't seem right to let him crawl over the place without asking Louisa.

Moving through to the back room, he called 'All right if I look in here?', now on a roll and not waiting for a reply.

She could hear him in the workshop, the low rumble of Gavin's response, hoping he might see fit to throw him out. But there was only the odd sentence drifting through the shop, no estate agent slung out on his ear, his folder following shortly behind.

Eventually Gavin appeared, moving slowly through the doorway as if he was one of the walking dead, tapping at his phone. 'Selling?' he said, his face slowly turning puce, cheeks puffed out. 'Woman's lived here for twenty years; she wouldn't just sell without saying anything. Would she?' He looked at Clara then, eyebrows pinched together.

Perhaps Louisa had spoken to Joe about it; Clara wasn't sure any more.

'She would have said something,' Gavin said, his voice sounding a little more certain.

The man was back, tapping his foot as he waited for her to join him. 'The flat,' he said, his voice a whine, as if she'd clean forgotten why he was there.

'Gavin, would you mind the shop? He wants to see upstairs.' Clara pointed in the man's direction.

Gavin nodded miserably, lowering himself onto the stool, his large legs bunched up beneath him. 'Selling,' he repeated, gazing at nothing, not even reacting to the bell above the shop door.

'I won't be long,' Clara said, feeling as dejected as he looked. She had worked so hard to try to turn the shop around, to prove to Louisa that it could be at the centre of things once more. She had started to believe that maybe, just maybe, she was managing it. And now here was this man with his nasty gelled hair and his shrewd eyes that seemed to be putting a price tag on every fireplace, mantelpiece and cornice.

'Are you a tenant?' he asked, following her up the stairs.

'House-sitter,' Clara said, standing at the door of the flat, watching him as he bent down to examine the wood-burner, admired the enormous mirror over the mantelpiece, measured widths, windows, period features. She regretted making it so welcoming, not enjoying hearing that it looked like a show home.

Lady CaCa had been watching him the entire time, beak opening and shutting as he walked past, only waiting until he was bending down near her cage to throw back her head and screech 'I CARRIED A WATERMELON!' which made him shoot up and hit his head on the mantelpiece.

Clara swallowed a small giggle, feeling a fraction better, until she realised that Lady CaCa might soon be homeless.

'Well,' he said, after an age, 'I think I've got enough to begin with. We can get something up on the website within the week. Now, where is Mr Alden? I should like to confirm how much we're putting it on for; he was keen for a quick valuation. His estimate wasn't far off.'

Clara felt a little sick thinking of Joe discussing the price of the shop and flat with this man, forging on ahead as if he owned the place. Was he protecting his inheritance? She knew it was a nasty thought, but she couldn't shake it. He claimed to be looking after his mother's interests, but was that really it?

The estate agent was still waiting for an answer.

'I'm not sure exactly when he'll be back,' Clara said, wanting to bundle him out of there.

'Well, here's my card; tell him to ask for Paul.'

'Paul,' Clara whispered, holding the card limply in her hand.

She followed him down the stairs, shoulders sagging. Paul took a last look round the shop before heading out, a decisive tinkle of the bell signalling his departure. Gavin was still huddled over the stool by the till, his earlier bonhomie gone as he sloped back through to the workshop. Clara didn't trust herself to speak. What could she say? It wasn't their shop, it wasn't their life.

Chapter 21

Switching off the engine, Joe sat in the driver's seat, drumming his fingers on the wheel, his mind still in the office, thoughts of the deal they were working on chasing each other round. The drive up had been a blur, the familiar roads passing in a flash.

As he looked up, he felt a sudden sense of relief that he was back here in the village. The office, the deal started to fade from his mind as he looked across the road. It had been the right decision to leave, he thought, suppressing the memory of his team's faces as he'd suddenly stood up, swept his things into his briefcase and left with a barely mumbled explanation. He'd only been there a couple of hours but suddenly he just hadn't wanted to face it all, had needed to leave. He could oversee things from here, he reassured himself. They'd be fine.

He looked across at the burgundy façade of the shop, the flashing lights of the robot display pulling the edges of his mouth into a smile. Clara had a real eye for detail, he thought. He realised that he was looking forward to seeing her, and it struck him that he should buy something for the dinner party that evening. He wondered if Roz's post office sold flowers.

It was a cold day and he leant his neck from side to side, feeling the pull on his muscles. Moving to the boot, he pulled out his bag, pausing before the side door to the flat and choosing to enter via the shop entrance instead. He could see Clara behind the counter. She was wearing her hair in a topknot now, a cream jumper over the flowered dress. He pushed open the door, pleased to see her look up at the sound of the bell.

He smiled, his hand moving to wave at her but freezing halfway as he watched her eyes narrow, her mouth purse closed. He almost looked behind him, confused by the coldness that seemed to sweep across the shop. Surely he was imagining it. He could hear the blood drumming in his ears, the noises of the shop whirring in the background, the sound of his own breathing heavier. His eyes darted over to her again. She turned away from him.

It was his paranoia. 'I'm back,' he smiled, moving towards the counter. Perhaps she was distracted by something in the shop? Maybe she was short-sighted and hadn't seen him? Perhaps it was all in his head?

'Great,' she said, her voice dull.

'Looking forward to later,' he added, wanting things to be as they had been, as he'd left them after pancakes in the flat above. He'd started to believe she was just being nice after all, that everyone was right about her.

She looked blank.

'The dinner party!'

'Oh ... that.' She could barely meet his eyes. What was going on?

'Well, I'll be upstairs,' he said, turning away from her, feeling his body grow hot as he fumbled for his key, wishing now that he'd arrived quietly, let himself into the flat, allowed himself a few moments to wind down.

'Ah, Joe,' came a voice. He almost dropped his leather bag. Roz was pushing her way into the shop, nearly tripping over a toddler clutching a soft toy, a duck almost as big as her. 'I thought I saw you outside. I'm glad I've caught you. I've just bumped into Paul from Strutt and Sons and he tells me they'll be handling the sale.'

Joe was watching her mouth flap open, hearing the words as if through a fog. Sale? Paul? Then he remembered the name, Strutt and Sons. So that was why Clara was giving him the cold shoulder. They weren't due to be here till next week; he'd cancelled their call this morning, had been going to call them back.

'He's given me a rough estimate, but we can discuss that privately. Apparently you haven't confirmed anything yet. I'm a bit frustrated that you've gone through an estate agent, we could have saved on fees, but ...' Her face broke into a wide smile; she had a dark red lipstick mark on one front tooth. 'I'm sure you can be generous. Shall we talk upstairs?'

He found himself nodding, not wanting to stay in the shop in the arctic presence of Clara, who was now clattering change onto the counter and glaring at him openly.

Roz yapped all the way up the stairs, and as Joe pushed open the door to the flat he felt a pang of regret for agreeing to talk to her now.

Lady CaCa obviously agreed, greeting him with a robust screech and a cry of 'I WISH I KNEW HOW TO QUIT YOU.'

'Sorry about that,' he mumbled, putting his bag down. On the counter in the kitchen Clara had left a batch of bread rolls on a plate, a smiley face drawn on a piece of paper next to it. She must have put it there before the estate agent came; God knows what emoticon she'd choose now.

Roz was moving through the flat, opening doors and cupboards, scribbling things down on a piece of paper. 'I'm so pleased she's selling. I thought that Danish girl might be here for good. The article in the paper made me worry.'

'Article?' Joe asked, confused.

Roz took the local paper out of her handbag as she marched past. 'Page six. She's very photogenic, of course, so they've gone with an enormous photograph. She'll be all over the website too. They call it clickbait, you know.'

Joe barely heard her next questions as he stared at the photo. Clara in the shop, surrounded by toys and children, grinning from ear to ear.

'Has your mother ever applied for planning permission to extend?'

'Is there a firewall to next door?'

'When was the boiler installed?'

What had he done? Why had he let Roz in here? He tried to answer the questions, realising as he did that he knew next to nothing about the flat. He kept picturing Clara's face in the shop below, the look she had given him. He pulled his arms across his body into a hug. Why hadn't he told her he'd been to see the estate agent? Then again, how was he to know they were just going to show up that day?

Roz was in the bathroom, running a finger along the surface of the bath, peering out of the window as if she could see through the frosted glass.

'Is it a power shower? Is there a water softener?'

'NO LIKEY NO LIGHTY.'

Roddy, clearly noticing the shift in mood, wound himself around Joe's legs, rubbing up against his calves.

'RUN FORREST RUN.'

'Is there a dryer?'

'Is that a built-in dishwasher?'

'Is the oven gas or electric?'

'FRANKLY MY DEAR I DON'T GIVE A DAMN.'

Joe felt an overwhelming urge to shout at them both to shut up. He hadn't asked for any of this. He thought of his mother in sunny Spain and experienced a flash of envy. He wanted to be on a beach, feeling the sun on his skin, not dealing with frosty looks and nosy neighbours and endless questions and the bloody parrot sounding like voices in his head.

'Where are the meters?'

'Is there a stopcock?'

He needed to explain things. He was answering Roz's questions in bumbling half-sentences, planning what he was going to say to Clara throughout, wanting to get rid of that expression on her face. He needed to tell her that he wanted his mum to have options, to know that she could have any life she wanted. She'd worked so hard for so long and he needed her to know that it hadn't been for nothing. He thought back to the uncertainty when they'd first moved here; how she'd worried constantly about bills and how he'd been so desperate to make sure she never had to worry like that again.

It seemed an age before he managed to remove Roz, promising to ring her when he'd discussed things with the estate agent, practically bundling her out of the front door and into the street. Then he took a breath and headed through the side door back into the shop, squaring his shoulders, preparing himself for Clara's disappointed looks, her scowls.

She was all warmth and laughter now, though, draped over the counter, smiling coyly up at the man who'd been here the other day, the local journalist, giggling at something he'd said, looking up at him with those big blue eyes.

What was *he* doing back again, hanging around the shop like a bad smell? He looked like an extra in *Point Break*, all long brown hair and holey jumpers. Joe could hear them talking as he stepped around a boy gnawing at a plastic Minion key ring, almost tripping over two girls playing with racing cars in the aisle. Clara's light laugh as she moved back around behind the counter, throwing a remark over her shoulder. Something about the way she did it made his fists clench and he walked across to her.

'So, were you going to mention it?' he huffed.

The journalist looked up, a frown forming. Joe didn't look at him, pointedly staring directly at her.

'Mention what?' She lifted her chin, a challenge to him.

Why was he behaving like this? He knew he should apologise, but something about their closeness wound him up: the smug way Mr Journalist was looking at him through his rectangular glasses as if he were auditioning to be a Specsavers model.

'Paul coming,' he went on. 'Did he take photographs? Measurements? What did he say, or did you just send him away?'

Clara looked affronted, her eyebrows knitting together, her eyes icy. He'd never seen her look like that before, and he stepped back.

'I showed him in and he took his photos and measurements and got his grubby hands all over the flat, and then he left you this.' She thrust a card at him; it missed his hand and fluttered to the floor.

He picked it up, already starting to feel foolish. 'Right. Good, I'd better be ringing him then.'

'You'd better do that,' Clara agreed, her cheeks two spots of pink. 'Now, if you don't mind, I'm talking to a customer, while there's still a shop to run.' She gestured to the man at the counter, who was staring openly at the exchange. 'And you should be thanking Sam for writing such a wonderful piece; everyone came to the workshop opening because of his article.' She turned a beaming smile on the journalist and twisted away from Joe.

'I saw it.'

'No problem, mate.' The journalist smiled at him, his green eyes piercing.

Clara still had her back to him. He had been dismissed. He felt his mouth open, a cutting response lost somewhere, no doubt to resurface hours later when he was replaying the conversation in his head.

He shouldn't have to justify himself to her. He'd just been doing what was best for his mother. He wanted her to be comfortable as she got older. She had always put him first and he wanted to be sure he was doing everything he could to look after her now. He looked back at Clara, all the prepared lines lost somewhere inside him. Why had he gone on the attack? Why had he taken it out on her?

He spun round, spotting the boy munching on the Minion. 'You'll need to pay for that,' he said, marching back through the shop and out of the door.

Louisa: Am refusing to recognise your QI – it is a silly invented word. Acceptable Q words include: QUEEN, QUIZ, QUINTESSENTIAL, but not QI, which means NOTHING.

Gavin: QUINTESSENTIAL would never happen.

Louisa: Don't be cheeky, of course it could if you had ESSENTIAL and then added QUINT on the next go. Anyway, stop trying to distract me from the fact that you are a complete and utter QI (I have made up my own definition for it).

Gavin: So does QI mean 'lovable and sexy rogue'?

Louisa: Only a QI would think that.

Gavin: ☹

Gavin: Also … do you really want to sell?

Chapter 22

Clara had closed the shop a little late, dragging herself up to the flat, spooning food into Roddy's bowl and topping up Lady CaCa's dish.

'THAT'S THE WAY A-HA A-HA I LIKE IT.'

She gave the parrot a weak smile.

Staring at the ingredients in front of her, she had the overwhelming urge to shove everything onto the floor, pack a bag and head out of the door. What a day: the shop had been busy throughout, the takings way up, and her legs ached from being on her feet. She'd even thought about restocking: the shelves were less crowded now, a few lines sold out completely. But what was the point? Her eyes flicked to Joe's bedroom door. Was he there? Was he drawing up spreadsheets? Working out profits? Contacting agents or potential buyers? She found herself inching across the kitchen on tiptoe, freezing as one of the wooden boards let out a telltale creak, lifting her foot to get closer.

'I AM YOUR FATHER,' screamed Lady CaCa as the door in front of her flew open and Joe appeared.

'Gah,' said Clara, hand flying to her chest, trying to pretend she wasn't lurking outside his room.

He raised an eyebrow as she knelt on the floor and rubbed at an imaginary mark. 'Cleaning,' she mumbled, hoping her face wasn't going red.

'LUKE, I AM YOUR FATHER.'

'Shut up, Lady C,' Joe said, causing an audible parrot huff and the fluttering of a number of feathers before she turned to the corner.

'ALL RIGHT, SHITHEAD.'

Joe held out a hand as if to help Clara up; she ignored it, scuttling back to the kitchen, back turned as she washed her hands. 'I'm going to make the fondue,' she called over her shoulder, not wanting to look at him. Why had she invited him anyway? Maybe he would go out.

There was a pause, and she wondered if he was still standing there.

'That sounds great,' he said. 'Can I help, do anything for it?' They were obviously not going to talk about what had happened earlier. Was he planning to apologise for snapping at her?

'No, all under control,' she said, remembering the hundreds of things she had to do but not wanting him working alongside her; hoping he'd get the hint and stay away.

'At least let me go out and buy some wine.' She heard him pick up his car keys, dared to look back.

He was shrugging on his overcoat and gave her a small smile. She looked away, reaching for a garlic clove to start chopping.

'Thanks,' she said, not looking up again, waiting for the click of the door. He loitered for a few seconds more before she heard the smallest sigh, and then he was gone.

She felt herself sag with relief, moving to turn up the volume on the radio, enjoying the simple task of preparing the meal, feeling better knowing he wasn't in the flat too. She kept picking from the enormous pile of grated cheese in front of her, waiting for the beer to start simmering. She'd added the chopped garlic and mustard powder and was reaching for the Worcestershire sauce when she heard footsteps on the stairs and Joe staggered in under an enormous box, patches of rainwater on his coat and hair damp.

He placed the box on the counter and removed more than half a dozen bottles. 'I wasn't sure what went with fondue,' he said, 'so I bought one of everything.'

She spotted champagne, prosecco, an expensive red wine, three different types of white, a pudding wine. She picked up the nearest bottle, reading the label as he continued to talk.

'I think that's for dessert,' he said in a rush. 'I'm not normally a fan, but I know you like sweet things.'

She looked up at him sharply. Was this a dig about her weight? His expression was neutral, though; in fact, as he raked a hand through his dark hair, she could almost have been fooled into thinking he was nervous.

'I'll lay the table,' he said, moving across to the sideboard and reaching for coasters, candlesticks, napkins. He arranged things in the same way she had done a few nights before, standing back to admire his handiwork before remembering what was missing and fetching a vase from under the sink.

'Won't be long.' He disappeared off, and Clara nipped into her bedroom, quickly pulling on a dress over leggings, dashing on some eye make-up on and spritzing her favourite perfume onto her wrists.

The fondue was bubbling by the time Gavin, Lauren and Patrick arrived. Gavin popped open the champagne and discovered that Louisa was the proud owner of some lovely-looking crystal glasses.

'Cheers,' he said, toasting Clara, leaning back against the kitchen counter to sip at his drink.

'Where's—' Lauren began just as Joe appeared in the doorway, coat now soaked through, hair dripping, clutching a bunch of twigs. He looked like Heathcliff back from the moors. 'They're for the table,' he explained.

'Here, let me,' Lauren said, rushing across the room to take the spindly branches from him.

Patrick looked at Clara and raised an eyebrow. Lauren became intensely focused on arranging the twigs in the vase in the centre of the table.

'What?' she mouthed when she finally looked up at her husband.

'So, Joe ...' and Patrick was off, asking him questions about work, about sport, moving across to the living room where Gavin was already sitting in the suede armchair looking right at home.

'Joe seems ... taller,' Lauren commented, pouring herself a glass of champagne.

Clara couldn't help a small giggle. 'I thought you loathed him,' she said in a low voice.

'Hmm ...' Lauren was looking over at the men distractedly. 'Oh, I do, he seemed so boorish, but ... well, he is quite easy on the eye, isn't he?' she said.

'You *tøs*,' nudged Clara.

'What does that mean?' Lauren asked.

'You don't want to know.'

'How rude,' Lauren said, reaching over and stealing a piece of cheese.

'Hey!' Clara narrowly missed her hand as she tried to slap it away. She couldn't help the warmth that stole over her. There were people in the flat, it was Sunday the next day and it was raining outside. This was how things were meant to be. So what if Joe had plans? She would make sure tonight wasn't ruined by that. She would just focus on everyone else, keep their contact to the bare minimum.

'Dinner's ready,' she called, ushering them all to the table.

The meal was a success, Gavin leaning back in his chair and patting his stomach, Lauren making some pretty obscene noises all the way through, Patrick covering a burp with a hand and Joe practically licking the plate clean. Clara was told to stay where she was as they all got up to help clear away and tidy, and she enjoyed sitting back, sipping at her glass of Chablis as she watched them. The others were chatting and laughing but Gavin was quiet, and she remembered his face in the shop earlier when he'd realised Joe might be selling. He hadn't spoken much that evening and was looking at Joe now with a funny expression on his face, as if he was planning something.

They returned to the table and Clara got up to start on the pudding, heading to the fridge to get the double cream. Lost in a rhythmic whisking, her mind miles away, she was distracted by Joe's laugh. She'd heard it so little really. It was an unguarded sound, a low, long, infectious rumble, and she found her mouth twitching in response. She realised this was the longest she'd seen Joe in any one place; normally he was darting off to talk on his mobile or link up to a conference call or check a screen for some share price. Here he was looking positively relaxed, his usually pale face softer in the candlelight, his grey eyes accentuated by the dark eyebrows. His hair had dried, the ends slightly curled. He was laughing at something Patrick had said, one flat hand smacking his thigh. Clara found herself staring at the hand for the longest time.

'Everything all right?' Lauren appeared next to her, peering into the saucepan. 'It's boiling.'

Clara snatched her gaze away. Lauren was right, it was

214

about to boil over. She dived on the knob to turn the heat down.

Lauren raised one eyebrow and glanced at Joe. 'You and him . . . getting on OK, are you?'

'Fine,' Clara trilled, bending down for bowls she had already brought out of the cupboard.

'Fine.' Lauren repeated in the strangest voice before drifting back to the table and topping up the wine glasses.

'Anything else to do?' Joe had got up and was standing in the kitchen, filling the small space.

Clara felt the wine going to her head. 'All good, just a few more minutes.'

'Thanks for this, for inviting me,' he said, his voice soft, at odds with the Joe she'd glimpsed in the shop earlier that day. Which was the real one?

'It's fine. You live here.' She shrugged, feeling a sliver of guilt as she watched his eyes dull. 'Not for long, maybe,' she added, wondering why she was ruining things, unable to suppress the anger she'd felt earlier.

'About that,' Joe said, taking a step forward. 'I should have said something to you about going to see them.'

'Or you could not have asked him,' Clara pointed out, her voice raised a fraction.

Joe opened his mouth to say something and then closed it again. 'It's not your decision,' he said quietly.

'I'm not sure it's yours either,' she said, switching the heat off and fetching a ladle.

'It's my mother's home,' Joe said quietly, aware of the

sudden hush around the dinner table. 'I need her to know what her options are.' His hands curled into fists as he waited for her to respond.

The word 'home' had deflated any desire Clara had to fight. This village, this flat wasn't *her* home. She used to know exactly where her home was, but that was gone now and she wondered if she would ever feel the same about anywhere else. Joe's chin lifted, preparing for battle. She shrugged wearily. 'You're right. It's none of my business,' she admitted in a small voice. 'She's your mother.' She stepped round him and called to the others, 'Let's eat pudding.' She looked at Joe, wanting to move on.

He nodded once.

They returned to the table, where Lauren was trying to teach Gavin how to say the word *hygge*.

'No, Gavin – it's *hoo-gah*,' she said, her mouth in an impossible shape.

'*Hue-gaa.*'

'No, *hoo-gah*.'

'*Hooooo-guurrrrrh.*'

They all fell about laughing, and Clara pronounced it again for them slowly, listening as they started copying her with varying degrees of success.

'What does it actually mean anyway?' Gavin asked, still opening and closing his mouth as he attempted it again.

'Well, there's no literal translation,' Lauren dived in, sounding like the Danish tourist board, 'but it means sort of cosy, doesn't it, Clara? It's why she's always lighting candles. The theory is that if things are cosy and beautiful and *hooooo-gaaaah* then you're happy, and Danish people are officially the happiest people in the world, so it must work.'

She turned to Clara as if wanting a pat on the head. Clara didn't feel like the happiest person in the world right then, but not wanting to break the mood, she joined in, trying her best to explain the concept that English people were so fascinated by.

'It's not just about candles and things, it's a way of life, I suppose, what you prioritise. The thinking is that if we stay inside our homes, surround ourselves with friends, family, good food and beautiful things, then we'll have a perfect *hyggelig* time.'

Joe was quiet, and Clara wondered if he was listening to her or whether he was still going over their conversation in the kitchen.

'See!' Lauren said. 'It's the secret to happiness.'

'Is that why you want to buy that absurdly expensive light?' Patrick said, turning to her. 'The one you showed me online.'

'It's an Arne Jacobsen,' Lauren said loftily. 'And as Clara will tell you, it's pretty vital to my well being.' She was waggling her eyebrows at Clara meaningfully.

Clara stepped in. 'Oh yes, absolutely, it's vital, Patrick. *Hygge* is all about lighting.'

'Absurdly expensive lighting,' Patrick grumbled, spooning up the last of his dessert.

'Don't you want a *hooooo-gaaaah* home?' Lauren asked.

'Not that fussed actually,' he said through a mouthful. 'I'm quite happy with the lighting we've already got. Won't something from IKEA do the job?'

'NO!' chorused Lauren and Clara.

Clara felt her spirits lift, and when everyone had finished eating she was happy to settle on the sofa with a glass of dessert wine, dipping her head onto Lauren's shoulder. Gavin had left with a quiet goodbye and Patrick and Joe were washing up.

'So,' Lauren whispered, 'how's it going with ...?' She jerked her head towards the two men, who were chatting comfortably at the sink.

Clara rolled her eyes in response. 'Gah,' she said.

'*Hoooooo-gah*,' Lauren giggled.

'No, definitely not *hooooooo-gaaaaaaah*,' Clara sighed. 'In fact' – she lifted her head and looked at Lauren – 'I officially admit defeat.'

Chapter 23

Joe was twitchy that night, hugging the hot-water bottle as if it might offer some answers. He thought back to Clara standing whisking cream in the kitchen, her blonde hair shimmering under the lights, the slight quiver of her body. She'd been cross with him, but he'd wanted her to understand. He did regret not warning her about the estate agent, but he also wanted her to realise that he needed to look out for his mother, his crazy carefree mother who did things on a whim.

It had all gone wrong, though: he hadn't explained anything, just watched the sparkle fade in her eyes. She had a right to be cross. She'd revived the shop, and watching her in there with the customers had made him realise that she really might just be there to help, because she was that kind of person.

He huffed and turned onto his side. Was he being naïve? She might look all wide-eyed, running around chatting and laughing with children, but was that all an act? A façade? Was she planning something? The way she had looked at him, as if accusing him of profiting from his own mother, made his fists curl even now. The little devil on his shoulder kept whispering as he turned this way and that in bed, the pill packet on the bedside table, unopened. He looked over at it for the hundredth time that night, but something stopped him from reaching out and picking it up.

He dreamt of Clara: her smooth skin, her straight teeth, her laugh as she explained another Danish phrase for the table. In between sleep and waking he replayed every conversation, thought back to the things she had done for him, the small kindnesses. He thought about her explanation of *hygge* and knew that was a philosophy for the way she lived her life. He had paid so many professionals to help him find a way of being happier with his lot. Had he missed something so simple?

When he started to see the outline of a new day edging around the curtains he pulled them aside to look at the hint of pink leaking over the horizon, the soft morning light resting on the fields, and felt for a moment as if he was seeing the landscape for the first time. No wonder his mother wanted to wake up to this view.

He found himself pushing on his trainers, grabbing his scarf and sneaking out of the bedroom. If *hygge* was all about cosiness and simple pleasures, he could *hygge* with the best of them. He paused at the door, looking back at the pill packet and his mobile phone on the bedside table. Then he turned and stepped outside, creeping past Lady CaCa – he could do without her announcing his presence – to the stairs beyond.

The morning was fresh, the pavement still damp from last night's rain, lightly dusted with droplets. He moved away from the shop, along the high street, dipping down a cobbled side street to a footpath he used to pound along as a young boy. The entrance to the field behind was narrower than he remembered. He squeezed himself through, his coat sleeve snagging on a bramble. 'Bugger,' he swore, causing a flock of birds in the field to flap upwards as a group and away. 'Shite.' Not completely *hygge*, then.

He didn't get far before he realised that the field was squelching beneath his feet, mud oozing over the sides of his trainers, but it felt good to be out as the sun was coming up, not another soul around, a thick line of trees in front of him reminding him of a carefree couple of years dodging and diving, screaming and racing with the other children in the village before he became a too-cool teenager. For the first time in years he wondered what had happened to the kids he'd played with then, who'd come into the shop to marvel at the shelves. Were they still around? Did they have their own kids? Did they still come to these woods?

The rumble of his stomach finally turned him around, and by the time he returned to the high street there were a few cars at the kerb, people moving about. He thought of

Clara and the constant meals she had produced for him, and ducked into the shop to buy some things for breakfast.

Roz was standing behind the counter flicking the pages of a magazine too quickly to be reading the articles, hair drawn back into a bun that stretched the skin on her face.

'Joe,' she said, one pencilled eyebrow raised. 'You're early, I've only just opened. Are you here to talk about the shop? Has Paul got back to you with a figure already? You know estate agents, though, greedy bastards, always overestimate. What did he say?'

He found himself shaking his head. He didn't want to talk about the shop. Seeing Roz had reminded him of the previous day, and all he wanted was to buy breakfast.

'I haven't spoken to him yet,' he said, whipping around the shop and throwing items into his basket as quickly as was humanly possible: part-baked rolls, butter, cereal, coffee, sausages. He was reminded of *Supermarket Sweep*; curling up with his mother on the sofa and screaming at the television as clueless people got lost in amongst the produce: 'IT'S NOT IN THE DAIRY SECTION, FOOLS.' The thought made him smile as he approached the counter.

'Someone's happy,' Roz said, swiping the first item over the scanner.

Joe wasn't about to explain, mumbling about the lovely weather instead.

'Hardly. No doubt your mother is seeing more sunshine in Greece or wherever it is she's swanned off to.'

222

He felt his face fall, turning back to the hiss of the frying pan. 'Right, sounds good,' he said in a faux-cheerful voice.

She seemed to be wavering near the bathroom. 'Any plans?' she asked, her voice softer. Was she feeling guilty?

'Just work: the usual.' His bark of laughter sounded forced.

'Oh, right, of course. Work,' she repeated. She headed into the bathroom, closing the door as he loaded up his plate with too many rolls and sausages. Of course she didn't want to have breakfast with him after what he'd said to her last night. Should he say something to her when she came out? He bit into a sausage roll, eyes on the bathroom door. He started when she came out, and a piece of sausage fell onto his plate.

Moments later, she'd emerged from her bedroom dressed in a baby-blue jumper and black jeans. 'Hope work goes well,' she said in a rush, not quite meeting his eye as she walked past him at the table. He barely had time to respond before she was closing the front door, her steps heavy on the stairs beyond. He looked around the flat, which seemed cavernous without anyone else in it, though Lady CaCa suddenly screaming 'NOBODY PUTS BABY IN THE CORNER!' reminded him that he wasn't completely alone.

He scraped most of the breakfast into the bin, feeling his shoulders sag as he moved across to his bedroom. He supposed he should work, catch up on the news from the City; he hadn't been keeping much of an eye on things this week and it was good to have a handle on share prices and recruitment. If anything significant was happening, his bosses would want them to be the first firm in there with a solution.

He sat on the foot of the bed, his earlier calm fading as his mobile announced that he had fourteen new emails. It was Sunday, though; surely he didn't need to respond to those now. If Tom asked, he could say he was working on a potential deal with a new client, or looking over some figures. He supposed some people were just having breakfast with their families, not thinking about their mobiles. Tom didn't have a family.

Decisively, he switched off the phone and flung it onto the other side of the bed. Then he grabbed his dressing gown from the back of the door, rifled through the bookshelf in the living room and headed to the bathroom.

'I SEE DEAD PEOPLE,' squawked Lady CaCa as he passed.

'Attention-seeker,' he grinned.

He had the place to himself, he remembered as he rested back against the door. He could have a completely *hygge* day. Spotting a box of matches, he lit the dozens of candles in jars that Clara had dotted around the room. When he pulled the blind down and switched off the overhead light, the effect was immediate and satisfying, with calming pools of light in every corner, dancing in the bathroom mirror and making his skin glow orange. He smiled at his reflection, feeling his good mood slowly returning.

As the bath ran, he rifled through the toiletries on offer, pausing for a moment to slather sea mud on his face before liberally pouring bubble bath into the steaming water. Lowering himself in, he rested his head back, picked up the book he'd found and started to read, enjoying the warmth and the silence as he slipped down into the water, feeling the tickle of the bubbles on the end of his nose.

Twisting the tap on and off with his foot to top up the hot water, he became immersed in his book. With no clock in the bathroom, he wasn't sure how much time had passed, but the ache in his muscles had eased and his hands were decidedly wrinkled as he relaxed back against the enamel. A sudden bang from outside made him lurch up in the water, spraying droplets. Had Roddy leapt from a great height? Had Lady CaCa escaped the cage?

The door handle rattled and Joe jerked to a sitting position, his hands covering his modesty where the bubbles failed to do so, just as Clara appeared in the doorway. For a moment she stared down at him, then she shoved one hand over her eyes and backed out again, closing the door behind her.

'God, sorry, I . . .'

Why hadn't he locked the door? What was she doing back? 'Just a second,' he called in a voice about three octaves higher than normal.

'No, it's fine, I'm sorry, I . . .' She was gabbling outside the door as he leapt out of the water and grabbed at his dressing gown.

'Hold on,' he said, shoving his arms into the sleeves and opening the door again, steam escaping in a cloud.

Clara's mouth fell open as she looked at him standing there dripping. He tightened his bottle-green dressing

226

gown, wondering what was so surprising. He was aware that the bathroom was still flickering with candlelight and that the bath was filled with a mountain of bubbles. The whole flat had also started smelling of lavender. Then, feeling the tightness in his face, he remembered the mud mask that he hadn't washed off. His cheeks flaming underneath it, he turned back into the bathroom and slammed the door.

Leaning against it, he closed his eyes. What a complete prat. He would have paid so much money to rewind the last five minutes. To emerge smelling of aftershave, leaving behind an immaculate bathroom, nodding calmly at her as he passed. He stared at his reflection in the mirror, his lips enormous, his skin tinged green, the whites of his eyes exaggerated. He scrubbed at his face, his jaw red from the effort, rinsing and splashing until all trace of the mud was gone and he could emerge back into the living room with his head held high.

'I had a bath,' he said in a small voice.

'Good idea,' she said, now sitting on the sofa, the remote in one hand, the TV still switched off. Was that the smallest shake of her shoulders? He stepped quickly towards his room, not trusting himself to say anything more.

'YOU CAN'T HANDLE THE TRUTH,' announced Lady CaCa.

I'm briefly forgiving you for the QI saga because I don't have anyone else to tell about Corralejo. It's marvellous, lots of restaurants and more of a buzzing nightlife here. I've made a lot of German friends and we all go off to the sandy beach together, which is so long you lose sight of it. I've tried bodyboarding because Klaus lent me his board, and although I swallowed half the sea I had the most amount of fun. There's no surfing in Suffolk, that's for sure.

We've taken a trip out to Lobos. It's a tiny island, uninhabited, just off the coast. We went there in a small fishing boat that rocked from side to side so violently I thought we might all be flung overboard, and I don't want to die before using the half-load on the dishwasher. I really must find out what it means. Does it only clean half the things? So we got to the other side just about intact and were released to roam around the island. It was a glorious day, a breeze lifting the back of my hair. I've entirely given up wearing hats and now sport lots of coloured scarves as headbands. I like to think I look a little like Greta Garbo, but I fear I look more like an ancient cleaning lady who has lost her way.

There's a volcano on the island – well, half a volcano, and you can climb up and peer down over the side where there's black sand below. It's really rather creepy. Then off back to the jetty where you can swim in shallow turquoise waters and see shoals of silver fish darting back and forth just below the surface.

What do you mean, sell? Did Joe really invite someone round? I don't want to sell, it sounds like things are going very merrily in my absence and I'm sure Clara is running it brilliantly. I have to say I'm a little bit jealous hearing about dinner at the flat. What do you mean, she has done a good deal with rugs and candles? What is *hygge*? It sounds very strange – is she in fact some kind of Danish cult leader? Will I return to discover you have handed over all your life savings and are living in a commune in a field behind the pub?

I must try ringing Joe, but it is such a bore always getting his rather depressed-sounding PA, who generally tells me he's on an international conference call, which sounds frightfully important, so I bottle things and never leave him a message. I can't imagine he'd be there to cause trouble, but he is protective and he's always had my best interests at heart. He can't help acting like the most frightful alpha male. I think I overcompensated when David left me, imagining that a young boy alone with his mother would turn out to be an outrageous sissy utterly bullied at school, so I used to take him to boxing matches and let him watch all the *Die Hard* films long before he was eighteen. Maybe I damaged him permanently? Tell him I do appreciate him trying to help, but I trust Clara, and you of course.

Chapter 24

She'd only returned to the flat for her purse – Gavin was taking her to Norwich to choose some things for the pub. They'd discussed ideas, taken measurements for new furniture, and he was now waiting, engine running, in the high street below, eager to get on and purchase his new look.

She had just thought she'd pop to the loo when she'd burst in on him. She hadn't seen anything much, just pink flesh and an absurd amount of bubbles. Then his startled face covered in that green mask had emerged, looking horrified. It was as if she'd caught him *in flagrante*, he was so tense. She felt the awkwardness of the night before fade away as she stood there staring at him. He was wearing his smart dressing grown with the embroidered emblem on the outside pocket, his hair spiked up and his face covered in mud, and had looked as if he wanted the ground to swallow him up. She thought it was the first time she might have glimpsed something of the real Joe.

She was thinking about it in the car all the way to Norwich, replaying the scene in her head, trying desperately hard not to giggle. He had lit all the candles, pretended not to notice the bath still covered in bubbles, the scent as if he'd crushed a hundred lavender plants underfoot.

She felt a glimmer of hope that perhaps he wasn't the lost cause she'd written off; perhaps he *was* able to change. She couldn't wait to report back to Lauren. She'd be careful not to tell her too much; there was something so helpless about him standing there in his bare feet, lost for words, that she didn't want him to feel she was mocking him. On the other hand, he was still about to sell the shop without consulting his mum. And he was still surgically attached to his mobile. His expression, though, as he'd stood in the doorway of the bathroom, surrounded by the scent of lavender . . .

'You all right?' Gavin asked, giving her a sideways glance.

She nodded, settling back into the passenger seat as she tried to help Gavin make a decent word out of four I's, a T, a U and an F.

'Futiiii . . . le?' she suggested.

'Not helpful.'

'Fuit.'

'Is that a word?' He sounded surprised.

'Probably. Somewhere in the world.' Clara shrugged,

feeling a lot more carefree, looking forward to the day ahead, overhauling the pub.

'Not helpful either.'

They loaded up the car with cushions, rugs, lamps and more, cramming items into the boot and lowering the back seats to jam everything in. They made slow progress back, stopping to pick up food, which they ate as they talked.

Back at the pub, they started by dragging all the furniture to the edge of the room, stacking stools and chairs on tables and going over the swirled carpet with a hoover. They'd brought rugs to cover it, in warm shades of red, touches of black. They polished the tables and rearranged the furniture, admiring the effect of the dark wood and the deep colours. The creamy walls and the dark timber beams blended brilliantly. The bare lights were covered in lampshades that muted the harsh bulbs and created an instant calm.

Gavin had cleared out the old fireplace and stacked logs in rows on either side, then reached into the enormous space to build a fire in the large iron coal pit. They placed cushions on the armchairs, wiped down dusty board games and displayed them on a wooden bookcase, along with a selection of novels and biographies that the villagers could borrow. They placed large clear jars on mantelpieces, tables and windowsills and filled them with enormous cream wax candles, their poker-straight wicks waiting to be lit. They hung a few pictures on the walls and hoisted a large antique mirror over the fireplace.

The day passed quickly and Clara was aware that the shop window needed dressing too. She still had to plan the finer details of the next display. She had plenty of time, though, and it was great to see Gavin completely absorbed, now cleaning every bottle behind the bar. The place did look fantastic, transformed into a gorgeous, warm and welcoming country pub. As the light faded, they lit the fire and the candles and sat drinking pale ale in the armchairs, their feet up on worn leather pouffes, toasting their aching limbs and enjoying the reaction as locals wandered in, drawn by the orange glow of the fire and staying to listen to the crackle of the logs and chat in cosy corners.

Clive walked in, talking on his phone, then looked up and ground to a halt. 'Wow,' he said, before remembering his phone call and hastily lifting the phone to his ear once more.

Gavin was serving a customer at the bar as Clara got up to leave. He looked across at her as she placed her glass on the counter.

'Hang on a minute, Clara,' he said, tipping a pint glass away from him and pouring a lager.

She paused, watching him slide the drink across the bar, wipe his hands and reach into his pocket. 'Something to say thank you. Just small. But wanted you to know I appreciate everything.' He handed her a package and she opened it to reveal a beautiful thin silver chain. 'So glad you turned up in our village,' he said, his voice gruff. 'You're a great girl. If I'd had a daughter, I'd have liked her to be just like you.'

Clara felt tears thicken the back of her throat as she

stared at the necklace. Unable to do much more than nod, she gave Gavin a one-armed hug and staggered away. *If I'd had a daughter.* The words rang in her ears all the way home. Would he have said that if he knew what kind of a daughter she *had* been?

She pushed her way into the shop, not wanting to go up to the flat, needing to be alone for a bit. The new display was the perfect distraction. Laying out all the items she'd need, she got to work on the backdrop, creating a wild forest from various rolls of green fabric and scattering leaves collected on her walks over the bottom of the shop window. Next she glued the figures into position, attaching a long plait to a Barbie, placing a Ken doll on bended knee. The story of Rapunzel was coming to life, the magic wrapping round her, allowing her to forget her mood, forget everything else going on in her life and simply create a scene.

Chapter 25

Clara was starting to become familiar with the trails through the woods. Even in winter there were things to see: bare spiked branches, curled leaves like a carpet on the ground. That morning she had stumbled across a patch of perfectly formed toadstools, their tops livid red scattered with yellow spots, like a scene from her latest window display.

She'd been in the shop all morning and needed this release, the new display finished. Frost was still clinging to the branches of the tree, the fields glistening with silver. Patches of the small stream had frozen, leaves and other debris stuck in the ice. She enjoyed the quiet of the forest, the small ticks and chatter of the insects around her, the call of a nearby bird, the flutter of wings, something rustling in the undergrowth. She sat drinking hot chocolate from her

Thermos flask, perched on a fallen tree trunk, her bottom growing numb from the cold but not wanting to move on yet.

The rustling grew louder, and behind her she heard a bark followed by a voice shouting, 'Gus, NO! No, Gus, leave.'

She stood up, spinning around in the direction of the noise: twigs breaking underfoot, the crunch of leaves, panting, another bark. Then into the small clearing bounded a cocker spaniel, a bush swishing as it snapped back into place. Clara smiled, stepping forward to crouch down, the dog racing towards her, ears flapping, burrs stuck to his curled fur, placing a paw on her jeans, leaving a muddy mark. She ruffled his head, grinning as he spun round her in excitement, left then right.

'Gus, I said— oh.' Sam appeared in the clearing, straightening as he saw Clara with his dog. 'Ah, you found him,' he said, pulling out a lead from the pocket of his waxed jacket. Today his hair was windswept, his cheeks pink with the cold and the exercise. 'He's immune to my voice,' he sighed, as Gus jumped up, placing both paws on Clara's thighs. 'God, I'm really sorry ... SIT, GUS.' Gus proceeded to hold out one paw as if he was begging.

Clara giggled. '*Sidde.*' Gus sat down immediately and she turned to Sam. 'Maybe he's Danish?'

'Bloody nightmare is what he is,' Sam said, moving forward to pop the dog's lead back on. 'Thanks. We didn't mean to disturb you.'

For a brief moment Clara wondered if he had followed her, then she dismissed the thought. Hark at you, Clara

Kristensen, you're no celebrity to be tracked down by random men. 'Not at all. I was heading back soon anyway. I'm exhausted; there's a new display up tomorrow.'

'Of course.' Sam nodded. 'Amber reminded me yesterday. I'll have to bring her down to see it. She loved your last one. Although they're costing me a fortune,' he added.

Clara smiled, watching his hand reach down to stroke behind Gus's ears.

'I'll walk back to the village with you. I don't want to spend the rest of the day chasing this one through the woods.'

She was still staring at his left hand, noticing an absence of rings. 'Great, great,' she said, a little too enthusiastically, feeling her skin warm despite the chill in the air.

They wound their way back down one of the narrow paths, Sam holding back branches to stop them snapping towards her, offering her a hand as they reached a particularly churned-up section.

'Thanks,' Clara said, feeling a little stupid, since the mud was stiff with ice and she could walked across easily, her boots not sinking.

They emerged from the line of trees, the sun hazy through a blanket of thick white cloud, the edges rimmed with pale pink.

'I love this light,' Sam said, echoing Clara's own thoughts. 'It's perfect for photography. I've taken so many pictures at this time of day.'

'You're a landscape photographer too?' Clara queried.

Sam nodded. 'All sorts of photography. It works well with the writing. I've sold a few pictures.' He shrugged, his face suffused with pleasure. 'And it's a great hobby when you're alone a lot,' he added, giving her a sideways glance.

Clara found her face growing warm under his gaze. 'How wonderful. I can't take a decent picture; I get too distracted, and I don't understand all the knobs and buttons.'

He raised one eyebrow then, making her look away as if she'd said something shocking. She laughed nervously, grateful that Gus decided to squeeze in between them, staring up at her as if waiting for a treat.

Sam was still looking at her, his head cocked to one side. 'You've got fantastic skin,' he said.

She felt her cheeks fill with heat, not used to compliments. She spluttered a thanks.

'I'd love to take your photograph again – an outdoors shoot, perhaps,' he said, smiling broadly. She noticed a spot of stubble on his chin that he'd missed shaving; wondered what it would be like to reach out and touch it.

'No, no, I'm not at all photogenic,' she said, pulling her hat down over her ears. 'I just freeze up or shut my eyes or both.'

'No, you're the perfect subject,' Sam said with a high laugh that didn't match his voice.

Clara walked on, Sam falling into step again beside her. They stepped over the stile, Gus running under it, getting the lead caught so that Sam was hauled back, as if he'd forgotten he had a dog on a lead.

'Well,' Clara said as the burgundy façade of the shop came

into view. 'That's me.' She pointed to it, wondering why she felt the need to do that. He knew exactly where the shop was; visited it often.

He stopped outside, staring at the drawn-down shutters. 'What is it?'

'You'll have to wait and see,' Clara said.

'Come on,' he said, his eyes roving as if he had X-ray vision in his glasses. 'Can I have a clue?'

Clara let out a small laugh. 'Let's just say I adore fairy tales,' she said, searching for her key. She sensed movement somewhere above her, distracted from looking by Sam.

'Amber will love it, then. Look,' he said, resting a hand on her arm so that she froze, staring at it, his fingernails cut perfectly square. 'Let me write another piece. This is bound to be great, and lots of people have shown an interest in the shop.'

'I'm not sure,' Clara said, biting her lip.

'I saw the estate agent in there the other day,' he said quietly. 'There's more of an angle on the story now. Let me help; it's really relevant at the moment, with high streets failing, shops being forced to shut. We can try and save yours.' His voice lifted at the end.

She pulled her arm away gently. 'It's not mine,' she reminded him.

'Well, let's see if we can't at least get some more trade in the run-up to Christmas,' he said, renewing the attack.

There was movement again; was that the curtain in the flat swinging back? A figure? She wondered if Joe was there, watching.

'OK, just a short article maybe,' she said. There was no harm in that, was there? 'Just to bring in customers for Christmas, nothing more,' she added in a warning voice.

'Of course, great, promise,' he said, leaning in and giving her a kiss on the cheek. 'And maybe I'll persuade you, then.' His green eyes twinkled at her.

Clara tipped her head to one side. 'Persuade me?'

He lifted his hands as if he had an imaginary camera and snapped at her. 'Goodbye, good luck with it,' he said, walking backwards, pointing at the window. Gus barked a goodbye too, and she held up one hand in a half-wave, watching them both disappear down the high street, Gus bounding next to Sam, barking in glee. Would she regret what she had just agreed to?

Chapter 26

She forgot all about bumping into Sam the moment she saw the package that had been left. Picking it up slowly, she stared at it for the longest time, holding it in her hand, turning it over, knowing what was inside, remembering when she had ordered it, desperate for home, the familiar. It had taken her forever to find online and the postage had cost a fortune. The day itself had passed a while ago and she'd thought about the package finding its way to her. Now it was here. She held it to her chest and climbed the stairs feeling her eyes sting.

She bit her lip as she entered the flat. Walking slowly over to the armchair, she sank into it, staring at the letters on the brown wrapping paper for an age. Then, drawing one fingernail across the opening, she tore at it, revealing the box inside, sliding open the box to draw out the brown beer bottle, paper shavings scattering everywhere.

She held up the bottle, staring at the label for a long time. Then she let out a sob and started crying, gulping in air and letting her face run with tears. What was she doing in England? How long would she be here for? She remembered this time last year, how different things had been. Wallowing in self-pity, she gave in to her emotions, the bottle and the flat both blurred by the tears pouring from her eyes.

Then, as if she were in a horror movie, she heard a creak as a door opened impossibly slowly. 'Clara?' said Joe in an uncertain voice.

'Oh, you're in,' she hiccoughed, frantically wiping at her wet face.

His eyes widened and he hurried over to her. 'Can I call anyone?'

She shook her head, unable to respond.

'Do you need a doctor? Are you unwell?'

Clara shook her head again. 'No,' she said, 'I'm fine.'

His voice went up a notch. 'Would you like me to fetch your friend, the woman from the dinner party?'

'Lauren,' Clara choked out.

'That's it,' he agreed. 'Of course, Lauren. Shall I fetch her?'

'No,' she said, aware of the tears streaking her cheeks. 'I'll be OK in a minute.'

He lingered next to her, placing one hand on the back of the sofa, then removing it, looking at her as if she was a wild animal.

'Tea,' he barked, as if pouncing on the word. 'I can make you some tea.' He didn't wait for her to respond but headed straight to the kitchen and flicked on the kettle.

'Milk? Sugar?' he called out, rapid-fire.

'OK,' she mumbled, dabbing at her face.

He waited in the kitchen, back tense, giving her wary looks every ten seconds or so, big false smiles when he caught her eye. 'It's on its way,' he chimed in a voice she didn't recognise. He was stirring the cup, still looking at her, tea sloshing over the side, as if she might dissolve in front of him.

She felt a small hiccough of laughter break through the tears at his unease. 'Great.'

He walked over carrying the mug as if it were the Crown Jewels and laid it on the table in front of her. 'Tea,' he smiled, pointing at it as if she was two years old and he was teaching her new words.

She picked it up and took a sip, trying not to wince at the sugar in it, then setting it back down as he stood by her like a waiter waiting for her verdict. 'Excellent,' she said, hoping he might leave her alone now.

'Right, so . . . ' He didn't go, but paused in front of the sofa before clearly making the decision to sit down. He stared at the floor, then looked back up at her. 'Better?' he said, probably hoping he could be released.

She nodded, feeling strangely moved by his expression. Oh no, the tears were starting again; she felt an errant one roll down her face. Joe slouched as he spotted it.

'What's happened? Can I help?' His voice was softer now, no edge, and she felt grateful for the fact that he was behaving like a human being rather than the manic businessman she always seemed to encounter.

'I missed a special day at home,' she said, reaching for the tea to try and distract herself.

He nodded, his expression confused. 'Your birthday?' he ventured.

She smiled, shaking her head. 'No, it was J-Dag, the sort of start of Christmas. It was a while ago now, but it's a big thing in Denmark.'

'OK,' Joe said, his fingers forming a steeple under his chin. 'So why the tears?'

She jerked her head at the beer bottle. 'I ordered that, I don't know why. We drink it on J-Dag.'

'Beer?'

'This exact beer,' Clara explained. 'Everyone dresses up in blue Santa hats and there are massive parties in the streets. There's foam and this beer is delivered by horse and cart.'

Joe was back to looking completely perplexed as he followed her finger to the beer bottle by her armchair.

'Right . . . foam . . . beer.'

'I know it sounds silly,' she said.

'Not at all,' he said, probably hoping she wouldn't cry again.

'No, I know it does,' she said, wiping at her eyes. 'It's just it reminds me of . . . of what's ahead.'

Joe didn't hazard a guess.

'Christmas,' she explained in a quiet voice.

'Not a fan?'

She sniffed, trying to stem the fresh tears. 'No, it's not that. I love Christmas, I just . . . '

Joe was biting his lip, clearly trying to keep up. 'So what's the problem?'

Clara swallowed, placing both hands on her thighs, trying to compose herself. 'There's no problem really, I'm being silly. I just . . . well, it reminded me of things.'

'The beer?'

'The beer.' She laughed, feeling marginally better for having had a cry. 'I'll be fine. Thanks for the tea.' She nodded at the mug, which was still almost full.

Joe's cheeks flushed pink. 'Glad to help,' he said, standing up as if she'd dismissed him. He paused before moving towards her, placing a hand on her shoulder. 'I hope you feel better later,' he said, then, with a quick cough, backed away. 'Right, I'm going to . . . I'll be . . . ' and he scurried into his bedroom.

She stared at his door long after it closed, then, shutting her eyes, she leant back in the chair, replaying the scene and groaning into her hands. Note to self: next time you want to cry, check flat is empty. As she thought back on the conversation, though, she found herself smiling. God, what on earth did he think of her? How could she explain? And then she was shaking with laughter, a bit of snot escaping just as his door was flung open once more.

'All OK?' He looked panicked again and she shot upright, wiping at her nose.

'Fine. I was just ... um ... laughing.'

Joe's eyes rounded further. 'Oh ... that's good,' he said, pausing only briefly before shutting the door for a second time.

Clara stayed where she was, a smile frozen on her face, until she heard the latch click. Then she smacked her forehead with her hand.

'DOH,' said Lady CaCa from behind her.

A makeover in the pub? How lovely. What have you done with it? Will you send me photos? I do miss the place. But enough of that. I am of course thoroughly enjoying being out here; the heat is fantastic and I am walnut brown. I look absurd, as if someone has painted me in mahogany varnish. Like a native. I am considering getting my hair dyed blonde at the ends, it's very fashionable with the Germans here – you see, I might have been out here too long on my own. I won't, of course, I've settled for wearing an ankle bracelet everywhere, which is just about curing me of doing anything too permanent.

Now let me just say right now that VAR isn't a word, Gavin. I have asked every German in my hotel, and they speak much better English than me, and all of them have confirmed that this is a terrible lie and you are winning through cheating. I'm sorry to be so blunt but I really must ask you to start defining the words you use if you insist on using some kind of entirely made-up language. Maybe you have set your version of the game on something that isn't English (UK). Do check. I will wait for your reply before playing again.

Chapter 27

He'd hadn't been back all week, stuck in the office for long days, overseeing the final stage of the merger: constant conference calls, updates to bosses, ensuring that Tom saw him issuing instructions to an overworked graduate trainee who really looked as if he could do with a square meal. He'd headed back to his flat, standing in the doorway as he took in the stark, cold surfaces. The cold grey outside seemed to seep inside. He'd stayed up late on his laptop, minimising spreadsheets to browse online, ordering lamps, rugs, candlesticks from an eye-wateringly expensive designer Clara had once mentioned, Verner someone, a furry hot-water-bottle cover, a new pair of slippers. The next day he'd left the office with an overwhelming urge to block out the stress of the day, get back to his apartment, cook a meal. He felt he was making changes and they were working: he had more energy, fewer headaches, felt better.

Now it was Saturday night and normally he'd be lining up a date from an internet dating app or heading to a casino into the early hours. Or working: scouring articles for insider news, going over the paperwork his team had prepared, replying to emails from earlier that week. Instead he found himself driving back to sleepy Suffolk, his heart lifting at the thought of finally getting back to the village after a long week, as if he was driving home. He was smiling as he parked, looking up at the windows of the flat and wondering whether Clara was in.

He hadn't seen her since Beer-Bottle-Weepinggate. He was still not absolutely sure what she'd been sad about – something about foam and blue Santa hats. It was obviously a Danish thing. Or a female thing. Or both. He would do what any self-respecting man would do and pretend it hadn't happened, he thought, as he stepped out of the car and reached for his leather holdall. Moving through the corridor and up to the flat, he readied himself for seeing her. He wished he'd spent some time there that week; witnessing her upset had reminded him that she wasn't always the contented, happy person she appeared. He'd spotted her out on the pavement with that journalist just before she'd been crying. He hoped she hadn't turned to him for comfort.

She wasn't in the living room; probably still shutting up the shop from earlier or working on another display. He would go and find her, see if she wanted a takeaway. Just as he was turning round to head back down the stairs, she stepped out of her bedroom. Normally she lived in cosy jumpers and jeans, but tonight she was wearing a black top with some shiny details on the shoulders over a pair of electric-blue trousers. Her legs seemed longer; he found himself staring as she shrugged on her coat.

'Oh, hey, you're here.'

'I'm here,' Joe said in a too-loud voice. He dropped his bag.

'Lauren's taking me to the cinema,' she said, gesturing to her outfit. 'I think it's overkill but I haven't been out in ages.' Her eyes were all smoky and dark, her lips glossy. Joe found his brain freeze until he realised he was definitely meant to respond.

'You look ...' The words hit him then. 'The cinema, GREAT,' he said, reaching to put a hand up on the mantelpiece in a casual way and missing. Righting himself, he nodded. 'Anything good on?'

'Lauren wants to see something with Ryan Gosling.' Clara shrugged.

Joe nodded. 'He's a good-looking guy. Smooth. And, you know, shiny.' What. Are. You. Talking. About. Joe? 'Well, I'll just be here. Waiting. I mean, not waiting for you but, you know, having a night in. Or maybe out, I haven't decided.' He knew he was gabbling. He wondered what had come over him. Was it the shiny things on her top? Hypnotising him?

'That sounds like a plan. It's raining again.'

251

Joe rolled his eyes and tsked. Before he could think of anything better than weather chat, she was picking up her bag and giving him a smile.

'See you later then,' she said, heading out the door.

'Yup,' he trilled, 'okaaaaay then.'

With a last puzzled look she left the flat and Joe sank into the sofa as if the last few minutes had exhausted him. Well, it was good nothing was still awkward between them. He got up to fetch a beer.

An hour and three beers later, he was feeling sleepy. Moving around the flat, he lit all the candles, and the woodburner, the living room a flickering calm haven. He changed into his pyjamas, shrugged on his dressing gown and unearthed a pair of oversized slippers in the shape of animal claws that his mother had bought him for Christmas one year. With his toasty new look he returned to the sofa with a tray piled high with bottles and snacks. He hadn't watched a DVD since the time he had been ill with a chest infection and had been bed-bound for three days. And even then he'd chosen *Wall Street* just to stay in the zone.

He riffled through his mother's DVD collection as he sipped at another beer; the choices were sparse. He'd never heard of Nicholas Sparks, but he'd give it a go. He noticed it had Ryan Gosling in it and couldn't help smiling. Clara hadn't needed to leave.

The rain was drumming against the windows, the wind a distant whistle as Joe snuggled under a rug, a hot-water bottle clutched to his chest, chocolate buttons melting in his mouth, the beer flowing freely. There was something to be said for Clara's *hygge* theory; staying in really was the new going out. He felt his body relax into the sofa, the whole world outside the flat dissolve away so that it was just him in his snug space with the DVD for company.

An hour and a half later, with the tears streaming down his cheeks and dripping from his nose, he failed to hear the chatter on the staircase outside, the door click open. He jumped as Lauren and Clara stepped into the flat and wiped frantically at his face. Nicholas Sparks had a lot of explaining to do. He felt his throat still thick with tears, his nose running as he dabbed at it with the sleeve of his dressing gown.

'Hey,' he croaked, his hot-water bottle falling out and landing in between his oversized claw feet.

Clara and Lauren both stopped short and stared at him.

'Why is one of us always catching the other crying?' Clara laughed, breaking the mood.

Joe found he still couldn't speak.

'What are you watching?' Lauren frowned, walking towards him, before spotting the DVD case.

'Oh my God,' she cried, scooping it up and waving it at him. '*The Notebook*. On your own. Are you MAD? You need a support network for that kind of thing, some good gal pals. Are you OK? Do you want us to hold you?'

Clara was giggling as Lauren stepped towards him holding out both arms.

Joe found himself backing away, the beer making him woozy, the candles throwing looming shadows round the walls. He never cried over movies. OK, aside from *Point Break*, but that was only because his mother had recorded an episode of *Neighbours* over it ten minutes from the end. 'I'm fine,' he said, straightening up, glad to see the end credits rolling. 'Fine,' he repeated, his voice more confident.

'I love that film,' Lauren said. 'That kiss in the rain is just ...' She was lost to a daydream.

'How was the cinema?' Joe asked, perching himself on the end of the sofa, folding his arms and trying to look as sensible as he could.

'Hmm,' Lauren said dreamily, still soaked and in Ryan Gosling's arms after a heavy storm in a rowing boat.

Clara moved towards the bathroom, calling over her shoulder, 'Lauren's in love!' She giggled.

Joe looked at Lauren, wanting desperately to escape to his own room.

Lauren was perhaps feeling the same, glancing around the flat, clearly struggling for something to say.

'It's looking very *hygge* in here,' she commented.

Joe followed her gaze, taking in the candles, the rug, the hot-water bottle. 'I thought I'd make it, you know ... nice,' he said, feeling a bit foolish.

Clara had left the bathroom and was heading to the kitchen.

'I was just saying to Joe,' Lauren called in a pointed voice, 'how very *hygge* it's looking in here. Don't you think, Clara?'

Joe frowned. Why was she giving Clara such a strange look?

Clara looked thrown by the comment, not speaking for a moment. 'It is very cosy,' she stuttered.

Something passed between the two women and Joe felt like an outsider, missing some punchline or joke.

'Hmm,' he said, walking around the room and blowing out candles, the sharp smell of smoke immediate, making his eyes water for the hundredth time that night. Were there any more tears in him? He must have red eyes, a swollen face. He needed to get out of here. The fact that he'd found Clara crying over a beer bottle and blue Santa hats didn't make him feel much better. He wasn't used to being caught on the hop in this way. 'Sleep well,' he said, his throat scratchy.

'You too,' Lauren called.

He heard Clara hiss something at her, and as he closed his door, he caught the snuffle of giggles.

Chapter 28

Clara woke to the sound of silence, and reached a hand out to pull back the curtain. The rain had gone and the sky was blue, clouds clinging to the horizon. She stretched, hearing a cough from the kitchen next door. Joe was up early. She had been relieved not to have seen him all week, embarrassed about her J-Dag meltdown, not sure what was happening with the shop, but she found she was smiling at the sound, sinking into the bed and listening out for him. Shrugging on a thick cardigan and opening her door, she was surprised to see him hunched over his laptop at the table, his chin in one hand as he stared at the screen, eyes bloodshot. Last night's *hygge* vibe was clearly long gone. She felt a little whisper of sadness.

'Hey,' she said, even her quiet voice making him start.

He tapped at the keyboard before returning to staring at the screen.

'Coffee?' she asked, moving past him to switch on the kettle.

'NICE TO SEE YOU, TO SEE YOU NICE,' Lady CaCa called out.

Clara dropped some pellets in her cage.

'LUNCH IS FOR WIMPS,' the parrot yelled, obviously picking up on Joe's vibe.

Roddy wound around Clara's legs as she added milk to the mugs and passed one to Joe.

'Thanks,' he said, taking it from her. She noticed his hand shaking as he drank. 'Everything all right?' she asked, feeling a wave of sympathy for him.

'Fine, busy – just having to unravel the mess that is my mother's accounts,' he said, looking with a frown at the kitchen table, where a pile of receipts, bank statements and dog-eared exercise books rested. 'Whilst simultaneously hoping my team don't screw up the biggest deal of the year tomorrow.'

'Sounds stressful,' she said, cutting a slice of malt loaf and slathering butter on it. 'Here,' she said, handing him the plate, 'breakfast. Have you been up long?' she asked, taking in a pile of empty crisp packets, three glasses containing the remnants of various coloured liquids and a thin silver packet, all eight pills popped out.

He took the plate without looking at her. 'Yeah. Sort of. I couldn't sleep after that film, and I knew I should have worked. I think I fell asleep for a bit.' Looking down at the plate in his hand and then up at her, he seemed to come round. 'Thanks,' he said, an unreadable expression crossing his face at the same moment that one of the many devices in front of him pinged.

Clara rested against the work surface sipping her drink, looking at the bags under his eyes, his grey expression. She thought he'd been trying a little harder to relax, to unwind, but the moment he was surrounded by the laptop and the phone he seemed completely sucked into another world.

'Let's go somewhere,' she said in a loud voice.

'What?' he said, simultaneously taking a bite of malt loaf and tapping at the keyboard with his other hand.

'Let's go somewhere. Out. Like normal people do on a weekend.'

The bread was clenched between his teeth as he tapped the keyboard with both hands. His eyes flicked up towards her but he obviously wasn't ready to talk.

At last he stopped, removed the bread and swallowed. 'Out?'

Clara nodded, pushing an errant strand of hair behind her ear. 'I want to see the sea.'

'GO AHEAD, MAKE MY DAY.'

Clara blushed, pretending she hadn't heard, as Lady CaCa stood watching them from her perch.

'The sea?'

Clara nodded. Joe looked unsure, staring at her as if she'd suggested they get a flight to another country.

'Come on,' she continued. 'It'll be fun.'

258

'OK,' he said slowly. 'I suppose we could.'

Clara clapped her hands together, feeling a sudden joy sweep through her. She hadn't realised she needed the release. 'Great. I'll just get dressed and we can go.'

Joe was closing his laptop. 'Right. The sea,' he repeated. He still seemed quite shell-shocked.

Clara started to walk back to her bedroom. 'Oh, one rule,' she said, turning back. 'No phone.' She pointed to the offending item in his hand.

'But what if work—'

'It's Sunday,' she said, cutting him off in a voice of old, a voice that had once been listened to. 'No one should work every single day of the week. In Denmark, people work a thirty-four-hour week in total; you do that in two days.'

'A thirty-four-hour week?' Joe said, shuffling papers and unplugging his laptop. 'How do they get any work done?'

Clara had moved through to the bedroom and was scooping up various things, throwing them into a bag. 'It's not all about work, you know,' she called. 'And actually, they think that if you can't get everything done within that time, then it's sort of inefficient.'

She was glad she couldn't see his face. There was silence as she reappeared. He was tapping at his phone.

'I'm serious,' she said, marching over to him and holding out her hand as if he were a toddler with a forbidden sweet.

'I can't. You don't understand. You've never had a job like mine,' he protested. She opened her mouth to say something and then closed it again.

259

'We're expected to be contactable at all times,' he stressed. 'Tom, the other managing director, is suspicious; I think he's ready to bury me.'

'But it's just not healthy,' Clara said, still holding out her hand. Joe was staring at it as if she were about to attack him.

'I'll put it on silent.'

'Nope.'

'I'll leave it in the car.'

'Joe,' Clara said, her voice exasperated now.

'You just don't get it,' he said, looking worriedly down at the item in question.

She dropped her hand and took a breath. 'Actually I do,' she said, and sighed. 'I used to be surgically attached to mine. I worked in London, as a trader, for six years.'

Joe had been about to say something, but now his mouth fell open.

'I was doing sixteen-hour days, all-nighters, didn't go home to Denmark for months, neglected my friends, my family,' she added in a quieter voice, staring off into the distance before turning away so Joe couldn't see her face.

There was silence for a while, and she wondered if he was back on his phone, tapping out another email, but when she peeked he was still just staring at her.

'Six years?'

She nodded.

'But why did you ... You worked as a ... But you're so ...'

It was almost amusing watching him struggle for words, but Clara hated talking about that time in her life. It had

260

been the reason she had changed everything. She still regretted not seeing how absorbed she'd been with it all, to the extent that she hadn't noticed important things happening to people she loved. Her mum, the visits to the doctor she'd brushed off, Clara not there to realise.

She swallowed. 'It was a while ago now, it doesn't matter.' She wished she hadn't brought it up. She was just fed up with Joe thinking she didn't understand, that she couldn't understand. She knew exactly what it was like to feel the bank owned you, that your mobile and laptop ruled your working life and your home life because there was no line any more: people could call or email at any hour and someone would expect you to answer, to jump to it. And if you didn't, someone else would and you'd be for the chop.

She moved to the door. If they weren't going to the beach, she could at least go outside. Then she heard him.

'Wait.' He placed his phone on the table and held up his hand. 'Give me two minutes,' he said. He went into his bedroom and she could hear him opening cupboards and drawers. 'You're not expecting us to swim, are you?' he called through.

'It's December, Joe.'

His head appeared in the doorway. 'So that's a no?' he asked uncertainly.

'Of course it's a no, it's like minus three,' she pointed out, staring at him as if he was mad.

'You seem the type to want to do that sort of thing,' he said, returning to his rummaging.

She wondered what he'd meant by that. Active? Impulsive? Clinically insane?

'Ready,' he huffed, emerging with a rucksack, wearing a beanie hat she hadn't seen on him before. He looked different, and for a second she couldn't put her finger on why, until she realised it was the first time she'd seen him dress really casually.

'I like your hat,' she said, feeling weirdly shy.

He touched it self-consciously. 'Thanks, haven't worn it in a while,' he said, picking up his keys. 'Well, come on then. The beach it is,' he said, and walked over to the door, opening it and waiting for her to step through.

'MAY THE FORCE BE WITH YOU,' Lady CaCa cried out as Clara glanced back. Joe's phone was on the table where he'd left it. She gave him a smile as she walked through and down the stairs.

He started asking her questions the moment they pulled out from the kerb. 'Which bank?'

'UBS.'

'They're big.'

'Yep.'

'What was the biggest deal you did?'

'What is this? A competition? I'm not telling you that. A lot. It was a lot.'

'Prove it,' he said, banging one hand on the wheel, a smile on his face.

'What do you mean?' Clara laughed, leaning back into the seat.

'Prove you really did it. Say something a trader would say.'

'What, like talk about the dealer board and how I spent my days observing the signs making up the price action, including price fluctuations and the liquidity of the order book ...'

'You *did* work as a trader.' He snuck a sideways look at her.

'I told you I did.'

'I thought it was just a lie to make me go to the beach.'

'It was to make you take me to the beach, but I'm not that manipulative.'

'So ...' Joe was clearly about to launch into another raft of questions.

'Look,' Clara said, cutting him off, 'I spent most of the six years shouting and swearing at people on the trading floor. Sometimes I miss that madness; that was what drew me into it. And I wanted to prove I could do it. But I really don't want to talk about it now. That bit of my life is over, I couldn't stay in it. I wasn't happy.'

'OK, but did you—'

She looked at his animated face. 'Enough now,' she said in a gentle voice.

Joe caught her expression. 'Enough,' he agreed. 'Can see how you might have been a bit scary on the trading floor,' he added, biting his lip.

Clara smiled and rested her head back on the smooth leather, focusing on the road ahead, the car pristine, her feet lost in the cavernous footwell, the sound of the tyres barely there as they twisted through narrow lanes to the coast.

Then there it was ahead, a thin strip of silver under brooding grey clouds, and Clara found herself smiling as she turned to Joe. 'The sea.'

They drove along the seafront, Joe tense at first as he fretted over whether parking was free, if someone would steal the car, whether he would need his hat. As they hit the stony beach, crunched over the pebbles, he seemed to grow quieter, start to look around him, and then they were walking along the shoreline, the waves rolling in, barely a breeze, the water sucked away before returning. A seagull hovering over the water, a ferry moving slowly past in the distance, a line of pink buoys like tiny heads bobbing just off the shore.

'Mum and I used to come here at weekends,' he said, eyes ahead. 'She used to skim stones with me, then we'd have fish and chips huddled on a single towel that smelt of vinegar for days afterwards.'

Clara held her breath. Joe had hardly said anything about his childhood, his mum, and it was so lovely to picture him as a young boy.

'What about your dad?' she asked, realising she'd never heard him mention his father.

Joe moved to sit down on the pebbles and Clara sat next to him, wondering if he'd heard her. He raked a hand through the stones. 'He left. When I was eight.'

'Oh,' Clara said. 'That must have been hard.'

Joe picked up one of the pebbles, turning it between his fingers. 'It was. We moved around a lot; my mum, well, she hadn't expected it, couldn't stay in any one place . . .'

Clara looked at him as he spoke, starting to understand a little more, his need to give his mother some stability.

'Do you see him?'

Joe shook his head. 'Not much any more. Once a year we have lunch. I used to be desperate to see him, to be like him, to show him I'd succeeded. I'd always wanted to work in the City, be important like him.' He laughed, but the noise was hollow and Clara felt the urge to reach for him.

'He should be very proud,' she said.

Joe looked at her then, his grey eyes trained on her face. 'Thank you.' Then, as if aware the mood had shifted, he got to his feet. 'Shall we keep walking?'

Clara stood up, followed him.

'How about you?' Joe asked. 'Do you miss your family?'

Clara was glad to be moving, could feel the familiar sting at the back of her eyes. 'My parents separated when I was small and my dad has his own life, but we've always got on, he's always seen me. I've got two stepsisters, twins, they're fourteen.' She hoped that was enough information.

'Your mum?' he asked.

Clara squinted out across the water that was the same grey as Joe's eyes, as if she might be rescued by a passing boat or a bolt of lightning. Nothing, of course, just the relentless noise of the waves and her own silence.

'She was ill,' she said at last, her voice almost lost to the wind. 'She was ill and she died, last year.'

Joe stopped abruptly; Clara had moved forward a few paces before she noticed.

'I'm so sorry,' he said, his expression aghast.

'It's OK,' she said, wiping at her face. 'Well, it's not OK, but thank you.'

'How did she ... do you mind me asking?'

Clara swallowed. 'She had pancreatic cancer. She had treatment but it wasn't found until it had spread to other sites, and the end was ... quick.'

Joe looked at her. 'I'm so sorry, Clara.'

She couldn't hold his gaze for long. 'She didn't tell me much about it,' she admitted, realising that now that she was talking, she couldn't stop if she tried. 'She knew I had my life in London and was worried about me.' She started to cry, unable to keep it all in. All those times she'd snatched brief phone conversations with her mum, boring her with the stresses of her life in the City, her upsets with colleagues, lost business, falling share prices, while her mum was on the other end of the line dying and saying nothing.

'She loved you,' Joe said, a hand on her arm.

Clara nodded, pressing her lips together. 'I loved her.'

'Of course you did,' Joe said, pulling her towards him.

She felt his arms around her, her face pressed against his chest. Her body relaxed into him as she got herself back under control. They stood there for a while as her breathing returned to normal, and she noticed that he smelt of woodsmoke and aftershave. Then she was blinking into his chest, not sure when to pull away.

He drew back, both hands on her upper arms. 'Do you want to carry on? There's a place selling doughnuts just over there.' He looked at her then, a slow, sad smile filling his face, clearly trying to make her feel better.

'A doughnut would be good,' she said, with a last wipe of her eyes.

They didn't talk about much else for the rest of the day, ambling along the seafront, past a merry-go-round and back to the car, Joe opening the door and letting her slide inside.

When they arrived back outside the shop, he turned off the engine and they sat for a moment in silence.

'Well,' said Joe at last, tapping a finger on the steering wheel. 'Thanks for getting me out in the fresh air.'

'I'm glad we went,' Clara said, catching his eye and seeing something new there. 'Thank you.' She felt the words were weighted with so much more.

Joe nodded before finally releasing his seat belt and getting out of the car.

They moved through the corridor and up the stairs without speaking. Was she imagining the momentary pause as they stood in the doorway of the flat?

'MY NAME IS MAXIMUS DECIMUS MERIDIUS, COMMANDER OF THE ARMIES OF THE NORTH!' Lady CaCa made them both jump. And then, as if she'd broken the spell, they moved inside, Joe picked up his phone, and whatever it was had passed.

An hour later, he was at the same spot at the table, the phone to his ear, the laptop screen glowing, and it was as if those few hours on the beach had happened to two different people, in a completely different world. Only the look he gave her as she said goodnight, his mouth half open as he lingered by his bedroom door, made her think anything had changed.

It's Lady CaCa's birthday today – do be sure to tell Clara to give her some extra treats. I think she hates having her birthday so close to Christmas. Perhaps I shall move it to June like the Queen. I think she'd like that.

I'm so pleased it's all going well and you're getting so many customers through the door. It takes you an age to reply to me so I know you must be run off your feet. Or struggling. Do you have a lot of vowels? It's very hard if you don't, although I always get too many Us, and what can you really do with a U?

We're experiencing a mini heatwave here – apparently the warm air is coming from the Sahara. It's just not feeling festive, there's too much sunshine around. How can you possibly think about gearing up for Christmas when you're sunbathing under a clear blue sky? Still, one mustn't fuss when one is spending the day in just a swimsuit and sarong. The manager has just popped by to ask me whether I am renting next month. He's a funny man, about three foot tall and with the most enormous beard.

If they ever remake those Hobbit films, he'd be entirely perfect. Now do send me some photos of the woods and fields behind the village, you know I love it in winter when everything is frozen white.

Chapter 29

Joe had planned to leave on Sunday night to be in the office first thing on Monday. The merger was being finalised, contracts signed; it was a huge day for him, for the team. But he hadn't been able to leave Clara that evening, wanted to stay in the flat, keep an eye on her. He'd crept downstairs when it was still dark on Monday morning, the whole of Suffolk sleeping, dawn leaking over the horizon as he raced down the motorway to London.

Now the deal was done. They'd signed the contracts. His bosses had waited in the outer office, ready to shake hands with the clients as they left the building. Joe had watched them talking as they milled outside the lift, Andy slapping one of them on the back, Karen looking like she'd won the lottery. Which she had. He should have been euphoric:

they'd just made billions of pounds for the company. They'd been working on the merger for months. Normally he'd be taking the whole team out for a celebratory dinner and drinks, on to a nightclub for champagne.

When he returned to the office, they were already downing shots, sliding a bottle his way, cheering and joshing each other. He found himself grabbing his coat, heading to the car park beneath the building, barely waiting to hear what they were saying. Within minutes he was in the car, heading out of the City, forgetting things the further he moved away, focusing on what was ahead.

He got back to find the flat empty, everything neat and tidy: the large dining table wiped down, a vase of fresh flowers in the centre, blankets folded and slung on the back of the sofa and armchair. It made him feel calmer just to look round the ordered space, Roddy the only blight on the scene, a large orange furball shedding on a rug in front of the woodburner, which was warming the room.

A babble of voices below him grew louder as he opened the flat door and peered down the stairs. Through the frosted glass of the side door he could make out the shapes of people moving past. The shop was obviously chocker, and he moved back inside to throw on some different clothes and go to help, bubbling with curiosity about the new window display. After they'd got back from the beach, Clara had spent the rest of Sunday in the shop, refusing him entry, announcing that he would have to wait to see it like everyone else. He stared at himself in the mirror.

Window displays? What next? And yet he was smiling goofily.

She was behind the counter, chatting to a woman with tight curly hair, when he moved inside the shop. He couldn't help heading straight over to peek into the window. The new display had clearly taken her hours. There was green cloth, mounds of it, creating the illusion of fields, divided by small lines of plastic fences. Animals grazed in the squares. She had found every type of farmyard animal – pigs, cows, horses, chickens and sheep – to scatter in groups. A farmer, a milkmaid, a shiny red tractor, a plough completed the scene. It was rural England, a brilliant glimpse of a summer's day on a farm. He could almost hear the snuffling of the pigs, the cockerel's cry, the whickering of the horses in the fields.

'I opened the shop on a Monday. I hope you don't mind, but it's busy?' She was babbling.

'Do you like it?' she added, standing close to him, biting her bottom lip, as if his verdict actually mattered.

He loved it; he should have told her at that moment. Something about it had touched him, reminded him of his childhood, his mum sitting on the floor of his bedroom revving up a huge yellow tractor, determined to give him the toys he'd wanted, to play with him when he was on his own.

'I—'

'Clara.' A woman was beckoning from the other side of the room. Clara was already moving away and he hadn't said a thing.

He looked back at the farmyard scene, catching the eye

of a father outside, holding hands with his son, who was gesturing at the shop. He felt the same flash of envy even now, twenty-five years later, as the man smiled and followed the boy inside. Joe moved back over to the counter, amazed to see yet more people milling around, many clutching brown paper bags holding their own painted toys. Clara really had created a buzz about the place, and he felt a pang that his mother wasn't here revelling in the atmosphere. She loved noise and people. He suddenly felt desperately lonely despite all the people pushing past him.

'Joe, Joe, do you mind?' Clara was calling across to him, snapping him out of his thoughts. He brushed at his face, suddenly worried that he could see inside her head.

'I just need to pop out into the workshop and get one of the toys.' She gestured at the till. 'I won't be long, a second or two. Well, a few seconds . . . ' She was babbling, pushing a strand of blonde hair behind her ear.

'It's fine, I've got it,' he said, walking down the aisle to take up her spot at the counter and holding out his hand, accepting the box, Holiday Barbie, from the smiling girl, head only as high as the counter. 'Take as long as you like,' he added, a small concession when he knew he needed to say a whole lot more.

'My birthday,' the girl announced, stepping back to point to a large badge on her coat with a glittering purple 6 on it.

'Oh. Happy birthday,' Joe said in return, feeling his own mouth tug into a smile in response to her wide grin, her button nose wrinkled.

Her mother passed over the money, a hand resting on the top of her daughter's head. 'We're going back to make a cake,' she said. 'In the shape of a spaceship.'

'Enterprising,' Joe said, giving her her change. He looked back down at the girl. 'My mum used to make me cakes in different shapes. One year she made an entire pirate ship, with a plank to throw people overboard and everything.'

He wasn't sure where that had come from, felt gratified to see her mouth form an 'ooh' of surprise. Cake-making, six-year-old girls' birthdays – this was not Joe's world. He was used to a lot of other men in suits, office banter that bordered on bullying; he shuddered as he thought of his team and what they would say if they saw him now, surrounded by small children, soft toys, dolls and balloons. He straightened up, feeling eyes on him, turning just in time to catch the back of Clara's head as she whipped back round. Had she been listening?

He stayed in the shop for the rest of the afternoon, helping behind the counter and collecting the toys from the workshop, marvelling at how many people seemed to come in and greet Clara. She appeared to have made more friends in a few weeks there than he had in London over the same number of years. He started to realise why his mother had always described the village as friendly; everyone just talked to you, as if it was normal, even if you were a stranger. In London, if someone spoke to Joe in that way he would assume they wanted money.

The afternoon went quickly, Joe now used to the shouts

and excited squeals. He lingered at the end of the day, finding more jobs, rolling the shutters down, sweeping the floor, locking the door behind the last customer. He'd barely thought about work, whether his team cared that he'd left. He just wanted to be in the shop, near Clara.

'Well,' he said, the room in semi-darkness, Joe suddenly uncomfortable at it just being the two of them. He opened his mouth to say something about the display, about the shop. Clara was sitting on a stool at the counter, separating piles of notes and coins, her hair falling forward as she worked. Joe had a flashback that made his throat feel tight. His own mother, curls bouncing as she bounded round the counter to show a customer a new toy, Joe himself sitting solemnly on a stool by the counter waiting for the clock to turn five. They would cash up together, Joe marvelling at the piles of coins that his mother would pour into small clear bags, the notes in a wallet that they would then put in his rucksack, walking out of the shop together to drop the day's takings at the bank in the high street.

'I thought I would make dinner tonight,' he said, his voice sounding smaller in the space. He cleared his throat.

Clara had looked up from what she was doing. He noticed violet shadows under her eyes that he didn't think had been there a couple of days ago. 'Are you sure? I don't mind.'

'I'm very sure.' He should be thanking her for all the other evenings when she'd cooked and waited on him, but perhaps tonight was his opportunity. He had never been one for words: best to show her.

'I won't be long,' he said in a loud voice, jangling car keys at her.

'Great,' she said, doing a pretty awful job of trying not to look surprised.

He could see her watching him through the glass door of the shop as he got into his car, and he felt his hand move into a half-wave. She nodded, her cheeks turning a deeper peach as she returned to the piles on the counter.

Half an hour later, he was wandering down a supermarket aisle, taking an inordinate amount of time before finally settling on two enormous fillet steaks, a bag of Maris Piper potatoes and some sugar snap peas. He was about to head to the checkout when he remembered that Clara had often produced a dessert. Heading to the refrigerated section, he panicked in the face of the enormous selection of pies, crumbles and cakes on offer. What would she like? He thought back over the things she'd produced, hand hovering over an apple pie. Something straightforward, no fuss. Then he spotted a large dark-chocolate cake covered in thick icing. He dallied for another few moments, earning himself a tut from an elderly woman, before deciding to buy both; she was sure to like one of them. He bit his lip, wondering why a pudding had managed to push him into such a spin. His hand reached automatically for his inside pocket, and the packet inside, before stopping halfway there.

His kitchen in London was pretty bare; he normally got takeaways on the rare occasions he was back in his flat in time for dinner. He wasn't even sure he had anything in his fridge aside from beer and champagne. But he used to cook – his mother had taught him when he was younger – and now he found himself humming as he moved around the kitchen, chopping and testing.

He was heating the steaks in the oven so the insides were warm, the griddle sizzling in preparation. He wanted to wait until the last moment to ensure they were perfect. Clara was still in the bathroom, had been for a good hour, moving through with a book tucked under her arm, a box of matches in one hand, a rolled-up towel in the other.

After another five minutes, he started to worry. He hadn't heard a sound. She might have drowned, fallen asleep in the water; she had looked tired earlier. He coughed loudly outside the door. No reply. He wavered, knowing she was fine really, just enjoying her bath. He strained to listen. No sound. No lap of water, no rustle of pages. He found himself calling in a high-pitched voice, 'Dinner ready in ten!'

There was a small splash. 'Lovely. Thank you.'

It startled him. She sounded close, as if she was just on the other side of the door, centimetres away. He sprang back, returning to watching his griddle. 'Excellent, excellent,' he called.

'TAKE ME TO BED OR LOSE ME FOREVER.'

'What?' asked Clara through the door.

Joe felt himself die inside, shooting Lady CaCa the filthiest look.

'Just, um, the parrot,' he called back, lifting a warning finger at the cage.

Lady CaCa turned on one claw and moved back across the perch. 'YOU CAN'T HANDLE THE TRUTH.'

Worried that Clara would find him standing there just waiting for her to be ready, he moved across to the large cupboard and unearthed the hoover. She had tidied the flat but it would be good to make things spotless. The hoover was ancient, still with a rocket sticker on the front from the days when he had hoovered round his mother's legs as a boy. Switching it on and plugging it in, he ran it across the carpet, nudging Roddy, who gave him a filthy look and simply rolled over onto his other side. He was sweating lightly by the time he had finished and Clara was standing in the kitchen, her wet hair in a high bun, a thick cardigan and knitted socks over leggings.

'Great, you're ready,' he said, moving across to the oven. 'Do sit,' he said, pointing to the table, which was laid for two people.

She raised an eyebrow as she took in the sight. 'You lit candles,' she said, her hands coming together as if she might clap.

He was glad to be bending down to the oven so the heat was on his face anyway. 'Well, I knew you were obsessed with them,' he mumbled, torn between embarrassment and pleasure.

'YOU HAD ME AT HELLO,' Lady CaCa shouted to the corner.

Joe dished up the food, pleased with the neat charcoal lines on the steak, the soft red inside as Clara sliced through it.

'Amazing,' she said, holding a hand over her mouth as she chewed. 'Perfect.'

Joe felt a rush of joy, his body finally relaxing. He reached for his glass of red wine, relishing the flavour of the meat, which seemed to taste better because he'd cooked it himself. He felt a peace descend on him for the first time in a long while.

Since the walk on the beach, he hadn't felt the need to make small talk with Clara, and now they were just enjoying the sound of the wind outside, winter whistling past the window as they sat snug inside in the glow from the candles. The light softened her face so that he felt an urge to reach out and touch her. He stared at her hand, resting next to her fork, for the longest time.

What was happening to him? He hadn't thought of work all night, and even stranger, when he did think about it there was no panic, no tightening in his chest, no urge to discover what was happening. They would already be looking for new business, another merger was always around the corner. The markets might be up, might be down, deals would come and deals would go, and tonight he just couldn't care less.

Clara had a slice of apple pie, had laughed as he'd produced both puddings.

'I've got an idea,' Joe said, scraping back his chair and getting up. Dragging the chair across the room, he popped open a trapdoor in the ceiling and pulled down the ladder folded up inside. 'Local knowledge,' he smiled, turning to her. 'Want to see?'

Clara nodded at him, standing up and reaching for her wine glass.

'Hold on, I'll go up first and you pass me these,' he said, walking round the flat and collecting up as many throws and blankets as he could find before clambering up the ladder, feeling the nip in the air as he stepped out onto the flat roof. Arranging the blankets on the ground, he turned to see Clara appearing through the hole, thrusting a bottle of wine in his direction before straightening up. She produced some tea lights from the pockets of her cardigan and proceeded to light them.

'You're like a boy scout,' he said, laughing as she looked at him in confusion.

They sat side by side, blankets around their shoulders as they stared up at the night sky. Aside from a wisp of cloud, the midnight-blue expanse was filled with stars, clusters spattered all around them. The high street was silent, a few squares of window lit up from the inside, a few chimneypots smoking, leaving the lingering smell of woodsmoke in the air. The flames around them flickered, marking their own spot away from everything else.

'Perfect,' Clara breathed.

Joe felt the same, finding it hard to remember what he'd normally be doing at this time, not caring that he'd left his mobile in the flat below, suddenly not caring if he never saw it again. He swigged from the wine bottle. 'I feel like

I'm fourteen again. I used to sneak up here with friends to drink and smoke. We thought we were so subtle until Mum left us ashtrays up here and we realised she'd known all along.'

'Your mum is brilliant,' Clara smiled, feeling a familiar stab of pain but pushing it away, not wanting to ruin things.

Joe nodded. 'She is,' he said, picturing her now somewhere in Europe. For the first time since she'd left, he felt a desperate urge to see her, to give her a hug, tell her to have an amazing trip. Why hadn't he done those things? Why did he have to hold everything in all the time?

'My mum was brilliant too,' Clara said, her voice whisper-quiet. 'I should have told her more.' She bit her lip and looked up at the sky again.

Joe stared down at his hands, imagining how he would feel. 'She would have known,' he said, placing his hand over hers.

Clara stared at it for the longest time. He felt the whole evening freeze as they sat there. Electricity shooting up through his arm, aware of her body inches from his. When he turned to say something to her, she was already looking at him, with an expression that made him cup her face in his hands, draw her slowly towards him.

Everything else faded away as they kissed. There was no nip in the air, no sounds from the high street, no wind at all. Just them, their lips together, her breath on his face.

'Darlings!' came a voice, a loud voice, a familiar voice. Joe squeezed his eyes tight; the kiss faltered. 'Cooeeee!'

He pulled away. He was imagining it; they'd been talking about her, he'd conjured her. This was definitely not the time. He begged his mum to get out of his head. Clara's lips, her pale-pink lipstick kissed away, were achingly close. Her expression matched his own confusion, and she drew back as they both looked towards the trapdoor.

Louisa's face appeared at the top of the ladder. 'Surprise!' she called, bustling out onto the rooftop. 'Oh,' she said, taking in the blankets, the candles. 'Have I interrupted something?'

Chapter 30

Louisa hadn't given either of them time to react. Caught on the rooftop snogging the face off her landlady's son, Clara thought she might die of embarrassment. She peered over the edge to see if she could make a leap for it. They were high up, but perhaps a broken leg might be worth it if it removed her from this awkwardness.

Joe had dived backwards as if she'd rubbed arsenic on her lips, and was running a hand through his hair as they both watched his mother emerge onto the roof, holding her arms out wide and staring up at the stars: 'How magical, this is just gorgeous.' His mouth was moving soundlessly. The whole scene seemed utterly surreal, as if the last few minutes hadn't happened, the kiss erased by the shock of the arrival. 'Clara, you are clever.'

'It was Joe,' Clara whispered.

Louisa barely seemed to notice, hustling them over to the blanket surrounded by tea lights and making herself at home. 'Amazing, come and sit here – and you, darling.' She waved at Joe, who was still doing an impression of a guppy. 'Clara, you've made it look so wonderful, my dear. I feel like the whole flat should feature in some winter chalet brochure, it's so Nordic-chic.'

'Clara's Danish,' Joe said in a low voice as he sat down on the other side of Louisa. Clara couldn't bear to look at him.

'Gavin had told me, of course, but I had no idea. And you found all those lovely rugs and blankets, and I adore the candles in the glasses. I felt so relaxed when I let myself in, almost dissolved into a pool. The flight was horrendous, and God, it's cold, but I just forgot everything and wanted to curl up on the sofa and snuggle down. You are clever. So ... tell me everything. Apparently you've been working miracles ...'

Louisa barely paused for breath and Clara couldn't focus on her answers. Discussing the displays, the workshop was a blur; all she was aware of was Joe, who had fallen completely silent.

Unable to answer any more questions, she stood up suddenly, glad that it was too dark to see Joe's expression as she stumbled backwards. 'I'm just going to pack up now, Louisa. I'm in your room, so I'll head to the pub ...'

Louisa was about to protest but got distracted almost immediately. 'Look, Joe, do look, the Plough is so bright tonight. Do you remember me pointing out Orion's Belt when you were small and we used to come up here? It's so wonderful to see you here, and you look gorgeous. I love that jumper. Cashmere just makes me want to cling on to you and never let go. I won't, of course, you'd hate that . . .'

Joe was almost mute; just one-word replies. Clara gripped the ladder as she descended.

'Wait!' Joe's voice. 'Mum, shall we . . . Clara,' he called, 'wait . . .'

Clara didn't give them time to stop her, but raced around the bedroom scooping up her belongings, stripping the bed and dragging her rucksack out the door. 'It's fine, honestly,' she rattled on. 'You have so much to catch up on, and I'm happy to stay at the pub. You know Gavin always says I'm welcome . . .'

'Oh, Gavin,' Louisa said, practically falling off the last rung of the ladder, clinging to Joe to right herself. 'He is so marvellous. Will you give him the most enormous hug from me and tell him I'll be over there tomorrow? I can't wait to see him.'

Clara nodded, pulling the cord on her rucksack, her coat dragging behind her, one arm in, the other out as she moved across the kitchen.

Joe had stayed frozen to the floor next to the rooftop ladder, watching her leave.

'So I'll be at the pub,' Clara called in her heartiest voice.

Lady CaCa chose that moment to reel off every movie line in her repertoire: 'HASTA LA VISTA BABY, SHOW ME THE MONEY, HAKUNA MATATA, SHITHEADS . . .'

Ignoring the parrot, Louisa dragged Joe over to the sofa, firing questions at him non-stop. Clara stood for a moment in the doorway, Joe looking across at her, before turning and heading down the stairs, feeling a stone in her stomach, a heavy weight that settled as she listened to their voices fading, as she opened the door out to the high street, as she closed it behind her.

By the time she got to the pub, she was aching and tired. She stared up at the familiar exterior, thinking back to her first night, looking at the difference now. The thick red velvet curtains that hung in the windows, the sprigs of holly, the wreath on the door, ribbons amongst the greenery, the flickering warmth from the roaring fire that hit her the moment she pushed her way through the door.

It was as if she was reliving that night all those weeks ago, standing there puffing, holding a heavy rucksack, Clive's bald spot at the same table to her left, bent over a pint once more. Even Roz was on the same stool at the bar, dark nails tapping her glass, lips stained red as she turned to stare.

Clara approached the bar, relieved to see Gavin looking at her with a question on his lips.

'Can I stay?' she asked immediately, ready to throw her rucksack to the ground and tell him everything.

Gavin's eyes widened. 'Here? But what about the flat? Have you and Joe fallen out?'

'No, I . . .' She couldn't face explaining. Where to begin anyway? She suddenly felt impossibly sad that her night had ended up here, that her adventure was over exactly where it had first begun. She felt herself sag. 'Can I take the room?'

Gavin bit his lip, his eyes rolling in panic. 'Oh, someone else is staying.'

Clara paused, her muscles protesting as she hoicked the rucksack up onto her shoulder. 'And there's no other room?'

Gavin paused for only a second, eyes flicking up and right. 'No, sorry,' he mumbled. He couldn't meet her gaze.

Clara felt a burst of anger. After all she'd done for him, for the pub. She pictured the closed door upstairs, not believing him. She turned to go, ignoring his calls, Roz's questions about Joe, the shop, the flat, pushing out of the pub and marching back down the high street.

As she neared the shop, she studiously avoided staring too hard. She couldn't ignore it though, a quick glance back over her shoulder as she passed, the windows still ablaze, picturing Joe with his mum, chatting warmly on the sofa, Louisa opening the shop up tomorrow without her. She felt the prickle of tears in her eyes, quietly admonishing herself for ever imagining things wouldn't have ended like this. She didn't belong here; she had been passing through. Louisa was back now and she would move on.

She was outside Lauren's cottage after only a few minutes, darkened windows on the first floor, a hopeful trail of smoke from the chimney, a glow behind the curtains of the front room. She knocked tentatively, rolling her shoulders, preparing herself to launch into an explanation, hoping Patrick wouldn't answer – she barely knew him. One fondue didn't warrant an overnight stay. No response. She knocked lightly one more time.

'Hello.' Lauren sounded uncertain on the other side of the door.

'It's me,' Clara whispered through the wood.

'Santa?'

'Er ... Clara,' she said, a little louder.

There was the sound of a lock being turned, one eye appearing in an inch-wide crack as the door was opened. 'Oh,' Lauren said, seeing Clara. 'What are you doing here?' She was holding a pot of nail varnish, one hand painted red, the other still bare.

'Can I stay?' Clara asked, standing on the doormat, fingers freezing, hair whipped to the side.

'Of course, of course. But what's happened? Are you all right? Come in, come in.' Lauren ushered her into the corridor, eyeing the enormous rucksack but not making any comment. 'Patrick's out and I'm halfway through a movie. The dog has just died so it looks like you're in the perfect mood to join me.'

She rushed about, going through to the kitchen for another glass, plumping cushions, sweeping aside magazines so that Clara could sink into the sofa, pouring wine without asking. Clara sat back, head resting on the cushions.

Lauren returned to painting her nails, giving Clara a chance to sip her drink. The moment she set her glass down, Lauren looked at her, a worried frown on her face. 'What's happened? Are you OK?'

Her expression was full of concern and Clara felt guilty for worrying her. 'It's not life-threatening; it's just . . . ' She paused, twirling the glass in her hand. Should she tell Lauren about the kiss? About how she thought things had changed between her and Joe? Last time she'd been here, she'd been swearing about him. That seemed a lifetime ago.

'What?' Lauren prompted, topping up her glass.

Clara took a breath. 'Louisa came back tonight.'

Lauren looked as though she was about to launch into a speech, mouth open. She snapped it shut. 'But . . . that's not too bad, is it?'

'I've left,' Clara said, as if to clarify.

'Oh, I see. Did she kick you out? She wouldn't do that, would she? Has she seen the latest article Sam wrote? Is she jealous?'

Clara frowned. 'What article?'

Lauren shifted on the sofa. 'It's nothing really, just very gushing. He called you a rare Danish gem.' She raised an eyebrow.

'Sam?' Clara couldn't concentrate, was too busy running over the night's events on repeat. What had Sam got to do with anything?

'I was worried, actually, that you might be falling for Mr Octopussy's charms. We've all been there,' Lauren sighed.

'Octopussy?' Now Clara was utterly confused.

Lauren leaned over towards her. 'That's what we call him. Because he has so many hands trying to get to your—'

Clara held up her own hands in surrender. 'Whoa – I understand.'

Lauren snorted a laugh. 'Don't say I didn't warn you. His poor wife,' she added as an afterthought.

Clara's mouth formed an O. 'He's married?' She thought back to their conversations; how she'd always seen him on his own or with his daughter.

'Oh yes, very married. She commutes and has carried on working full-time. Didn't he mention her?'

Clara shook her head. 'Wow, I had no idea.'

Lauren shook her head. 'Pretty standard from Octopussy. Did he offer to take your photograph, by the way? Did he tell you you had great skin? Which you totally do. But did he?'

Clara felt her toes curl at Lauren's questions. She nodded slowly. 'Yes, he told me I'd make a perfect subject.'

Lauren grimaced. 'Oh dear, I'm sorry. I should have warned you about him. He's tried it on with half the mothers in the village. He told my friend Cressida she had skin like a freshly opened oyster, which doesn't even make sense, and she almost left her husband there and then. So don't be down about it.'

Clara shook her head. 'No, it's not Sam, nothing to do with him.' She took another sip of wine. 'It's just . . . well, now that Louisa's back, I needed to leave.' She'd decided she wasn't ready yet to tell Lauren about Joe.

'OK,' Lauren said slowly, but if she suspected there was more going on, she didn't say.

'She had lots to catch up on with Joe.'

291

'Of course,' Lauren said, stroking on more nail polish, the pungent smell making Clara's head swim in the small living room.

'So she'll run the shop again and I'll ...' Clara trailed away, feeling her mouth turn down, the hopeless feeling from earlier wash over her, 'I'll move on again.'

Lauren looked up, cocking her head to one side. 'Is that what you want?' she asked, all jokiness evaporated.

Clara paused, bit her bottom lip. She nodded slowly. 'I've been here long enough. I wasn't planning to stay anywhere too long.'

Lauren reached across with one hand. 'And why's that?' she probed.

Clara felt tears build at the back of her eyes. She found she couldn't speak.

'Why are you always on the move, Clara?' Lauren wouldn't release her from her stare, and Clara felt the whole room suck in a breath as if waiting on her next words.

'I'm always looking for somewhere that feels like home,' she whispered, feeling the tears spilling over, marking a trail down one cheek.

'Like Denmark?' Lauren's nose screwed up in a question and Clara let out a hiccough of a giggle, wiping at her face.

'Somewhere I'm loved,' she said, realising the simplicity of what she wanted, and how hard it was to achieve. 'I love Denmark, but my dad has his own family now. Until last year it was me and Mum, but now she's gone, it's not the same.'

Lauren looked at her. 'I'm sorry, Clara, I didn't know.'

'She was ill for a while. I was always working. Then I missed ... missed ...' She couldn't finish the sentence, crumpling under the words, the tears coming faster now, the room blurring as she thought back to the last time she'd seen her, the visit cut short so she could get back to London for a client meeting. She couldn't remember if she'd kissed her goodbye. Her mum never asking her for anything, always proud of her busy daughter, showing photos of her to friends, telling them about the awards Clara had won. Then the decline, so quick, and Clara sitting upright in a plastic bucket seat at London City Airport, waiting for the first flight home, watching dawn leak over the horizon, knowing that every second was precious. Arriving home to her mum's friend Freja reaching for her, face tear-stained, her mum prostrate in bed upstairs. Too late to say goodbye.

Lauren had scooted to sit next to her on the sofa, pulling Clara's head onto her shoulder. 'Oh, poor you. She knew though, didn't she, Clara, she knew you loved her.'

Clara nodded, unable to speak, her top damp from her tears. Joe had said the same. They were both right. 'She knew,' she agreed, a small light inside her, glad she was here.

They sat for a while in the living room, not speaking, and Clara felt something lift in her as she got up to go to bed. She hadn't realised she had needed to talk about it. She followed Lauren up the stairs, smiling weakly at the sight of the room she'd be sleeping in: a camping mattress rolled out on a play mat covered in large letters of the alphabet; a Peppa Pig duvet that would barely cover her.

Chapter 31

Clara was on her second beer of the day and it wasn't even midday. Outside, the pavement was dusted with a thin layer of snow and she couldn't help thinking of home. What was she doing here in Suffolk? She didn't belong here. And yet the last few weeks had sparked something in her: she felt she belonged somewhere again, that the village had needed her. She had needed the village. She thought of the displays, the children she wouldn't see any more, the giggling in the workshop as they painted and created, the chaos and mess, the delighted faces when they turned to show their parents what they'd produced, the small crowds collected on the pavements when she turned the countdown to zero.

Lauren had woken her earlier with a cup of tea and a KitKat Chunky before flying out of the door with Rory to nursery. Clara hadn't wanted to stay in the house alone but realised she had nowhere else to go.

Gavin had been polishing the same glass forever, his eyes flicking over to her. He had apologised repeatedly when he'd appeared on Lauren's doorstep that morning, dragging her along the pavement to the pub, plying her with free drinks to make up for kicking her out the night before.

'I was so worried. I should never have let you leave like that. I checked everywhere. The bus shelter, the garden shed, Joe and Louisa joined me, we even searched the woods, she was wonderful ... ' He tailed off then, looking all misty-eyed.

Clara found herself distracted from asking more about Joe. 'Are you and Louisa ... ?'

Gavin nodded slowly. 'I think we're "an item",' he said, doing the quotation marks. 'We stayed up all night.'

Clara raised an eyebrow.

'Talking.' Gavin had practically shouted it as they reached the door of the pub. Clara couldn't help the giggle that escaped.

'And look,' he'd said as they'd bustled inside, pointing to the window. He had upholstered the window seat, lining it with cushions, bookshelves set into the wall, the perfect spot to curl up in and read.

'It's lovely,' Clara said grudgingly, because it really was, and she found herself wandering over there, running a finger along the spines of the books. Perhaps losing herself to reading and beer was the only way to go. She'd been there ever since.

Louisa appeared in the doorway and Clara heard a startled yelp and then a smash as Gavin dropped the glass he'd been cleaning.

'Gavin!' She bounded into the room, her skin deep brown, her eyes twinkling, snow clinging to her red coat. 'Mulled cider. What a wonderful idea. Yes please,' she said.

'It was Clara's idea, proving popular,' Gavin called from where he was crouching on the floor behind the bar, sweeping glass into a dustpan.

'Clara?' Louisa spun round to where she was sitting, shoulders sagging. Clara felt dreary next to Louisa's bright coat, straightening up and trying not to hiccough from the early drinking. 'You found her! Oh Gavin, well done, you are wonderful.'

A red stain crept into Gavin's cheeks as he handed her a drink.

Louisa skirted round the bar to press her lips on his, and Clara looked away.

'Clara,' Louisa said, moving away from Gavin, who now had cherry-red smears all round his mouth, 'I'm so, so sorry for the desperately rude way I burst in last night. I should never have let you go, but it was so darling to see Joe. I never see him and he looked so relaxed and happy I just couldn't resist. And then when Gavin appeared and told us he'd turned you away and I realised you'd actually gone, upped and – poof! – left, we looked for you. Joe was terribly ups— Gavin, darling,' she started to laugh as he moved across to join them, 'you've got lipstick all over your face ... So, as I was saying,' she turned back to Clara, clearly having lost her thread, 'it's just heavenly to see you back here now.'

She took a sip of her mulled cider. 'I think Lady CaCa is in mourning too. She has been quite out of sorts all morning. Usually I put on *Top Gun* and she cheers right up, but not even Maverick could make the old thing perky. And she'd shedding feathers; it's desperately sad, you must visit her.'

'It's been less than twelve hours.' Clara felt her mouth lift.

'She's a very sensitive bird,' Louisa said.

Gavin had moved across to the bookshelves and was taking down board games, ready for the customers that afternoon. Many had taken to playing the games by the big fireplace.

'Oh, did you hear?' Gavin said, his head emerging from behind an armchair. 'Bertie's is opening up again. A restaurant back in the village. Isn't it great?'

Louisa clapped her hands. 'How wonderful! I always adored his dessert trolley,' she said, a dreamy expression on her face. 'He would never tell me how he made his meringues so light. Mine are always flat as a pancake, and so chewy.'

Clara felt her heart lift at the news, then fall as she realised she wouldn't be around to see it opening. She couldn't stay on now, there was nothing for her here. She thought quickly of Joe, whether he was still in the flat, allowed herself a flicker of hope.

'So will you be moving on now?' Louisa asked, as if reading her mind, 'We must give you a proper send-off if so. Something spectacular. Don't you think, Gavin?'

Gavin was sitting with both legs stuck out in front of him, surrounded by board games. He nodded to the carpet. Then, after a pause, he looked up. 'Actually,' he coughed, getting slowly to his feet, 'I think I'd better show you both something.'

Clara looked at Louisa and frowned. Gavin looked impossibly shifty, as if he was about to tell them a terrible secret.

Louisa clearly felt the same, laughing as she teased him. 'Very mysterious.'

Gavin fiddled nervously with the cuff of his jumper. 'It's, um, upstairs.'

Louisa raised an eyebrow. 'What's upstairs?'

'The ...' Gavin stuttered to a stop. 'Oh, just come on, I need to show you.'

Clara had shot off the window seat, heart thumping as she realised she might finally find out what was behind the closed door upstairs. That had to be it. She hadn't dared asked him; he'd always seemed so impossibly jumpy about it. She'd imagined a mad wife in a torn nightie, a room of skeletons, a secret sex dungeon. None of the options had quite fitted with what she knew of gentle Gavin. All her other worries disappeared and she trotted dutifully up the stairs behind him.

'I'm getting a bit nervous, Gavin,' Louisa called up as she followed Clara. 'You're not going to ask us to start calling you Gail, are you?'

Gavin was completely silent as he stood outside the door in the corridor. Unlocking it, he lifted the latch, took a deep breath and stepped back, gesturing silently that they should go inside.

Clara wavered in the corridor, not sure she really wanted to know any more. A man was entitled to his secrets, and poor Gavin seemed so nervous, pulling at his jumper and looking anywhere but at them.

'Go on,' he said gruffly. 'I should have done this ages ago. Turning you away last night, Clara; it was unforgivable.'

Clara curled her clammy hands together before tentatively pushing on the wooden door and stepping inside, Louisa so close behind she could feel her breath on her neck.

'Oh my,' said Louisa.

Clara nodded mutely. So this was the big secret. There was so much to say but she found that all she could do was laugh in relief.

The room was jam-packed with hundreds of different-sized teddy bears. Teddy bears with clothes on, teddy bears missing eyes, teddy bears in browns, blacks, greys. Gavin must have been collecting them for years. Somewhere underneath them was a bed, patches of carpet bare in between teddies on rugs, teddies in different poses.

Gavin appeared, ashen-faced, behind them.

'Surprise!' he said, looking so weak he might fall down.

Louisa looked at him for a long moment, then held out her arms and grinned. 'You great big gorgeous softie,' she said, and launched herself at him.

They were still laughing about it half an hour later when Louisa checked her watch and stood up, spilling mulled cider all down her top.

'Darn, I'm late,' she said, grabbing the back of Clara's chair to right herself. 'Wow, that stuff is potent,' she said, staring at her glass as if it contained diamonds.

'Where are you off to?' Clara asked, nudging Gavin. 'Your move.'

Gavin stared at his tiles once more.

'A good game is a fast game, et cetera,' she chided for the millionth time. She felt this game of Scrabble might go on forever. Louisa had had the right idea.

'I'm off to see Roz,' Louisa said, rolling her eyes. 'Dreadful woman.'

'Louisa,' Gavin said in a warning voice, looking up. 'It's a good offer.'

'I know, I know,' Louisa said.

Clara found herself freezing, her tiles forgotten. Before she could ask about what Roz was offering, and for what, she was distracted by Louisa's next sentence.

'And Joe said he'd handle it all for me, with the agent.'

'Joe,' Clara repeated, blushing deeply as she realised she'd just blurted his name out loud. She coughed, attempting to conceal her interest. 'Where is he?'

'Joe?' Louisa was shrugging on her coat and getting one arm caught in it. 'Oh, he's back in the flat. I don't think he slept. After our search for you, he got a call from a colleague and disappeared into his room on his phone, tapping on his laptop. Typical Joe,' she smiled. 'He'll probably already have left for London. That boy doesn't stay anywhere for more than a second. It was heavenly to see him last night but I assume it will be back to the grindstone for him. I must text him and tell him we found you.'

'London,' Clara repeated, the thought causing her to panic. She stood up abruptly. She couldn't just let him go back to London without seeing him. Did he even know she was still here? She cursed herself for staying in the pub for so long.

'All OK?' Gavin said, raising an eyebrow, watching her fumble with her coat.

'Need to go . . . ' Clara mumbled, doing up the buttons all wrong. 'Must see . . . remembered . . . something,' she said, not meeting his eye.

'But your tiles!' Louisa cried. 'I know you've got the X,' she added.

'Have it,' Clara called as she headed for the door.

'Ooh goody.' Louisa dived on her tray.

Clara hurtled down the high street, her heart lifting on seeing the burgundy paint of the shopfront. She fumbled with her keys, letting herself in and bounding up the stairs to the flat before pausing to take a breath, smooth her hair, readjust her top. This was it. She turned the key in the lock and stepped inside.

'Joe,' she called out, not wanting to surprise him in the middle of a mudbath or a conference call. 'Joe,' she said a second time, already feeling the weight of the silence around her.

Then a rustle of feathers alerted her to the sole occupant of the room, Lady CaCa peering at her from her position on high. 'HOUSTON, WE HAVE A PROBLEM,' she called.

The flat was empty, washing-up done, wine glasses drying upside down on a tea towel. The counters had been wiped down and Clara moved across to read from a single sheet of paper left on the side: *Mum, have left for London. Will call later. Love you, J x*

She sat down heavily on a bar stool, picking up the note and reading the words over and over again. He had already gone back to London, without even waiting to say goodbye to his own mother – or to her, a little voice added in her head. She felt her whole body wilt, all the things she wanted to say draining out of her, all the excitement she'd felt on the way over leaking away. He had gone, back to the City, back to his job. Maybe she'd been wrong about the change in him; maybe he was the same as he'd ever been.

Then something on the table caught her eye: a newspaper, open on a large photo of Clara herself, grinning behind the counter of the shop, children scattered around her, the place looking colourful and alive with joy, noise and people. She peered at it, tracing the outline of her own face. She looked impossibly happy, her smile, her face totally content. She really had loved her time in the shop, seeing the children's expressions when she changed the display, chatting with the local parents. With a sting, she realised that all that was over. She would be moving on too. There was nothing keeping her here.

Suddenly she noticed the headline of the piece – SAVE OUR SHOP! – and a growing sense of unease filled her as she began to read Sam's new article. It was a call to arms to stop the shop from being sold, a lot of quotes from locals bemoaning the closure of yet another high-street shop, the rise of online shopping, the damage it was doing to communities. *To think some toffee-nosed Londoner can come up here and sell it off, it's part of the village, the beating heart*, an anonymous source was quoted as saying. *'It's not my shop,' Clara Kristensen said, standing wide-eyed in front of the doomed store. The Danish woman who has breathed life back into this toyshop, created a magical place for children in the village, looks heartbroken at the thought of it closing its doors for the last time.*

'Oh no,' Clara whispered, hand to her mouth as she read to the end. It was damning, and she pictured Joe reading it, seeing her picture, knowing she'd spoken about the shop to a journalist.

She got up slowly, not wanting to believe he had really left, that she couldn't fix this. As she moved across to his bedroom, she saw that his leather holdall had gone. He had left and she had missed him, and she wasn't sure when, or if, he'd be back. She leaned against the door frame and stared ahead, at a loss as to what to do next, just wanting to rewind time.

Chapter 32

Everything was back to normal. Joe stepped out onto the pavement, turning to tip the driver, who looked startled but pleased. Pigeons scattered in his wake as he moved towards the revolving doors. He craned his neck, looking up at the blank glass windows, sunlight bouncing off them, unable to make out which was his amongst the uniform rows. Someone swore on a mobile behind him; a cyclist swerved around him, trousers tucked into socks. Joe tried to summon the energy required to take the last few steps towards the building.

He thought back to the previous night, the scene on the rooftop happening in another lifetime now. Clara's face in the candlelight, her hand resting on the blanket. He'd stared at her fingers for the longest time, plucking up the courage to reach across the space and kiss her. Then his mother's shock appearance and the way he'd just frozen, knowing already that everything was about to change again. Clara's face as she'd dragged her backpack across the kitchen, his feet planted as he'd watched her leave.

He pushed through the revolving doors, nodding to the porter and heading towards the lift. He tapped in the floor number and held open the door for someone racing to catch it.

'Thanks,' the man huffed, tie askew, bags under his eyes.

'No problem.' Joe smiled, unable to rush today, unable to focus, still lost somewhere in Suffolk. He wondered where she'd gone; they'd searched for a while. Why didn't she have a mobile? His mum had texted to tell him she was still there but he'd already left.

The lift had reached his floor, the doors opened, and then he was striding across the familiar reception area, holding up his ID to be scanned as he pushed open the door.

The sound of raised voices, shouts, keyboards tapping, phones ringing, a photocopier whirring hit him like a wall, and he almost turned on his heel and went straight back the way he'd come. No one looked up as he walked across the space to his desk, everyone too focused on their jobs, shouting down the phone, slamming the receiver down, swearing into space.

The energy, the excitement had been what had first attracted him to the job; no more sleepy Suffolk, no more evenings with just his mum. Here he could be the man he wanted to be, the man his father was, making deals, handling millions of pounds, important. Now the thought of the day ahead, a day that probably wouldn't end before the early hours, exhausted him: his overflowing in-tray, the emails he hadn't responded to, the taut faces of his team, eager like greyhounds in the starting blocks, wanting to share their updates first.

He let them rattle on, sipping at his coffee, not switching on his computer, half listening to their words, praising their efforts but looking over their shoulders to the windows behind them, the clear blue sky, a perfect winter day. He wondered if Clara was walking, wellingtons on, cheeks pink, through the woods behind the village. Then he thought of the newspaper article, what she'd said to that journalist. Is that how she'd really felt? He had needed to get out of there. Clearly he didn't fit in; it had all been a strange, momentary pipe dream of an alternative life. It was over now. His mum was back and he was in London.

'And Pam is leaving in the new year, of course, so we've lined up interviews for your new PA . . . '

Joe came to. 'Leaving? Pam's going?'

Mercer looked at him as if was stupid. 'She's retiring. After forty-five years.'

Pam herself appeared at that moment, carrying files, her hair pinned back, skirting an errant office chair.

Joe jumped up, face flooding with shame as he removed the files from her arms. 'Pam, I had no idea. Retirement!'

Her eyes widened before she collected herself. 'Oh, that's

quite all right. I put it in your calendar, but you're a busy man.'

Joe felt terrible. He'd always taken Pam for granted, her stable presence, her no-nonsense approach, her ability to screen calls, make clients feel welcome, never a day off sick or a favour asked. Why hadn't he valued her more?

'You're amazing. How will we ever replace you?' he said, watching her face flood red at his words.

'Don't be silly,' she huffed, pulling on the cuff of her shirt. 'We'll find someone more than capable.'

'Well, it won't be the same.'

'Tsk,' Pam said, scooping up a dirty mug nearby. 'The moment I take one of these away, another one appears,' she added, clearly keen for the focus to be shifted away from her.

Joe made a mental note to think of something they could get her, something that would really show her work had been valued, noticed. Then his cheeks coloured again as he realised he didn't know the first thing about her, had only ever spoken to her about work, deadlines, clients. He'd allowed her to bat his questions away so that he had stopped asking and only ever treated her in their stiff, professional way. He regretted that now; he hoped she was going to do something fabulous in her retirement.

'Andrew has been asking to see you when you're in, Joseph,' she said on her way past. 'He's asked twice, in fact.'

That was one more time than he liked to ask, and Joe found himself hurrying over to the lift. He straightened his tie on the way up, already starting to forget the other things on his mind, running through the latest deal, ready to dazzle, to smooth-talk. He cleared his throat, tapping his foot impatiently. With every floor he passed, Suffolk seemed further and further away.

He stepped into the polished foyer, a marble fountain in front of him, a glossy desk opposite, manned by a woman wearing a telephone headset. She had bright red lips and smooth dark hair. A few weeks ago he might have asked for her number. Now he simply asked to be buzzed into the room.

They left him waiting a while, twitching on the sofa, idly flicking through the *FT*, unable to concentrate on the articles. Shares going up, companies going bust, money being made, same old, same old. He felt a sharp shock at that thought, returning to tapping his foot, realising he'd left his phone downstairs. After an age, the smooth-haired woman beckoned him through.

Andy was there, seated behind his enormous glass desk, Karen perched on the edge of it as if Joe had just interrupted them chatting casually. He knew them better than that, knew she had wanted to be here, that the casual stance was a carefully thought-out pose. Andy looked up and acknowledged him. Karen stood to shake his hand, bracelets jangling, the lines on her face reduced by recent surgery. Joe found himself staring at her hand, the liver spots and slight creasing of the skin the only hints to her age.

'So fire away,' said Andy, a man who could only talk in clichés and figures. 'Tell us about this latest merger and what's next.'

Joe brought them up to speed on developments, pausing every now and again to dredge up the finer details, slipping up for a moment when he couldn't recall the name of one of the companies they'd just closed the deal with. Karen corrected him, scratching at her neck with one pink talon.

'Well, Joe,' Andy said at last, ' it's been a good year, a good year, but we're concerned about this latest deal. The rumour mill has been whirring, and as you know, we tend to feel there's often no smoke without fire.'

Joe wondered what the rumours were, starting to feel sweat prickle on his hairline.

'We thought Matt's formal warning might help streamline things, but we've been told it's not been completely smooth sailing since. You've spent a bit of time away from the office in the last few weeks and your team have had to really roll up their sleeves to keep things on track. Some of them tell us you've been visiting clients a lot ...' Andy paused and lifted an eyebrow, 'yet your diary seems strangely empty and you've not mentioned any new clients.'

Joe found himself leaping to his own defence, used to having to fight for survival in this industry. There was always someone snapping just behind you, desperate to take your place. 'I've been directing operations, updating the team all the time, and we've discussed the importance of delegation before. I need my team to all be aware of the whole process from start to finish, and they have been more than capable of running things, as was evidenced when we pulled the deal off.'

He wondered which of them had slunk up here to the bosses to whisper in their ear about his absences. He thought of their faces waiting downstairs. He didn't blame them. He'd have done the same himself a few months ago.

'So this working remotely – that will all be coming to an end, will it not.' It was not a question. Andy stood, staring down at Joe, using his not unimpressive height to intimidate, an old trick. He placed his hands behind his back, an expectant look on his face, a man not used to waiting. 'We wouldn't want to lose you,' he said, giving his bark of a laugh.

Joe noticed the warning in the sentence. He found himself nodding automatically, watching as if from afar as his life picked up pace, as if he were getting on a roller coaster and the bar was coming down over him. No more thoughts of heading back to Suffolk, no more dreams of taking his foot off the pedal. This wasn't a job you could do out of town; you had to protect it, be available twenty-four hours a day. The thought used to get him leaping out of bed in the morning, proud to be chauffeured to one of the finest buildings in London, complaining in a loud voice about the eighteen-hour days, the overnight stays, the takeaway food, the client meetings that ended up in Mayfair nightclubs. Suddenly he felt weary thinking about it all, knowing he'd need to find that energy again, that spark.

He was dismissed soon afterwards, Karen staying behind so she and Andy could discuss him. They watched him in silence as he left the room, their heads cocked to one side.

He wondered what they were thinking, whether they could sense the shift in him.

He got through the day on automatic: answering emails, checking figures, laughing with colleagues. A split second late, perhaps, responses sometimes dredged up from where his mind had wandered off to. It was dark as he left the building, the pavement slick with rainwater, a damp smell lingering in the air. He rested his head back on the car seat and tried to will away the headache that had emerged at lunchtime.

He paused outside his block, feeling as if everything had changed since he last stepped through the doors. Then, taking a breath, he headed up in the lift, feeling his heart sink at the thought that he would step out into an empty flat.

He stood for a moment as the lift doors froze on either side of him, the whole place in darkness, the chill whistling through the place. Then he turned on his new lamps with a decisive push, moving across from the living room to the kitchen, every surface polished, the place spotless, his belongings tidied away.

He searched for a box of matches in every drawer, unable to light the many candles he'd bought. He moved back to the living room, his leather sofa too stiff to get comfortable. He switched on the television, flicked through the channels, not settling on anything, watching programmes zip past, faces come and go, music burst and then silence.

He couldn't settle, got up to stare at the bathroom. He had had the bath taken out when he'd first moved in, replaced it with a double shower. A bath had seemed pointless; there was no time to lounge about. The room couldn't be more different from his mum's small bathroom. The walls lined with black onyx, the chrome heated towel rail sparkling, the mirror surrounded by spotlights, the underfloor heating just coming through. It was worth about ten times as much for a start. So why did he miss the free-standing bath, the window that looked out on the fields behind the village, the bottles and tubs on the side that all made the water smell so good, the loo you needed to flush twice in quick succession to make it work?

He moved back through the living space, not sure what he was doing, ending up in his bedroom. He pulled out a brand-new pair of pyjamas from their box, and changed into them, feeling instantly more relaxed. Normally he went to bed in just his pants; sometimes even fell asleep on top of the duvet fully clothed.

He sat up in bed and stared ahead, thinking about the day, the past few weeks' happenings zipping around each other, muddled. He reached out a hand for the emergency pack of pills he kept in the bedside table, popping two into his hand, staring at them for the longest time.

He shifted under the duvet, realising what felt wrong: no hot-water bottle. Clara would often leave him one out to take to bed. His feet felt chilly, the bed enormous. He wondered for the tenth time that day whether she had left the village.

He'd got an email from his mum earlier: she was going to sell the shop. Roz had made a decent offer and she didn't have the energy to run it by herself. He was relieved she seemed to know what she wanted, had seen the way her face had lit up when Gavin had appeared. Still, he hadn't been able to stop himself scanning the high street as he'd left that morning, looking out for a curtain of shiny blonde hair, a purple hat and a chunky knit jumper. She hadn't been there, though, and he cursed himself again for letting her walk into the night.

Now he was back in London, where Clara had once lived and worked. He wondered whether they had ever walked past each other in Canary Wharf, attended the same conferences, talks. He couldn't imagine her in that world, in a sharp suit and spiked heels, it seemed all wrong. Would she stay in the village? Had she already moved on? He needed to sleep, to get his head in gear. Taking one last look at the two pills in his hand, he swallowed them both in one mouthful.

Chapter 33

Clara knew she should feel more grateful. Gavin and Louisa had taken her out for a wonderful farewell dinner the night before, and had been working on a surprise when they got back and all through this morning. She'd heard rustling and giggling from the corridor and had a sneaking suspicion it involved Gavin's spare room. Louisa couldn't do anything quietly, knocking glasses over with her wildly flailing hands every time she told a story. Clara already adored her.

She'd felt lonely, though, staring at them both across the table, their easy joking, Gavin placing a hand over Louisa's, his face constantly breaking into a smile, his eyes creasing when she spoke. Clara was happy for them, but their togetherness had seemed to accentuate her own single status. She'd never minded life without a boyfriend before, had always chosen to be on her own, free to do her own thing, rather than remain in a half-hearted partnership. Now, though, she felt the tug, had glimpsed a future in a moment of pure happiness on the rooftop of the flat under the stars.

She kept returning to that night, the dip of his head, how right it had felt. Then she thought back to when she had felt something shift, remembering how he'd emerged from the bathroom, utterly at ease with himself, a broad grin on his face, and then the wild-eyed panic as he realised that his face was covered with mud. She grinned at the ceiling, then, with a pang, remembered that that was all over now. She wasn't back in the flat with Joe in the room next door, trying his damnedest to be *hygge*. He had left and she was back where she'd begun, in the single room under the eaves in the pub.

A knock on the door roused her. 'Thirty minutes and we'll see you at the shop,' Louisa trilled. 'In this, please.' A pink satin blindfold appeared under the door and Clara couldn't help smiling at it.

'I'll be there,' she called back.

She needed to get a grip, put on a big smile, shake off this mood. They'd been so generous, Louisa offering to pay her for her time in the shop, Clara adamantly refusing the money, but touched by the gesture.

'It was never about that,' she'd insisted. 'It became home.'

She'd bitten her lip after the words had left her, realising as she'd said them that it was exactly how she felt. Quietly allowing Louisa to give her the largest slice of tiramisu instead of money, the pudding sticking in her throat as she swallowed each mouthful.

She dragged herself to the bathroom, staring at her face in the mirror and reaching for her make-up bag. Bronzer, mascara, lip salve: she felt better with each stroke, emerging into the bedroom a glossier, shinier, more together version of herself. Pulling on one of her favourite dresses, she looked at herself in the thin strip of mirror on the back of the door. The dark-green material brought out the blondes in her hair. She smacked her lips together, reached for her coat and scooped up the blindfold, ready to head into the high street, determined to enjoy her send-off.

'She's here.'

'That's her.'

'There!'

The whispers hit her as she approached, amazed to see such a swell of people outside the shop. The little boy whom Joe had drawn a duck for gave her an energetic wave. Gavin was handing out drinks on a tray; she could make out mugs topped with marshmallows, which he almost dropped on seeing her.

'Blindfold, Clara, NOW!' he called.

She hastily obliged, pulling it over her eyes, feeling more than a little silly as the world was plunged into darkness and she inched her way along the pavement, waving both arms in front of her so she didn't bump into anyone in the crowd.

With relief, she felt an arm looped through hers and smelt

basil as she was steered down the pavement by Louisa. 'Take it slowly ... I am sooooo excited ... Oh, watch out for that child, that was a close one ... '

'Louisa,' Clara protested, feeling people squeezing past her, the brush as she knocked against someone.

'Don't worry, it's only Roz. It would be a desperate shame for her to spill her drink down that camel coat of hers. Chocolate is notoriously difficult to get out ... Oops, I think she heard. Hi, Roz ... '

Clara found herself giggling quietly. 'Is the blindfold quite necessary?' she asked.

Louisa ignored her, of course, keeping up her spiel. 'Oh ... there are children everywhere, it's such heaven, and they're all delighted by Lady CaCa. Gavin carried her cage down from the flat but she does keep calling them all shitheads so he's thinking of taking her back upstairs ... So thoughtful,' she breathed, pausing to sigh like a lovesick teen. 'He can't bear the thought of missing your reaction, such a big heart ... '

Clara had started giggling again as they came to a halt. She could hear Lady CaCa screeching 'SHOW ME THE MONEY.'

'Go on, then,' Louisa nudged her, 'this is it, take a peek.'

Slowly Clara removed the blindfold. She was standing in front of the shop, surrounded by the crowd, and she gasped as she took it all in. The entire window was crammed with Gavin's vintage teddy bear collection, piled high with soft toys in every colour, stitched-on smiles all facing out to the street, where children were pressing their noses against the glass to see them all. Bears in clothes, bears sitting in a variety of poses, bears piled higgledy-piggledy on top of each other. The effect was incredible, and Clara couldn't help grinning as she moved inside to see shelves of teddies lining the store, jaunty music piped through speakers in the corner.

'It's wonderful,' she said, catching sight of a group of teddy bears sitting on the counter having a tea party with some Barbies. Lauren gave her a quick thumbs-up from behind the till, inundated with customers in a queue that snaked all round the shop.

'It's all been inspired by you, my darling. Look,' Louisa said, sweeping an arm around, bracelets clashing. 'Packed, smiling, laughing, you've brought the place back to life. It was like this when we first moved here, just me and Joe running the place . . .'

Clara felt her face fall at the mention of his name, the familiar sting she was already growing accustomed to. He would love to see this, to see his mum looking so fired up, back in love with it all. How sad that she was really going to sell.

'Actually, there was something I want to ask y—'

Louisa didn't finish, interrupted by Gavin appearing with a shy smile on his face. She had clearly forgotten all words and was just staring up at him as if she'd never seen him before. 'Looks better than them being scattered all over my spare-room bed, doesn't it?' he said, a blush moving up over the tattoo on his neck.

'It looks brilliant,' Clara said.

'It was silly of me to keep them hidden away all these years. They should be shared. The kids love them.'

'DO YOU FEEL LUCKY, PUNK? WELL, DO YA?'

'God, we must ban that bird from watching telly,' Gavin said, cringing as the call came through the shop. 'We'll get complaints,' he said, snaking an arm round Louisa.

'She can't be tamed,' Louisa said. 'She's a free spirit, like me.'

'Just less pretty,' Gavin said, kissing her hair and then blushing a deeper red as he remembered that Clara was standing there.

'We've got you a little something actually, Clara,' Gavin said, pulling away and heading to the counter, where he produced a bear holding something in its paw.

Clara laughed as she realised it was the Danish flag. 'I couldn't,' she said, hugging the bear to her.

'Course you can. We can't thank you enough really. And all you've done for the pub, too. You know we've been asked to have a wedding there in the summer, and Clive says there's talk on the parish council of the Christmas market returning next year. You've saved our village, Clara, it's no mean feat.'

Clara found herself glowing inside, happy that she had given something to the village, knowing she would always love the place.

'And that's why . . .' Gavin looked at Louisa. 'Have you told her?'

'No,' Louisa sniffed, 'I haven't been able to get a word in edgeways with you rabbiting on.'

Gavin grinned at her. 'Apologies, Your Majesty, do go ahead.'

Clara suddenly saw Roz hovering in the corner of the room and frowned. What was she doing loitering here? Louisa had started to speak and Clara found herself zoning out as she heard the first few words. 'I was selling it to Roz ... a good offer ... but then ... '

She felt a wave of nausea hit her. No wonder Roz was here, surveying her new territory, planning to tear out the old, redesign the place.

' ... she's seriously peeved I've found a new buyer—'

'A new ... ' Clara interrupted, head spinning with it all. So Roz wasn't buying the shop. A new buyer had snapped it up.

'He's in the back, actually, checking up on his investment ... '

Clara frowned, feeling her insides grow cold. All the effort she'd put in, the room bursting with excited children, and Louisa had really sold it, was leaving the place. She wondered if the new owner would even run it as a toyshop.

'I'm moving into the pub.' Louisa couldn't keep the smile out of her voice. 'But we were wondering if you might want to discuss a possible partnership with him ... '

Clara couldn't think, had to get out of there, get out of the village before her heart broke again. Louisa was moving in with Gavin, leaving the shop, letting this new owner run amok. How could she? She had seemed so happy to see it crammed with people.

' ... he's keen to discuss his future plans with you ... '

She felt tears building at the back of her eyes as they steered her towards the door of the workshop, her legs wanting to run in the other direction. She didn't want to meet the new owner, wasn't interested in his plans for the place. He probably wanted to smash it down, build luxury apartments, turn it into something entirely different.

'Really, I ... ' She was twisting away, desperate to get of there.

Louisa and Gavin weren't letting her leave, though, and she found herself in the doorway of the back room. The table was scattered with paints, children sitting on the stools, brushes in hand, squinting in concentration at their toys, sunlight streaming through the windows as they worked. She couldn't believe that all this was going to end, that the room would once again be turned into a dusty storeroom, neglected, full of broken furniture.

The new owner had his back to her, was bending over one of the children at the table, a great rumble of laughter bursting out of him as the little boy looked up and dabbed him on the nose with his paintbrush.

Then Clara felt all the breath leave her body as he stood up and she took in his profile: the straight nose, the dark brown hair, the long eyelashes. He was dressed in black jeans and a russet-coloured jumper and now he turned towards her, the smile lighting up his face as he caught her staring at him.

They stood for an age just looking at each other.

'But I don't understand . . .' Clara whispered, turning to Louisa and Gavin, but they had already melted away, back into the shop.

Joe stepped across to her, drawing her into the corner of the room, both her hands in his.

'Hey,' he said.

Clara found that the words had frozen somewhere inside her. She had so many questions, looking over his shoulder suddenly as if she'd made a terrible mistake, as if she'd assumed something impossible and a small, balding new owner was in fact in the room, Joe merely overseeing the sale. But there were only children and mothers, and now she found herself biting her lip, daring to hope.

'I've bought it,' Joe said, 'for a steal.' He grinned. 'Some old lady let me have it off her way too cheap.' He sounded nervous, his words tripping over each other.

'But I . . .'

'She wants to retire, she wants to travel – well, mostly she wants to snog Gavin's face off . . .' He shuddered at that, and Clara couldn't help smiling. 'It makes sense, the shop's doing brilliantly, and, um, I was hoping you might agree to stay on to run it. It only works because of you; you've made it this way.' He looked back at the room, at the children crammed round the table.

Clara felt her heart sink again. So that was it. A business

transaction, was that all this was? She would run the shop and Joe would return to London, to the City, to his pills and his serial dating and his busy life.

'Where will you ... ' She didn't want to know, found her mouth snapping shut.

Joe let go of her hands, and she felt the shock of it, curling her fists together.

'I've left my job,' he said slowly. 'It was killing me and they've given me a generous redundancy package. I thought perhaps we might make some plans together. Lauren's agreed to help if we decide we want to go somewhere else, travel, or ... '

She didn't hear any more, his words spinning round her head as she started to take in the enormity of what he was saying. He had left London, he was back here for good, he was asking whether she would make plans with him. She felt her whole body lighten as she looked at him, his eyes so serious, trained on her.

'Wow,' she said, unable to say much else.

'Is wow a yes? Because if it is, I got you this,' he said, holding out a small box.

Clara found she couldn't think. Everything was moving too quickly. How could you be so miserable one moment and so happy the next? Her hands shook as she took the box from him, opening it slowly, and then, with an enormous grin, felt her body relax with the relief of it all. It was true, he was really here to stay, and she could stay too.

She drew out a scented candle in a glass jar. 'You shouldn't have,' she laughed.

'It's for the flat,' Joe said, smiling. 'Our flat,' he finished. Then, reaching down, he cupped his hands on either side of her face and kissed her. And Clara knew she'd finally found home.

First of all I want to say a huge thank you for choosing to read *The Hygge Holiday*. I imagine the cool rose-gold foil on the front lured you in but I hope you enjoyed the book once you started reading. If you did enjoy it and have yet to do your good deed for the day – you're in luck! It would be AMAZING if you could review the book on Amazon or Goodreads. It's easy to do and doesn't have to be long and gushing, its very existence is enough to make a difference. I do read all reviews and appreciate the time it's taken you to leave one. If a review is too much please feel free to just tell everyone you've ever met both online and in real life how much you loved the book. Or if you have the cash and want to make a big show of things feel free to rent one of those aeroplane banners. These are just IDEAS; it's really up to you how you run with things.

If you want to get in touch/become Best Friends Forever/ tell me stuff that I didn't know about people that have appeared in the first three seasons of *Love Island* then please do feel free to track me down online. Follow me on Twitter (@RosieBBooks) particularly if you like useless trivia, book recommendations and photos of kittens in mugs and stuff. I'm on Instagram too (@RosieBBooks) if you like pictures of babies, rivers or the sky. I am also on Facebook as Rosie Blake and my website is www.rosieblake.co.uk. Really, there is no excuse not to get in touch.

Thank you once again, in all sincerity; it really is humbling to have your book read when there are so many amazing books out there. I hope to keep writing them for many, many years.

Rosie x

Acknowledgements

This was such a joyful book to write and I had plenty of help along the way. To Paddy Burrowes an enormous thank you for an extensive session on tales from Canary Wharf and cool City jargon. To Fabio Priori for his banking knowledge. To Isabelle Broom for explaining to me how Tinder works. To Will Round for explaining time zones to me. To Luc Golding for originally telling someone to 'punch my willy'.

To Maddie West, my amazing editor, who has made this whole process fun rather than work. I am so glad to be working with you at Little, Brown. Thank you to the rest of the team for working so tirelessly on this book. In particular to Thalia Proctor, Desk Editor, Jane Selley for her copy edit and Cath Burke for her warm welcome to the company and her excitement. To the Rights Team for wanting to get it into the mitts of other editors and spread the love of *hygge*. To Hannah Wood for the absurdly gorgeous cover.

As ever I want to thank the team at Darley Anderson too. To Clare Wallace, my fab agent, for all that you do.

To Kristina for making emails about tax forms actually fun to read and to Mary, Emma and Sheila in the Rights Department for continually talking up my writing. I am always grateful to be represented by such an excellent literary agency.

To my writing buddies I just want to give you all a big, squishy hug – thank you. A special high-five to Kirsty Greenwood for saying nice things about my writing when I'm wobbling. To the book blogging community: you guys absolutely rock. Thank you so much for endlessly sharing posts and reviews about my books, getting in touch and making me giggle on Twitter and generally being awesome.

To Aleksandra and Lauren who looked after Barnaby while I was writing about all things *hygge*. Thank you for being so loving. To my parents for always getting excited about any book news. Lastly I have to say a huge thank you to Ben for 'allowing' me to steal his workshop and turn it into the world's loveliest writing shed. I'm sorry. If it makes you feel better I've really shot myself in the foot as this year is our fifth wedding anniversary and that means it's 'wood'. I assume I'm getting a shop-bought spoon. I love you.

This book had to be dedicated to Barnaby for making each day such a crazy joy. Despite your regular diva outbursts you really are the most wonderful child. We love you so much and are so grateful we get to be your parents.